### *"Were you in on this?"*

He took a step back. "What do you mean?"

"Did you know Seb was going to leave the *Beacon* to both of us?"

Her outrageous accusation chased away all thoughts of offering comfort. "No. If you're suggesting I somehow influenced him, you're dead wrong. Why would I want a mess like this?"

"Half owner is better than being totally cut out, isn't it?"

"Not if I have to work with you," he ground out.

Dear Reader,

I love visiting small towns and making up stories about people who might live there. What are their lives like? What are their hopes and dreams, their joys, their disappointments and tragedies?

*Eva's Deadline* is such a story. The drama takes place in Willow Beach, Washington, a fictitious town on Washington's coast. Many times I've driven the same route that my heroine, Eva Sinclair, drives as she travels from her new home in Seattle to her hometown of Willow Beach. But, unlike Eva, I have always made these trips in happy anticipation.

Eva makes the trip to Willow Beach not for a vacation, as I have done, but because her father, Sebastian Sinclair, has suddenly passed away, and so for her, the trip is a sad one. The one saving grace is that she will soon be back in Seattle, where she can continue her promising career as a writer for a prestigious magazine.

Imagine her distress when Eva learns that her father had found a way to keep her in Willow Beach. Why, she wonders, would he do this, when he knew that what happened there eleven years ago caused her so much pain?

Mark Townson's life has also been changed by Sebastian's death, for it throws him and Eva together in ways that he finds difficult, if not impossible, to accept. But Mark loves his life in Willow Beach, and his job as editor of Seb's newspaper is the fulfillment of a dream he's not about to abandon. But, like Eva, he has a past that haunts him.

How these two deal with their challenges and, oh, yes, manage to fall in love, too, is what I envisioned happening in Willow Beach. I hope you enjoy reading the story.

Visit my website at www.lindahopelee.com. Email me at linda@lindahopelee.com or write to me at P.O. Box 238, Edmonds, WA. I am also on Facebook and Twitter (@LindaHopeLee).

Linda

# Linda Hope Lee

*Eva's Deadline*

MILLS & BOON

Published in Great Britain 2014
by Mills & Boon, an imprint of Harlequin (UK) Limited,
Eton House, 18-24 Paradise Road, Richmond, Surrey, TW9 1SR

© 2014 Linda Hope Lee

ISBN: 978 0 263 24497 7

33-0514

Harlequin (UK) Limited's policy is to use papers that are natural, renewable and recyclable products and made from wood grown in sustainable forests. The logging and manufacturing processes conform to the legal environmental regulations of the country of origin.

Printed and bound in Spain
by Blackprint CPI, Barcelona

## LINDA HOPE LEE

lives in the Pacific Northwest. She likes traveling to new places, especially to small towns that might serve as settings for her novels. In addition to contemporary romance, she writes in the romantic suspense and mystery genres, as well. When she is not writing, she's busy creating watercolor paintings or drawing in colored pencil or pen and ink. Another pastime is photography, which she uses as inspiration for her art and for her stories. She also collects children's books and anything to do with wire-haired fox terriers.

**To my new friend, Billy.**

# CHAPTER ONE

"I'M SORRY TO BRING you bad news," Mark Townson said, "but your father is dead."

"What?" The pen Eva Sinclair held slipped from her fingers and clattered onto her desk. When she'd answered the phone, the last person she'd expected to hear on the other end of the line was someone from her hometown. "No, no…"

"I'm afraid so."

"When? How?"

"Early this morning. When he didn't show up at the office or answer his home phone or his cell, I came over here to his house. I found him and called nine-one-one."

"Do you know what happened?"

"Not for sure. He was slumped over the kitchen table where he'd been eating breakfast. My guess would be a heart attack. I'm sure someone official will be in touch with you soon. I just thought you should know right away."

"Yes, but a heart attack… I didn't know he had a bad heart."

"I suspect there's a lot you didn't know about him."

His reproachful tone stung. Yet, the statement was true. She hadn't spoken to her father more than three or four times in the past five years, and those occasions had been short and strained.

"He told me about your, uh, disagreement," Mark Townson said. "And that you chose moving to Seattle over staying in Willow Beach and working for him at the *Herald*."

The *Willow Beach Herald*. Why would she want to write for a small-town weekly newspaper when she could work for a prestigious magazine like *Seattle's Best?* But, of course, that wasn't the only reason she didn't want to stay in Willow Beach.

She wondered how much Mark Townson knew about the reason for her leaving. Not the entire story, she'd bet, because her father didn't like to talk about the past any more than she did.

What Mr. Townson knew or did not know

was not important now. His shocking news took precedence. At the age of fifty-two, her father, Sebastian Sinclair, was dead.

"I'll drive to Willow Beach right away." She checked her wristwatch. "If I leave by noon, I should be there by six."

"Come to the *Herald*'s office when you get into town. We can get started on plans for a memorial."

"Yes, I suppose there should be some kind of service, but you don't need…"

"I want to be involved. Seb meant a lot to me and to the entire town. Everyone will want to say their last goodbyes."

"Well…all right. We'll talk about it when I get there."

An hour and a half later, after informing her boss of her father's sudden death and then driving to her Queen Anne Hill condo to toss some clothes into a suitcase, Eva headed south along the I-5 Freeway to Willow Beach. The blazing June sun turned the downtown skyscrapers into silver towers and glittered off the pewter waters of Elliott Bay.

As she left the city behind, her father dominated her thoughts. The most vivid recollection was his voice, deep and resonant when he was in a good mood and sharp and biting when he was angry. All too often, especially after her older brother, Brett, died, he'd been angry—and he'd taken out his anger on her. He'd pin her with a laser gaze and make his demands. Finally, after the ultimate battle over whether or not she would stay in their small town and work for him, she'd walked out.

At the thought of Brett, she fingered the silver chain she wore around her neck. A silver medal attached to the chain was hidden under her blouse. She visualized the words embossed there: *First Place*. Brett won the medal in a footrace on the beach the summer he was fifteen. Three years later, he was dead. Now she wore it. Although the memories were painful, she didn't want to forget him, ever.

When she reached Olympia, Eva focused on taking the exit leading to the coast. A few miles later, a turn south swept her past logging operations where stacks of timber waited for transport to paper mills. The acrid smell of the mills filled the air. The towns grew farther and farther apart as the road wound through thick evergreen forests and flat stretches of undeveloped land.

The last leg of the journey took her directly west toward the ocean, where a string of towns dotted the coast like beads on a necklace. Soon the sign for Willow Beach, Population 3,521, greeted her. On Main Street, familiar establishments popped into view: Bon Ton Bakery, Barnett's Drugs, Cooper's Hardware. So far, nothing had changed in the five years she'd been gone. Had time really stood still for her hometown?

The question didn't concern her, though. Her stay here was only temporary. Soon she'd be back in Seattle, where she belonged. Her father had been her last tie to the town, and now that fragile, final connection was broken.

A lump formed in her throat and her eyes misted. She blinked back the tears before they fell. Now was not the time to get emotional. Save that for later.

AT 6:00 P.M., in anticipation of Eva Sinclair's arrival, Mark Townson cleared his desktop and turned out the lights in his office at the *Herald*. He was the only one left in the building. The shock of Seb's sudden death had paralyzed the staff, and he'd sent them home early.

Instead of heading directly down the hallway to the reception area, on impulse he turned in the opposite direction, toward Seb's office. He opened the door and, with his hand still on the doorknob, let his gaze sweep the room. He could still see the man in his high-backed black leather chair, head bent over his work, or leaning back, gesturing expansively while he talked on the phone.

Mark wouldn't change anything about this room, not until after the funeral anyway. Maybe then Seb's death would seem more real. Right now, it was as though he'd stepped out for a moment and would soon be back.

His gaze landed on the two gold-framed photos on the desk. He walked over to see them better. One was a picture of Seb's son, Brett. Mark didn't know much about him, except that he had drowned in a boating accident eleven years ago, when he was eighteen. Seb never wanted to talk about the incident, and Mark had respected his wishes.

Judging by the photo, which showed the teenager standing with feet apart, hands resting easily on his hips, a gleam in his eye and a tilt to his chin, Brett had been confident, fun-loving and maybe just a bit arrogant.

The other photo was of Eva, who was two years younger than Brett. It had been taken, Seb had told him, on her graduation from the University of Washington. She was dressed in traditional cap and gown, with the university's buildings in the background. She smiled into the camera, her dark hair curling around her shoulders, her eyes sparkling with the enthusiasm of someone about to embark on a grand adventure. He guessed Seb had chosen this photo because he wanted to remember her as a happy person, rather than the angry daughter who'd left town five years ago.

Leaving the office, he walked to the reception area and stood looking out the front window. Traffic flowed smoothly along Main Street as shoppers and workers made their way home and tourists returned to their motels.

Mark checked his wristwatch. Almost six-thirty. Even with heavy freeway traffic, Eva should be here by now. He wanted to get their initial meeting over with so he could pick up Sasha and go home himself.

A late-model blue compact pulled into a

parking space in front of the office. A young woman in a tan jacket, knee-length skirt and high heels got out. She had an oversize purse slung over one shoulder. Eva Sinclair. He'd bet on it.

Sure enough, she headed directly for the *Herald*'s front door. He walked over and pulled it open. "You must be Eva. Come on in."

She nodded, and as she stepped inside, her perfume wafted past his nose.

"I'm looking for Mark Townson."

He extended his hand. "I'm Mark."

Her eyes widened as she slipped her hand into his. Her skin was soft, yet her grip was firm. At her continued stare, he asked, "Is something wrong?"

"No, it's just that you sounded older on the phone." She pulled her hand away.

He couldn't help smiling. "I was thirty-one my last birthday. Some days, that feels mighty old."

He took a moment to study her. Not surprisingly, she had changed since the day she'd posed for her graduation photo. Her dark hair was pulled back in a fancy twist. Her eyes were outlined with dark pencil and mascara, and the bright red lipstick she wore matched her fingernails.

He wasn't sure he liked this more sophisticated version of Eva Sinclair. He shrugged off the thought. Whether he liked her or not made no difference. Their association would last a week or two at the most, and then she'd return to her life in Seattle.

"I see you found the place okay," he said and then could've kicked himself for the lame remark.

She shrugged. "No problem there. Nothing's changed in Willow Beach."

Mark was immediately defensive. "Oh, I don't know about that. You stay here long enough, you'll see plenty of changes."

Eva adjusted the strap of her purse more firmly on her shoulder. "I'm here only for as long as it takes to bury Seb and settle his affairs. I'm hoping everything can be wrapped up in a week, tops."

Her businesslike tone grated. They weren't discussing a stranger; the dead man was her father. But then her shoulders sagged and she ran a hand over her forehead, and he pushed away his impatience. After her long drive to the coast, she must be tired. Not to mention still in shock over her father's sudden death.

"Why don't we talk over dinner?" he suggested. "Or did you eat on the way?"

She shook her head. "I threw some things in a suitcase and came straight here. I'm not really hungry, but I'd better eat something."

"Me, too. So, fancy? Casual? What's your preference?"

Judging by her outfit, he figured she'd want someplace upscale and was surprised when she said with a shrug, "Casual is fine."

"Charlie's Fish House is casual."

A smile touched her lips, the first he'd seen since she arrived. "Charlie's, my old teenage hangout. Sure, why not?"

"Okay, I'll drive. My car's out back."

He locked the front door and then led her down the hallway, past the staff's cubicles and his and Seb's offices to the back door. His SUV, still covered with dust from his last camping trip, sat in the unpaved parking lot that bordered an alley. He opened the passenger door for Eva, then went around to his side and climbed in. She settled in the seat, her purse on her lap, charging the air with her perfume.

One of Sasha's stuffed toys, a Pekingese with a faux-jeweled collar, lay on the console. He picked up the toy and tossed it into the backseat.

Noticing Eva's raised eyebrows, he said, "My daughter's."

"You're married, then."

He started the engine and shifted into Reverse. "I was. Diane died three years ago. Sasha's our only child. She'll be six in a few weeks." He checked the rearview mirror as he backed out of his parking spot. "Single parenting can be a challenge, but Sasha has a great caretaker. And she's a good kid."

The mention of his daughter made him wish he were on his way to pick her up instead of spending time with Eva Sinclair. Gripping the steering wheel, he vowed to do his best, though—for Seb's sake.

EVA TOOK A BITE of the halibut she'd ordered at Charlie's Fish House. Even with little appetite, she had to admit the crisply fried seafood was as good as she remembered. Charlie's decor hadn't changed since her high-school days, either—the same plain wooden tables and chairs, the same counter with red vinyl-covered stools, the same chalkboard menu on the wall. Outside, the surf sang as soft waves rolled onto shore, and the warm breeze carried the aromas of salt and seaweed and wet sand.

The one unfamiliar element was the man sitting across from her. Mark Townson. As she'd so tactlessly blurted out earlier, he wasn't what she'd expected. Over the phone, his deep voice had sounded as though it belonged to someone older than a man in his early thirties. But Mark was definitely young—and fit. His blue knit shirt stretched across a broad chest, the short sleeves showing off impressive muscles. His hair was a dark brown and his eyes a deep sea-blue. He could've been a model for one of the outdoor recreation companies that advertised in *Seattle's Best*.

He looked up and caught her staring. She scrambled for something to say. "So…you've worked for the *Herald* for about five years now?"

Mark finished chewing a bite of his burger. "Right. Since shortly after you left town. I started out doing ads and column writing, some general stuff. You know how it is on a small newspaper—everyone does a little of everything. Then three years ago, Seb decided he wanted to back off a bit and suggested I take over as editor." He dipped a French fry into a pool of ketchup. "I take it you like your gig in Seattle?"

"Very much. I interned at *Seattle's Best* when I was at the University of Washington. Went to work there shortly after graduation. Started out as copy editor. Now I'm a staff writer but hope to be assistant editor soon. The current assistant is leaving, and I'm pretty sure I'll be taking her place."

"Good for you. What you write is different from newspaper writing."

"Vastly. Our aim is to discover the best Seattle has to offer in restaurants, fashion, housing and entertainment and get it out to our readers. I love what I'm doing."

"Like I said on the phone, Seb told me how you didn't want to stay here and work for him."

"There's no way I could be writing the kinds of articles here that I'm doing for *Seattle's Best*."

"Big disappointment to him, though."

She leveled Mark a gaze. "But after I left, he found you, didn't he?"

Mark frowned. "I guess you could put it that way. Or I found him. I was the one who came looking for a job."

Eva just stared at him. "Whatever. Maybe we'd better get down to business. You want a big memorial, you said."

"No question. If you don't want to be involved, my staff and I can pull it off."

"No, no, I'll go along with that. There are other things to take care of, too, though." She pulled her iPad from her purse and switched it on. "Forest Lawn can do the service and the reception. I'll call them." She tapped the keyboard.

"We'll need an obituary. You're the logical one to write that. We'll put it on the website, too."

She looked up and raised her eyebrows. "The *Herald* is online?"

"Yep. We're not as backwoods as you think."

"Good to know. Okay, how about flowers?"

Mark pulled a notebook and pen from his shirt pocket. "I'll get April on that. She's on our staff."

Details about the memorial carried them through dinner. When they finished, they both had to-do lists. "I do appreciate your help," she told him, slipping her iPad into her purse.

"You're welcome." Mark studied her a moment. "So, you'll be here about a week?"

She nodded. "I can't afford to be away any longer than that."

"No, I suppose not."

On the drive back to the *Herald*'s office, Eva gazed out the window at the growing darkness. Here and there, lights blinked on, but unlike in Seattle, they barely penetrated the rapidly approaching night. She'd forgotten how dark Willow Beach became once the sun dipped below the horizon.

When they reached Main Street and the office building, Mark drew up behind her car. Leaving the engine running, he stuck his hand in his jeans pocket and pulled out a leather key ring. "This is for Seb's house…."

At the sight of the familiar key ring, memories crowded her mind. She pressed her fingers to her lips. "Oh, no, I couldn't…not tonight. Besides, I have a reservation at The Gables."

He raised his eyebrows. "Oh, yeah, the

fancy B and B off the highway. Okay, but take the key. You'll need it eventually."

He was right. Sooner or later, she'd have to visit the house where she'd lived with her family. So many memories. So much pain.

She took the key ring, slipped it into her purse, then opened the car door.

He snapped his fingers. "Oh, I almost forgot. Did you know Seb had a will?"

Eva frowned. "He never discussed a will with me. He and my mother always kept financial matters to themselves. I'm not surprised, though. Why do you ask?"

"His lawyer, Lawrence Prentiss, has a copy. His wife called this afternoon when she heard the news. She said Lawrence is out of town. He should be back in a couple of days."

Eva shrugged. "I can wait. Considering how we parted, I doubt the will has anything to do with me."

"Just thought I'd mention it."

"Well, thanks for dinner and for all you're doing for my dad," Eva said as she got out of Mark's SUV.

"Of course," Mark said as he waved, then he waited for her to drive away.

As she headed out of town, Eva passed

the road leading to the freeway. Her fingers itched to turn onto it. She'd drive all night, if she could, to get away from here and return to Seattle. To her condo, her job, her friends—to all that was familiar, all that mattered.

A heavy blanket of fatigue settled over her. How was she ever going to get through the next couple of weeks? Then she thought of her father, whose weeks, days and years were used up too soon. *Oh, Dad, why...why did you have to die?*

# *CHAPTER TWO*

As soon as Eva's car was out of sight, Mark took a deep breath and leaned back against the seat. Even though their meeting had not been as stressful as he'd expected, his shoulders ached with tension. Probably an accumulation of the entire day's events, beginning with the discovery of Seb's lifeless body slumped over his kitchen table.

He straightened and slapped the steering wheel. Enough brooding. He had a daughter to pick up. He started the car's engine and headed down the street.

Five blocks later, he reached the Dugans' yellow frame house, the porch light sending a bright glow into the night. He smiled as he pulled to a stop at the curb. It had been one lucky day when he'd found Eileen Dugan. After Diane's death, he'd had no one to care for Sasha, and then a friend introduced him to Eileen and her husband, George. Already looking after three grandchildren, Eileen welcomed his Sasha into her brood.

Eileen answered the door. "Come in, Mark."

He stepped inside and paused to sniff the air. "Ah, chicken and dumplings for dinner."

Eileen chuckled and smoothed a lock of red hair from her forehead. "Your nose is right on, as usual. There's plenty left over, if you're hungry."

"Thanks, but I've already eaten. Eva Sinclair and I had a bite at Charlie's."

Eileen pursed her lips. "So she's back, is she? Couldn't be bothered to come while her father was alive."

"Yep, she's back. But not for long."

Eileen harrumphed. "I don't know all that went on between those two, but it seemed to me she could've been more of a daughter to him. Janice passing quick like she did, and then Brett's terrible accident. Only the two of them left. And what's wrong with working at a fine newspaper like the *Herald*? You work there. You like it."

"I do, very much. And, no, I don't know what went on between them, but at least she's here now."

Sasha appeared in the hallway, arms outstretched. "Daddy, Daddy!"

"Hey, sweetheart." He leaned down and swept her into his arms. Smoothing back Sasha's fine blond hair, he planted a kiss on her soft cheek, inhaling her sweet, little-girl scent. "Were you a good girl today?"

"I'm *always* good. Aren't I, Grammy Eileen?" Keeping one arm hooked around Mark's neck, Sasha looked to her caretaker for confirmation.

Eileen patted Sasha's shoulder. "That you are, my dear." She turned to Mark. Behind her rimless glasses, her brown eyes shimmered with tears. "I still can't believe Seb's gone."

Mark nodded and shifted Sasha in his arms. "Shocking, all right."

Sasha's brow wrinkled. "What happened to Mr. Seb?"

"I'll tell you on the way home, honey."

While Sasha collected her backpack, Eileen bustled into the kitchen. She returned with a plastic container, which she handed to Mark. "We made chocolate-chip cookies today."

"I put in the chips," Sasha said, "and stirred, too."

Mark exchanged a grin with Eileen. "Good for you, Sasha. These will hit the spot with a glass of milk when we get home. By the way, any news from Dan and Rilla and the kids?"

Dan and Rilla were Eileen's son and daughter-in-law. They were on a road trip to visit Rilla's parents in Montana.

Eileen grinned. "They're having a great time. I sure miss my three grandkids, though. Good thing I have Sasha." She gave Sasha a hug. "Bye now, darlin'. See you tomorrow."

"Bye, Grammy Eileen." Sasha planted a smooch on the woman's cheek.

Eileen walked out with them onto the porch. Then Mark tucked Sasha into her booster seat and they were on their way. The clouds parted to reveal a half-moon on the rise. Tall evergreens were silhouetted against the silvery sky. The salty smell of the ocean drifted in through his open window.

"What about Mr. Seb?" Sasha asked from her seat behind him.

"He died this morning."

"Why?"

"Well, because his body stopped working and the doctors couldn't fix him."

"Like Mommy?"

Her forlorn voice tugged at Mark's heart. "Yes, like Mommy."

Sasha had been only three years old when Diane had died. He'd explained death as best he could, but doubted his daughter really understood. Then last year she began asking why she didn't have a mommy like her friends. He'd given her a simplified version of the truth. The bus Mommy was riding in had an accident. Mommy was hurt so bad her body wouldn't work anymore.

"I miss Mommy," Sasha said now.

"I know, honey. I do, too."

And he did. Even though she had betrayed him, he missed her presence, missed being part of a complete family. Since Diane's death, he'd more or less stayed away from women. He had a date now and then, mostly when someone set him up and when accepting was easier than refusing, but nothing came of these encounters. He didn't want to risk being hurt again. Or having Sasha hurt.

He'd never told their daughter why her mommy was on the bus or where she was going. No need to burden the child with the awful truth. Maybe when she was older.

Then again, maybe never.

Later, after they had their cookies and milk, Mark tucked Sasha into bed. He kissed her forehead and pulled the covers up around her chin.

She smiled at him. "'Night, Daddy."

"'Night, honey." He gazed at his precious child, his heart full of love.

In the living room, he settled into his recliner, the one Diane had insisted on buying because the blue upholstery matched the sofa she'd picked out. He'd rather have had a leather chair, but, no, blue cloth it had to be. After she died, he'd kept it, as he'd kept nearly everything else in the house that she'd had a hand in. For Sasha's sake. He didn't want her to forget her mommy, and having things around that reminded her of Diane would help to keep her memory alive.

Switching on the TV, he tuned in the local news to see what they said about Seb. The TV crew had been at the newspaper office that afternoon, interviewing him and the other staff. Sure enough, there he was, being quoted about what a shock Seb's death was, and what a great newspaperman he'd been, and how much he'd be missed. Mark slowly shook his head. He still had trouble believing the man was gone.

He knew that despite their estrangement, Seb had loved Eva. He always spoke of her with pride and said what a good writer she was. But, as far as Mark could tell after meeting Eva this evening, she still seemed to harbor resentment toward her father. Indignation tightened Mark's chest. Seb deserved better.

Yet, what right did he have to judge Eva? Wasn't he still angry with Diane for what she'd done to him and Sasha?

He turned off the TV and headed for the bedroom. As he lay in bed, the thought of dealing with Eva, even for the brief time she'd be in Willow Beach, kept him tossing and turning.

EVA'S CHEST TIGHTENED as she watched the pallbearers lower her father's casket into the ground at Forest Lawn Cemetery. Up until today, his death didn't seem real, not even when she was making plans for this very event. It was as though she were talking about someone else, not her father, who had always been so energetic and full of life. That the life had gone out of him didn't seem possible. Yet, this last goodbye was about to happen.

She let her attention stray to the nearby markers for her mother, Janice, and her brother, Brett. Her whole family gone now. Tears burned her eyes. She blinked them back. Now was not the time. Save that for when she was alone.

The pallbearers, including Mark, moved back from the edge of the grave. He walked over to join the rest of the *Herald* staff standing nearby. Eva surveyed the crowd gathered to pay Seb their last respects. At least four hundred people had been packed into the hall for the service preceding the burial, and more were expected to attend the reception following. Mark had been right: Seb had a lot of friends in Willow Beach. Eva recognized many of the crowd, including some of her old classmates at Willow Beach High, but there were a lot of mourners she didn't know, newcomers to the town.

Pastor Jordan stepped forward. "Let us pray," he began, and along with the others, Eva bowed her head.

Half an hour later, she stood in the middle

of Forest Lawn's reception room, holding a plate with an egg-salad sandwich and a scoop of pasta salad, refreshments provided by the funeral home's catering service. Now that the burial was over, her tension had eased, but only a little. She still had to greet the guests and talk about her father and receive their condolences. They meant well, of course, but her alienation from Seb made talking about him difficult—and painful.

She looked over at the picture of him on an easel near the door. The *Herald*'s photographer, Cody Jarvis, had made the enlargement. The photo must have been taken recently because Seb's hair had more gray than she remembered, and new lines bracketed his mouth and his eyes.

"He looks so lifelike," said a voice behind her.

Eva turned to see her high-school friend Fran Oliver. "He does. Larger than life."

"He'll be missed." Fran put her arm around Eva's shoulder. "That was a beautiful service."

"It was. Pastor Jordan did a wonderful job officiating."

"It's sure good to see you again, Eva." Fran

dropped her arm and stood back, regarding Eva with solemn eyes.

Eva nodded. "Good to see you, too. How's the teaching going? Still love it as much as you did at first?"

Fran's solemn expression relaxed, and she smiled and smoothed her short blond hair. "You bet. Chasing those high-school kids keeps me in shape."

"Thanks so much for coming. I appreciate your and Jason's support." Eva looked around. "Where is your husband? I should thank him in person."

"He's over there talking to Mark. They're basketball-team buddies." Fran nodded toward the other end of the room. "But we're not your only support. Alison and Trudi came, too. And some of the others from our class."

"Yes. I spoke to them at the service."

"You have more friends here than you might think."

Eva looked away. "I know I haven't been in touch much since I left…."

"I understand, but you've been missed." She tilted her head. "Any chance you'll be coming back?"

"No. I love my life in Seattle."

"I'm glad you've found the place you want to be, hon, but that doesn't keep me from wishing you were still here. Uh-oh, Jason's waving at me. We need to pick up the twins from the babysitter's."

After Fran moved off, a man about her father's age, with thick white hair and black-rimmed glasses, stepped to Eva's side. "Hello, Eva, do you remember me?"

"Of course, you're Hal Barnett. I've been in your drugstore many times. Your son was a year ahead of me in high school."

Hal nodded. "I haven't seen Carson for a couple years. Left town, same as you. What is it about our town that makes our kids want to leave?"

Eva shrugged. "Some of us just want to explore the rest of the world, I guess." She thought of Brett, and her stomach twisted. That was what he'd wanted to do, but tragedy struck before he had the chance. Thinking of her brother prompted her to reach up and finger the silver chain that held his medal.

"We'll sure miss Seb." Hal slowly shook his head. "He did so much good for our town, 'sides publishing the news. Will you be comin' back to help out at the paper? Not that Mark isn't doing a bang-up job, but it'd be nice to keep the newspaper in the family, doncha think?"

"'Fraid not, Hal. I've found my place elsewhere."

Hal's mouth turned down. "What's gonna happen to the *Herald*?"

"I don't know. I haven't thought about it."

She spoke the truth. She hadn't been involved with the *Herald* in the past, so she hadn't given any thought to its future.

They chatted for a few more minutes, and then Hal excused himself to return to the buffet table. Eva finished her food and set the plate on a nearby cart. She turned to see Mark and a tall, slender man in his fifties heading toward her.

"This is Lawrence Prentiss," Mark said when the two men reached her side. "He was your father's attorney. I mentioned him the first night you were here."

Ah, the man who had Seb's will. She'd been so busy with other matters she'd all but forgotten about that. "Hello, Mr. Prentiss. I don't think I remember you…."

Lawrence Prentiss extended his hand. "You

wouldn't. My wife and I moved here from Portland three years ago. I took over Sam Lambert's business when he passed away."

"I do remember the Lamberts." Eva shook Lawrence's hand, which seemed more bones than flesh.

"My condolences for your loss, Eva. Your father was a fine man."

"Thank you, Mr. Prentiss."

He cleared his throat. "As you undoubtedly know, Sebastian left a will."

"I didn't know until Mark mentioned it. My father was a very private person. There was a lot he didn't share with me."

"I understand, but now that I'm back in town, we need to schedule a time when the three of us can sit down together and read it."

Mark raised his eyebrows. "The three of us?"

Lawrence nodded. "You need to be there, too, Mark."

"Why do we need a reading of the will?" she asked, folding her arms. "I thought that was something done only in the movies."

Lawrence's thin lips cracked a smile. "I know it sounds dramatic, but your father re-

quested that you and Mark meet with me. I'm
only following his instructions."

"But I'm leaving for Seattle as soon as this
reception is over. Can't you just send me a
copy?"

Lawrence shook his head. "No, I'm obligated to honor Seb's wishes."

Eva was tempted to stand firm on her "no."
But the man was only doing his job. She
heaved a sigh. "Can you see us tomorrow?"

"I can. How about one o'clock?"

"Fine."

Lawrence turned to Mark. "How about
you, Mark?"

Mark rubbed the back of his neck. "Saturday? I'd planned a hike with Sasha, but, yeah,
I'll be there."

"Great," Lawrence said. "I'll see you both
in my office at one o'clock."

AFTER HE'D TUCKED Sasha into bed that evening, Mark settled in his recliner with a cup
of coffee. Satisfaction brought a smile to his
lips as he thought about the day's events, all
fitting tributes to Seb.

Lawrence Prentiss's insistence that he be
present for a reading of Seb's will left him

scratching his head, though. Why would he be in Seb's will? Then again, why not? Their relationship was more than boss and employee. They'd gone fishing together and played pool on Friday nights at Durango's Tavern. Mark had become involved in some of Seb's charity projects, such as helping out at the community center's free Thanksgiving dinner.

Seb had often told Mark he was like a son. "I had a son...once," he'd say. If they were in his office, his gaze would stray to the photos on his desk.

His thoughts returned to the will. Seb had probably left him a token of appreciation for his friendship and loyalty.

No surprise that Eva was in the will. Even though they'd been estranged, she and Seb were still blood. What a shame the two hadn't spent Seb's last years together in harmony.

"'I, SEBASTIAN FRANKLIN SINCLAIR, of sound mind, do declare this as my last will and testament...'"

Seated at an oval table in Lawrence Prentiss's office, Eva listened to the lawyer begin the reading of her father's will. After waiting nearly half an hour for the meeting to get under way, and then having to sit through the lawyer's small talk about the weather, she realized her nerves were more on edge than ever.

She glanced at Mark, who was seated across from her. His attention was on Lawrence, but he didn't look any happier about being here than she was.

The first bequests were to charities, including the local hospital, the animal shelter and the University of Washington's School of Journalism. The last designation didn't surprise Eva; both she and her father were alumni.

The bequest to UCLA was puzzling, until Lawrence said to Mark, "I believe that's where you studied journalism, isn't it?"

Mark nodded. "That was nice of Seb to give them something."

Lawrence turned to the next page. "'To my daughter, Eva, I bequeath my property at 880 Oak Avenue and all structures thereon and all personal and tangible property contained therein.'"

The house she'd grown up in was to be hers? Why had Seb bothered to leave her the house? She didn't want it and would never live there again.

She expected that to be the end of the reading, but Lawrence continued, "'To my daughter, Eva, and to Mark Townson, I bequeath the entire holdings of the *Willow Beach Herald*. Each shall receive 50 percent of the total assets comprised by the newspaper…'"

Eva gasped, unable to believe what she'd heard. Besides the house, her father was leaving her 50 percent of the newspaper? Why, when she'd refused to work there or to have anything to do with his publication?

Lawrence cleared his throat. "'…subject to the following provisions. One, that both Mark and Eva assume coeditorship of the newspaper for the period of one year.'"

"What?" Eva blurted and half rose from her chair.

Lawrence held up his hand. "Let me finish, please."

"Sorry," she mumbled and sank back into her seat.

"'Two, if either party declines to accept the terms, neither inherits and the *Herald* shall be auctioned to the highest bidder. Neither party may bid on the *Herald* or in any way be associated with a bidding party.

"'Three, after assuming coleadership of the *Herald* for the proscribed year, both parties are free to do as they please regarding their involvement with said newspaper.'"

"What on earth was Seb thinking?" Mark said, obviously as shocked as she was.

Eva shook her head in disbelief. "He must have been crazy. But it won't work."

"I'm afraid the will is ironclad." Lawrence tapped the sheaf of papers with his forefinger.

"But the terms are impossible." Eva looked from one man to the other. "I have a life, a career in Seattle. I can't give up everything to come here for a year. It's different for you, Mark. You already work at the *Herald*."

He folded his arms. "I can't see us working together."

"Me, neither. No. Never. Not in a million years. Newspaper writing is not what I do."

"And fluff pieces aren't what *I* do."

Eva drew back and stared at him. "I beg your pardon. *Seattle's Best* is every bit as serious a publication as…as a rag like the *Herald*."

"The *Herald* is not a *rag!*"

Lawrence spread his hands. "People, people, please. This is not the time to argue about who writes what."

Mark leaned forward. "Okay, but are you sure there isn't some way out of this?"

The lawyer shook his head. "You're both free to obtain your own counsel, of course."

"I intend to," Eva said. "There is no way I will spend another year of my life in this town."

"I understand your position," Lawrence said. "But don't forget that Mark's future depends on what you decide. If you don't accept the terms, Mark loses his inheritance, too, and the newspaper goes on the block. Is that what you want, either of you? Think about it."

MARK STOOD OUTSIDE Lawrence's office, scanning the adjacent parking lot for Eva. When she'd stormed out, he'd impulsively followed. He wasn't sure why. What was there to say? That he didn't want his half of the newspaper? That wouldn't be true. The *Herald* and its future meant everything to him. From the day Seb had hired him, Mark had devoted himself to the newspaper and its success.

He ran a hand through his hair. What a disaster.

Eva's blue outfit made her easy to spot. She marched along, head high, her straw purse swinging from her shoulder. A woman on a mission. He watched her for a moment, debating whether he really wanted a confrontation, and then he ran after her. Just as she reached her car, he caught up.

"Eva!" He grabbed her arm, jerking her to a halt.

She looked down where he gripped her arm and then up at him. "What do you think you're doing?"

He let go of her and stepped back. "I, uh, look, I know you're upset—"

"*Upset* doesn't begin to cover my emotional state. I'm devastated. But Seb's will isn't going to happen. I'll call my lawyer. He'll know what to do."

He was about to say he'd do the same, but before he could, she said in an accusing tone, "Were you in on this?"

"What do you mean?"

"Did you know Seb was going to leave the *Herald* to both of us?"

Her outrageous accusation left him momentarily speechless. "If you're suggesting I somehow influenced him, you're dead wrong. Why would I want a mess like this?"

"Half owner is better than being totally cut out, isn't it?"

"Not if I have to work with you." He turned and strode off.

## CHAPTER THREE

"I HOPE YOU HAVE good news." Eva was back in Seattle sitting in her cubicle at the magazine. She'd given a copy of Seb's will to her lawyer, Nolan Cramer, and he'd finally called.

As he spoke, her spirits sank. "You're sure there's nothing I can do?" she asked when he'd finished.

"I'm afraid not, Eva. Sorry. My advice? Accept the terms. You might like the experience better than you think."

Eva doubted that.

She ended the call and slumped over her desk, head in her hands. Nolan had just confirmed what Lawrence Prentiss had already told her—the will was ironclad. She'd held out hope that the will could be broken, but now that door had closed.

Was there no way out of this?

She sat there, her mind spinning, and sure enough, an idea popped into her head. If her boss, James Forsythe, would take pity on her, she could at least soften the blow. She picked up the phone and called him.

Luckily, he had time to see her, and half an hour later she sat in his spacious office. As she waited for him to finish a phone call, she gazed around the room, taking in its warm brown-and-yellow color scheme, the desk, the credenza, even an armoire for storing coats. Someday, this office would be hers. She just knew it. Whenever she was in here, she mentally ran through the changes she would make. For starters, she'd replace the hydroplane photos—James's son was a champion driver—with the colorful giclée flower prints she'd seen in a Pike Place Market gallery. Add a runner to the top of the credenza, and place her pewter umbrella stand, shaped like a half-open umbrella itself, by the door. Personal touches that would put her brand on the office.

Today she didn't dare play her little game. Too much rode on convincing James to accept her plan. She knew her boss liked her and valued her as an employee. Surely he would help her through this crisis.

He finally finished his call and turned to

her, his back to the picture window. The incoming sunlight glinted on the silver highlights in his dark hair.

"I'm glad you're back, Eva. I've been thinking about you down there in Willow Beach and hoping everything was going okay."

"I appreciate that, James. Yes, I think my father would have liked his memorial service and the reception afterward. But now I have a new problem." Clasping her hands and leaning forward, she explained about her father's will. "I don't want to leave the magazine," she concluded. "I like working at *Seattle's Best*. I think I have a good future here."

"You do, Eva."

"So I thought if you could grant me a year's leave of absence, then I could return when I finish my obligation in Willow Beach. I'll miss out on any promotion this year, but at least I'll still be in the game." She leaned back and held her breath. He would accept her plan. He just had to.

But he shook his head and looked apologetic. "A year's leave? Much as I'd like to help you out, I'm afraid that's impossible."

Her heart sank, but she wasn't ready to give up. "Why?"

"A year is way too long. I might get the board to agree to a month, but a year? Never. I'm sorry. You know I'd do anything I could to help you, but my hands are tied."

Her last hope crushed, Eva looked down to hide her reaction.

James rose, came around the desk and placed a fatherly hand on her shoulder. "I know you're disappointed, but why not consider this an opportunity?"

"An opportunity?" she said. "Living in a nowhere town and working for a weekly newspaper? I don't think so."

Of course, James didn't know about Brett and the terrible accident and the memories that haunted her, and she wasn't about to tell him. She'd never brought her personal problems into the workplace. Absently, she reached up and ran her forefinger over the silver chain. As usual, the medal itself was concealed under her clothing, but she knew it was there.

James clasped his hands behind his back and paced to the window. He looked out at the Seattle skyline, then turned back to her. "You know where I started out? Writing restaurant reviews for a newspaper in California, in a town about the size of your Willow Beach. The experience was the best I could've had."

"But I'm not just starting out," she complained. "I'm five years down the road. And being exiled to Willow Beach feels like going backward."

"Your life has taken a different turn. Look on the bright side. Running a paper could be a great opportunity."

Eva shook her head. "I appreciate what you're trying to do, James, but you'll never convince me that this situation has a bright side."

Instead of returning to her desk, Eva bypassed her cubicle and continued on to the large window at the end of the hallway and its sweeping view of Elliott Bay.

She folded her arms and leaned against the window frame, idly tracing the progress of a green-and-white ferry on its way to the Olympic Peninsula. Her last option was to refuse the terms of the will. But that would take away Mark's inheritance, and if the new owner chose to not keep him on, his livelihood, too. He had a daughter to support. Sure, he'd be able to find work somewhere else, but, if she'd understood him correctly, the *Herald* meant a lot to him. And her father had wanted him to have a part of it.

Eva scrubbed a hand over her forehead. She wouldn't be able to live with herself if she denied Mark his inheritance. She had no choice but to give up her own career opportunities and spend a year in her hometown.

With a resigned sigh, she returned to her cubicle. Lying on the top of her desk was the latest issue of *Seattle's Best*. The cover featured the title of an article she'd written, along with her byline. A lump formed in her throat. She stared at the cover for a minute or two, then picked up the phone and punched in Lawrence Prentiss's number.

AS SOON AS MARK received the news that Eva had accepted the terms of Seb's will, and because his own efforts to break the will had proven just as useless as hers, he called an emergency meeting of the staff. Such as it was. Only four people worked for the newspaper full-time and the rest were freelance. The employees dutifully filed into the lounge, poured themselves coffee and sat at the vintage Formica-topped table.

The fragrant aroma of the coffee mixed

with the sugary smells from Bon Ton Bakery's doughnuts. Mark bought the pastries especially for the occasion, hoping to soften the news they were about to receive. He'd filled his mug and taken a couple sips, even though he had no desire for either coffee or sweets.

"What's up, Mark?" Bernie Sanchez, in charge of advertising, gripped his World's Greatest Husband coffee mug, a present from his wife, Maria.

Dora Winters, circulation manager and, at sixty, their oldest member, looked up from the multicolored scarf she was knitting. "This meeting is about our future, isn't it?"

"I bet it has to do with Eva." Underneath eyebrow-grazing blond bangs, April Hensen's eyes shifted warily. In her mid-twenties, April did double duty as receptionist and compiler of the Police Beat column.

Their photographer and webmaster, Cody Jarvis, also a twentysomething, fingered the digital camera hanging around his neck. "I thought she went back to Seattle."

"She did," Mark said from his seat at the head of the table. "But she's coming back."

"What?" everyone chorused.

He held up his hands. "Simmer down and

I'll explain." He launched into his prepared speech, beginning with Seb's will and ending with, "Both Eva and I tried to find a way out, and neither one of us was successful. So she and I will be coeditors for the next year."

A stunned silence filled the room, setting Mark's nerves even more on edge. But maybe silence was a good sign, and they were only taking time to digest the news.

Bernie was the first to speak. He looked at Mark, a frown wrinkling his forehead. "I was kinda hoping you'd continue to be our leader. Why do we need two bosses?"

"The only answer I have for you is that it's what Seb wanted."

"I got the impression she doesn't want to be here." Cody folded his arms over his chest, covering the *Herald* logo on his T-shirt. "And if that's true, then what kind of a boss will she be?"

"She has a job in Seattle that she really likes," Mark said.

April flipped her long hair over her shoulder. "Yeah, she thinks she's better than we are because she works for a big-city magazine."

"Now, April." Mark leveled what he hoped was a reproving look at her. "I think you're being a bit unfair. She prefers the magazine because that's the kind of writing she wants to do, not because that kind of writing is better than what we do here."

April's scornful expression indicated she wasn't buying Mark's lame excuse for the impression Eva had made.

Bernie took his mug over to the coffee urn for a refill. "Didn't she and Seb have a falling-out?"

"My understanding is, yes, they did," Mark said. "Dora, you're the only one of us who was working here at the time. Can you help us out?"

Dora put her knitting down on the table and smoothed a hand over it. "I was here. I've been working for the *Herald* for almost twenty years. I'm a real old-timer. Why, I remember when I hired on. That was when Seb and Boyd Carlstrom were partners, and, oh, my, did we have a time getting this operation off the ground—"

Mark cleared his throat. Sometimes, keeping Dora on track was a challenge. "I'm sure you did, Dora, but about Seb and Eva?"

Dora looked away. "A bad time, that was. It goes back to when Eva's brother, Brett, died.

He drowned in a boating accident, you know. On Pine Lake."

"He was older than Eva, right?" Bernie slipped into his seat. "I heard some of the guys at Sam's Garage talking about him. Said he was kinda wild."

Dora nodded. "He liked a good time. And, yes, he was two years older than Eva. Seb had his heart set on Brett following in his footsteps here at the *Herald*. When Brett died, Seb went into hiding, and Boyd had to run the show. It was awful. Seb never got over losing his son. Never."

"What happened to Seb's wife?" Cody asked. "I've never heard much about her."

"She died two or three years before Brett. Pancreatic cancer. Nasty stuff. Can take you just like that." Dora snapped her fingers. "Janice was a lovely woman. Quiet and unassuming. Kept in the background. Seb definitely has been the boss in that family."

"But what exactly caused Seb and Eva's split?" Mark asked.

Dora shrugged and picked up her needles again. "Seb never wanted to talk about what happened with Eva. Maybe she just didn't want to be second choice."

"That doesn't mean she has to take out her bad attitude on us," April said.

"Not gonna be too good for morale around here," Bernie grumbled under his breath.

"Remember, this is what Seb wanted," Mark said. "And the terms are only for a year. We can handle it."

A tension-filled silence descended on the group. Bernie drank his coffee and stared into space. Cody pulled a cloth from his back pocket and dusted the lens on his camera, while Dora concentrated on her knitting. April pouted and studied her fingernails.

Finally, Mark said, "I know you're all upset about this turn of events. But I gotta say again, it's what Seb wanted. He must've had his reasons. We'll welcome Eva and do the best we can while she's here. For Seb's sake. For the *Herald*'s sake. Can I have your cooperation on that?"

The staff nodded their agreement.

When the meeting was over, Mark rinsed out his mug and hung it on the mug tree. Maybe Eva's disappointment at being her father's second choice to take over the business was the reason for her reluctance to accept the terms of his will.

Still, something told him there was more to the matter than that. Would he ever know? Judging by their relationship so far, he couldn't see them becoming friends, much less confidants.

In the meantime, he must be careful to live up to the standards he'd set for the others. It wouldn't be easy. As coeditors with different viewpoints, he and Eva were sure to clash over how to run the paper. Yes, the coming year promised to be challenging indeed.

"IS THIS ALL?" Eva glanced around the apartment's combination living, kitchen and dining rooms, then shifted her gaze to Mrs. Halsey, the building's owner.

Mrs. Halsey frowned and brushed a lock of gray hair from her forehead. "I'm not sure what you mean. What more do you want?"

"It's just so…small."

The apartment was on a corner of the town's Main Street. It was on the second floor, above a mini-mall, with stores and antiques shops geared for the tourist trade— what there was of it in Willow Beach.

"Don't forget the great view of the ocean." Mrs. Halsey gestured to the picture window.

Eva walked over and gazed out. Mrs. Halsey had a point. From here she could see the ocean in all its glory, waves breaking on the sand, and she could even make out a couple of clam diggers trudging along with their buckets and shovels.

Still, she much preferred the view of Elliott Bay from her fifth-floor Seattle condo. Fortunately, she'd be able to return to the condo when her exile here was over. Her leaving coincided with her coworker Susan Jensen's need for new living quarters, and Susan had happily sublet Eva's unit. Plus, Susan said Eva could stay there whenever she returned to Seattle, something she looked forward to. She was homesick already.

"And this apartment is furnished," Mrs. Halsey said. "You won't find many furnished places around here."

Eva tore her gaze away from the view to focus on the lumpy maroon sofa and two stiff-looking chairs upholstered in 1950s lime-green. Once again, she thought of her condo, with the beige sectional couch she'd purchased from Sigma Design, the fashionable furniture store on Queen Anne Hill.

Still, Mrs. Halsey was right about the dearth

of furnished apartments in Willow Beach; Eva had searched all the ads she could find, and this was the only one offered.

There was always her father's house, which was now hers. She could live there until she finished cleaning out the place and put it on the market. She shook her head. Better to stay here in this dingy rental than to be surrounded by all the painful memories.

She turned to Mrs. Halsey. "All right, I'll take the apartment."

Mrs. Halsey beamed, then opened a file folder she'd been carrying under one arm. Extracting two sheets of paper, she handed them to Eva. "Here's the lease. First and last month's rent due up front."

"Of course." Eva scanned the lease, then signed her name to both copies. She gave one to Mrs. Halsey.

The older woman squinted at her signature. "Eva Sinclair." She looked up. "Are you Seb's daughter? Heard you were in town."

"Yes, that's me."

"Had to miss his memorial. Had to take care of my sick mother in Morganville." She slowly shook her head. "I'm sorry for your loss. Seb was a wonderful man."

"Thank you," Eva said. Was there anyone in this town who did not think her father wonderful?

"You're here to take over the *Herald,* then?" Mrs. Halsey tucked the lease into her file folder.

"Uh, no, just helping out for a while."

"Good to keep it in the family."

"Yes, well, I'd better start unloading my car," Eva said hurriedly, not wanting to continue a discussion that made her uncomfortable. She stuffed her copy of the lease into her purse and headed for the door.

TWO DAYS LATER, Eva sat at the kitchen table in her new apartment, lingering over toast and coffee and putting off reporting for work at the *Herald.* When she could delay no longer, she stacked her dishes in the sink and collected her purse from the bedroom. On the way out, she glanced in the mirror on the bathroom door. She smoothed her chocolate-brown top over her beige slacks and tucked an errant lock of hair into the faux-pearl clip at her nape. At home, she would've worn a skirt, but this outfit ought to do just fine for the *Herald*. From what she'd seen of the staff, she doubted the newspaper had a dress code.

Leaving her car in its designated spot behind her apartment, she headed for the *Herald*'s office on foot.

Willow Beach hadn't changed much, not the stores anyway. The window of Barnett's Drugstore still displayed the same duck holding a placard that said Get Your Prescriptions Filled Here. And she would swear Macon's Diner sported the very same café curtains in what was still an ugly black-and-white checker pattern. The Bon Ton Bakery still kept its door open, allowing enticing aromas to drift along the sidewalk.

Two blocks later, she arrived at the *Herald*, located between The Book Nook and Mac's Barbershop. As she placed her hand on the doorknob, her fingers froze. Then, filling her lungs with a deep breath, she opened the door and stepped inside.

The receptionist, whose name Eva remembered was April Hensen, looked up from her desk situated behind a semicircular counter. She had pale blond hair as fine as corn silk and high cheekbones any model would envy. Unfortunately, her checkered, sleeveless blouse was more appropriate for housecleaning than for meeting the public. Eva was right. The *Herald* had no dress code.

She shut the door and crossed the room. "Good morning, April." She hoped her cheerful tone sounded authentic rather than forced.

"Morning," April said in a flat voice. "I'll let Mark know you're here." She picked up the telephone and punched a button. "He'll be right out," she said when she'd hung up. She turned back to her computer.

Feeling more like a customer than the new coeditor, Eva gazed around. She hadn't taken much time to survey the place the night she'd arrived. The shock of Seb's death had preoccupied her.

The reception area was as drab as it had always been, with half a dozen molded plastic chairs bracketed by two small tables. In one corner, a terra-cotta tub held a tired-looking philodendron. She thought of *Seattle's Best*'s reception area and its elegant black leather sofa, matching side chairs and glass-topped coffee table with its bouquet of fresh flowers provided weekly by a local florist.

Spotting a stack of the latest edition of the *Herald* on the counter, she walked over and picked up a copy. Tabloid-size, with *Willow Beach Herald* printed in big letters across the top, the paper had at the most ten or twelve pages. Compared to *Seattle's Best,* a publication of at least fifty glossy pages, many in color, the *Herald* seemed hopelessly dull.

At the sound of footsteps, she turned to see Mark walking down the hallway. He wore his usual jeans and short-sleeved shirt—today's was blue—that showed off his tanned, muscular arms.

Mark's long-legged stride quickly brought him to her side. She thought he was going to reach out and shake her hand, and she braced herself for his touch. But he rested his hands on his slim hips and let his gaze sweep over her.

"Looks like you're all ready to go to work."

"That's what I'm here for," she said with the same forced cheerfulness she'd used on April. She had the feeling she'd be calling on that voice a lot in the coming days.

"Right. First, though, we have a little surprise for you."

Eva narrowed her eyes. "What do you mean?"

"Don't look so worried," he said with an

easy grin. "It's a nice surprise. In the staff room. You'll see." He glanced over his shoulder at April. "C'mon, April. You, too."

April frowned. "I need to be here to answer the phone."

"Did you forget about the extension in the staff room?"

"Oh, all right."

April stalked around her desk, arms hugging her slender waist, lower lip thrust out, and fell into step behind Eva as Mark led the way. Her flip-flops slapped on the tiles as she shuffled along.

Mark took them down the hallway, past the staff's cubicles—all empty, Eva noticed— to the employees' lounge. A yellow banner stretched across the ceiling. Welcome, Eva! proclaimed the bold red letters.

Eva stared. She hadn't expected anything like this on her first day. Unexpectedly, she choked up. Were they really welcoming her? Did they really want her to be here?

Several tables had been pushed together to make a large square. In the center sat a tray of doughnuts and a stack of red paper plates and yellow napkins. The scent of fresh-brewed coffee filled the air.

"I think you know everyone." Mark gestured to the three people standing near the tables.

"I do. You're Cody." She nodded at the tall twentysomething man wearing a T-shirt bearing the *Herald*'s logo and then turned to a stocky dark-haired man. "Bernie, in Advertising, right?" Bernie nodded. "And of course I know you, Dora Winters. You've been Dad's circulation manager forever."

She focused on the gray-haired woman, who barely came up to Bernie's shoulder. The yellow tote she clutched had knitting needles sticking out the top. "Still knitting, I see. How many scarves have you done?"

Dora smiled. "Too many to count. Good to see you again, Eva."

"Have a seat and dig into the doughnuts." Mark strode to the table and pulled out a chair, motioning to Eva. "Bon Ton Bakery's best. April picked them out. She's our official doughnut buyer. Aren't you, April?"

April scowled. "If you say so."

Ignoring the ill-humored response, Mark pointed to the chair. "Come on, Eva. Sit and enjoy."

Eva had no desire to add any food to her

already queasy stomach, but she dutifully sat. Mark picked up the plate of doughnuts and held it out. She selected one with white icing and sprinkles. He crossed the room to the coffeemaker and picked up a mug. "You take anything in your coffee?" he asked over his shoulder.

"Black is fine."

At home, she'd have stopped on her way to work to buy her favorite hazelnut latte. But she wasn't at home. She was in Willow Beach having coffee and doughnuts with her new staff. With the possible exception of Dora Winters, a staff that obviously wasn't any happier about her being here than she was.

Dora sat across from Eva and began adding stitches to her scarf. Bernie grabbed a mug that said World's Greatest Husband and stood behind Mark at the coffee urn. Cody pulled out his phone and studied the screen. April heaved a sigh and rolled her eyes.

Mark brought Eva's coffee and one for himself. Bernie joined them, then Cody and finally April, who sat as far away from Eva as she could.

Eva had to give Mark credit for trying to build a conversation, but each attempt drifted off into uncomfortable silence. She nibbled her doughnut and sipped her coffee.

Finally Cody looked at his wristwatch, and his eyes widened. "Hey, I've got a shoot scheduled. I need to get going." He grabbed his camera, jumped up and, with long-legged strides, headed for the door.

Chair legs scraped the tile floor as the others mumbled their excuses and fell in behind Cody. They disappeared out the door and down the hallway.

Eva glanced up at the banner. So much for a welcome. "Well, you tried," she said to Mark, forgetting to use her cheerful voice and resorting to sarcasm.

Mark rubbed the back of his neck. "They'll loosen up when they get to know you." He drained his coffee cup. "We'd better get you set up with an office."

"Right." Eva stood and carried her cup to the sink. This was going to be a long day.

## *CHAPTER FOUR*

"This is where I hang out." Mark pointed to the open doorway of a small office near the back of the building. He nodded at an adjacent closed door. "You can have this office." He stepped forward and put a hand on the knob.

"Wait," Eva said. "Isn't that my father's?"

"Yeah, it is…was."

Eva raised both hands. "No. No way am I going to use his office. Why don't you take his and I'll take yours?"

Mark frowned. "Why should I move, when you could just as well use his?"

Eva shook her head. "You're not hearing me. I said no."

They glared at each other.

Eva's heart thudded, but she wasn't going to back down. She didn't belong in that office. She would never belong there. A lump rose in her throat.

She swallowed and tried again. "Why don't you want to take my father's office now? You'll eventually be there anyway. Once I'm gone, you'll be on your own here."

"We don't know that for sure," Mark said.

"That still doesn't explain why you don't want to move into his office now."

"You haven't given me a reason why *you* won't take it," Mark pointed out.

No, and she wouldn't, either. Eva expelled an exasperated breath. "We're going around in circles."

"It's his or a corner of mine."

"What about the broom closet?"

"We don't have one."

"We do, too. I remember one down that way." She pointed to where the hallway angled off to the right.

Mark jutted out his chin. "Don't be ridiculous. The paper's editor working out of the broom closet?"

"Works for me."

Mark shook his head. "You are something else."

Neither said anything. Mark stared at the floor. Eva crossed her arms and tapped her foot. In one of the cubicles, a phone jangled.

Mark finally looked up. "Okay, there is one other possible place for you. We have an extra cubicle that freelancers use. You can park there."

"Where will the freelancers work?"

"I'll fix up a corner of Seb's office. Somebody will get some use out of it."

"All right."

Mark led her down the hall to the cubicle. Eva peered at it. About half the size of the one she had at *Seattle's Best,* it contained a desk with a computer and a phone and a two-drawer file cabinet. "Pretty basic, isn't it?"

Mark shrugged. "You had your choice."

"Okay, now that I have a place to park, as you put it, what am I supposed to do?"

"We need to discuss that. Come on into my office."

Mark's office was considerably larger than the cubicles but as simply furnished, with the exception of a high-backed black vinyl desk chair. Her father had had a chair just like that, she remembered. A worktable near the window held a stack of file folders and several books.

He directed Eva to a straight chair on the other side of his desk and then sank into his chair, swiveling around to face her. He picked up a copy of the *Herald* lying on the desktop. "Seen our latest issue?"

"I glanced at it when I first came in, but I haven't read it."

"Don't suppose you've seen any back issues, either." He picked up a thick file folder.

"Not a one."

"Didn't think so." He slid the newspaper and the folder in her direction. "Take a look. I think you'll find the paper has changed a lot since you worked here."

Eva laced her fingers together in her lap and, with studied patience, said, "I never worked here. I helped out summers when I was in high school. Opening the mail, mostly."

Mark shrugged dismissively. "Whatever."

Eva picked up the paper. She turned the pages, scanning the headlines: "Local School Board Loses Longtime Member," "Facts About Home Buying," "Traffic Increase Prompts Study."

Bor-ing. Aloud, she said, "Looks like quite a variety of articles."

"*News* articles. The *Herald* reports important happenings around town."

She met his stern gaze. "What are you trying to say, Mark? That what I write at *Seattle's Best* isn't news? What did you call my writing when we were in Lawrence's office? 'Fluff' pieces?"

"A publication like *Seattle's Best* has its place."

"But obviously a less prestigious place than a newspaper like the *Herald*."

Mark shook his head. "I'm not trying to pick a fight. I just wanted to make our mission clear."

"Trust me, you have," she said crisply.

Mark cleared his throat. "Getting back to your role here, I figured the closest to what you've been writing would be the Our Town column. Notices of club meetings, food drives, activities at the senior center, that sort of thing."

"Who's been doing that up to now?"

"One of our freelancers. A sweet lady named June Baker. She was very disappointed when I told her we wouldn't be needing her anymore."

"I don't want to take anyone's job. Isn't there something else I can do?"

"Besides the Our Town column? You can help me with the overall layout and editing.

And I'm sure we'll find some other tasks to keep you busy."

Eva raised an eyebrow. "So that's the main objective—keeping me busy?"

Mark ran a hand through his hair. "Come on, Eva. This is tough for both of us. You've given me the impression you don't want to become involved while you're here, that you're only marking time until your year is over." He studied her closely. "Am I off base on that?"

Eva looked away. "No, you're not."

"I'm trying to make the year as easy for you as I can. You want some other assignment, okay, you pick it."

"Never mind," she said. "I'll do the column."

They spent the next few minutes going over various routines and procedures. At last, Mark leaned back and said, "That about covers it. Any questions?"

"No. I'll go to my cubicle now."

"June's files are all there. They should help you get in the groove."

Before she could make her escape, voices sounded in the hallway, and a little girl burst into the room. Except for her white sandals, she was dressed all in pink: blouse, skirt and tights. Looped over one arm was a pink plastic purse with a large daisy stuck to the side.

"Daddy! Daddy!" Arms outstretched, she ran to Mark.

He swiveled away from his desk just in time for her to jump into his lap. "Hey, sweetheart! I didn't expect a visit from you today."

An older woman, presumably Sasha's caretaker, hurried into the office. "We're on our way to our ballet lesson," she said. "And she insisted on visiting first. She's her daddy's girl, that one."

"I'm always glad to see my girl." Mark bestowed a kiss on the child's forehead.

Eva had little experience with children, but judging by her impression of Sasha at Seb's memorial, the child was a charmer. She obviously had her father twisted around her little finger.

Eileen turned to Eva. "Your first day on the job, I bet. I'm Eileen."

Eva smiled. "Nice to meet you. I'm Eva."

"Heard you rented Lola Halsey's place. Seems strange, when you could be staying in Seb's house."

Eileen reached up to her topknot and adjusted the chopsticks, or whatever they were, that were stuck through it.

"I'll be getting the house ready to put on the market," Eva said.

"If you need an agent, see Morgan's Realty on Main Street. Jeb's my cousin. Tell him I sent you."

Eva smiled indulgently. "Thanks, Eileen, I'll make a note of that."

Mark turned Sasha around to face Eva. "You remember Eva from Mr. Seb's memorial, don't you, honey?"

Sasha beamed her luminous blue eyes on Eva. "Yes, I 'member."

"I remember you, too," Eva said. "How are you today?"

"Fine. I have a new purse." She pointed to the purse hanging over her arm.

"Very nice. It matches your outfit. I bet pink's your favorite color."

"Uh-huh." Sasha grinned shyly.

"She always has to be color-coordinated." Eileen favored her charge with a smile. "Not like me," she added, pointing to her orange blouse and red cardigan sweater.

"I like my outfits to match, too." Eva gestured at her brown shirt and slacks.

"You look pretty," Sasha said.

"Why, thank you."

"Hey, Sasha, I thought I heard your voice."

April Hensen, clutching a piece of paper in her hand, entered the room. Her flip-flops slapped across the floor as she headed for Mark's desk. Leaning down, she gave Sasha a hug.

As April straightened, her free hand brushed Mark's shoulder in a gesture that seemed intentional, rather than accidental. April always seemed to hover around Mark. Were they more than boss and employee?

Mark and April's relationship was no business, or concern, of hers.

"Here's the flyer for the picnic." April laid the paper on Mark's desk. She looked around wide-eyed. "I'm not interrupting anything, am I?"

"No problem, April." Mark lowered Sasha to the floor and turned his attention to the paper April had brought.

Sasha danced over to Eva. "Are you coming to the picnic?"

"What picnic is that?"

"The Fourth of July picnic. Huh, Daddy?" Sasha looked to Mark for confirmation.

Mark sat back in his chair. "Right, sweetie." He looked at Eva. "It's at the City Park and sponsored by the Chamber of Commerce. The entire town is invited. We're including these flyers in the next edition of the paper." He tapped the sheet in front of him. "We're covering the event, of course."

"You *have* to come," Sasha said. "There are games and prizes and fireworks!"

Eva didn't want to spend the Fourth of July—or any holiday—in Willow Beach. This occasion would be a good time to take Susan up on her invitation to stay in Seattle. "Yes, the picnic's always been a popular celebration. It sounds like fun, but I plan to go home that weekend."

Sasha's brow wrinkled. "Home?"

"To Seattle. That's where I really live."

"Eva's only here in Willow Beach for a year," Mark said. "Then she's going back to her home in Seattle." He turned back to Eva. "But about the picnic—you're writing the Our Town column, right?"

"Yes, but—"

"And doesn't the picnic sound like an event for your column?"

"Ordinarily. But it's the Fourth of July.

Won't that rate a front-page feature? And wouldn't that be you?"

She glanced at the others. Eileen and April had their gazes glued to Mark, anticipating his answer. Even Sasha, who'd been fussing with her purse, was now focused on her father.

Mark folded his arms and glared at Eva. She set her jaw and glared back.

Seconds passed. Finally, he shrugged. "Go to Seattle. We'll get along just fine without you." He turned away and shuffled some papers on his desk.

"I'd already made plans before I knew about the picnic," she felt obliged to say. True enough, even though she hadn't yet checked with Susan to see if that weekend would work for her, too. But Susan had said to come anytime, hadn't she?

"I wish you could come to the picnic," Sasha said.

"Never mind, honey." April patted Sasha's shoulder. "We'll have a good time."

Eileen grasped Sasha's hand. "We need to go, honey. We don't want to be late for your ballet lesson."

"Bye, Sasha." Eva waved. "Nice to see you again."

"Bye."

After Sasha and Eileen left, Mark turned to April. "Was there something else, April?"

"I need to talk to you." She rolled her eyes and tipped her head in Eva's direction.

Seizing the blatant hint as a chance to escape, Eva stood. "If you'll excuse me, I'll get to work."

"Have a seat, April." Mark nodded at the chair Eva had vacated.

April sidled to the chair and perched on the edge. The slight flush to her normally pale complexion sent tension rippling across his shoulders.

"What's on your mind?" he asked.

"I, um, thought you and Sasha might want to come to my place for dinner tonight. I'm making spaghetti, and my housemate has a night class at the junior college."

Yep, as he'd suspected, her reason for lingering was personal. "That's nice of you, April, but I'll be working late. I'll only have time to grab a bite at the deli."

April's forehead wrinkled. "Sasha could

come, though, couldn't she? She and I always have fun together."

"Sorry, I've already arranged for her to have dinner at Eileen's."

April lowered her gaze and shifted in her chair. "I hope things between us won't change now that Eva is here," she said in a low voice.

At the mention of an "us," Mark inwardly cringed. A few months ago, he and April had seen each other at a concert on the beach, and he'd invited her for a bite to eat afterward. Since then, she'd had the idea he was personally interested in her. As gently as he could, he'd tried to make it clear that wasn't the case. She was a valued employee and a good friend only, and he didn't want to hurt her feelings.

"I'm still your boss," he said carefully, "but Eva is a boss, too."

"I'll take orders from her if I have to," she said in a petulant tone. "But that's not what I meant. What about us?"

Mark spread his hands. "I've explained that I'm not ready for a new relationship. Don't take it personally."

April pushed out her lower lip. "It's been three years since your wife died. I'd think that would be long enough to wait before moving on."

Mark kept his voice firm. "I'll decide when I'm ready, okay? Now, what about your Police Beat column? I'll need your copy by the end of today."

April huffed, "I know when my deadline is."

After she left, Mark leaned back in his chair and took a deep breath. Dealing first with Eva and then with April had drained him of the energy and enthusiasm he usually brought to the job.

Seb created this mess, he realized, and for a moment, he shared some of Eva's resentment toward the man. Had he really thought Mark and Eva would get along and be able to keep the *Herald* running smoothly?

EVA SHIFTED FROM side to side in the green vinyl chair, trying to get comfortable. No luck; the seat part was too short for her long legs, and the wooden arms extended at an awkward angle so that her elbows kept falling off. The small TV set that had come with the furnishings was broadcasting the evening's news, but she wasn't watching. She was mulling over her first day on the job at the *Herald*. She'd read June Baker's files, which, as she'd suspected, were full of the kinds of articles that appealed to the citizens of a small town: local woman bank teller promoted to manager; high-school graduate awarded scholarship to prestigious school; local truckers lamenting the high cost of gasoline.

At lunchtime, instead of eating alone at one of the town's diners, she'd walked back to her apartment and made a tuna sandwich.

In the afternoon, Mark had emailed her an article from one of their freelancers to edit. The topic was a recent quilt show at the community center. Eva had to admit the accompanying photos were bright and colorful, but the article itself was, in her opinion, pedestrian. Still, she'd performed the best editing job she could do without drastically altering the text. When she'd ventured to suggest to Mark that the article was uninteresting, his response was that Lettie Snow, who'd written the piece, was, in *his* opinion, one of their most talented writers and suggested that if she thought she could do better, she was welcome to try.

This terse exchange had taken place in the hallway in hushed voices. Still, Eva had noticed Dora's and Bernie's heads popping up from their cubicles to see what was going on. She'd told Mark no, thank you, and marched back to her own cubicle.

After work, not feeling like cooking and not being much of a cook anyway, she'd stopped at the supermarket and bought the makings of a salad.

Now the evening stretched before her like a yawning hole. She'd never be able to last an entire year. Never.

At least she could escape for the Fourth of July weekend. She was sure Mark and the others no more wanted her at the picnic than she wanted to be there. Which reminded her that she'd better let Susan know she was coming.

She picked up her cell phone and punched her friend's number on the speed dial.

"How'd your first day go?" Susan asked when she came on the line and they'd exchanged greetings.

"Stressful, but I managed to make it through to the end. What's new at the magazine?"

"Rolling along at high speed, as usual. Today a bunch of us went to lunch at the Four Seasons."

"Oh, one of my favorite places."

"I know, and you were missed."

"Has anyone been hired to replace me yet?"

"Nope. Still interviewing."

"I'd like to think it's because my shoes are hard to fill," Eva joked.

Susan laughed. "No doubt."

They chatted for a few minutes, then Eva said, "Okay if I come up for the Fourth? Trying out my own guest room will be fun."

The silence that followed raised an alarm. Then Susan said, "Oh, Eva, I'm sorry, but my cousins Julie and Lanette are coming for the holiday. You could sleep on the sofa, though."

Eva pictured the curved sofa in her living room, comfortable to sit on but hardly suitable as a bed. "No, I don't think that would work."

"How about the weekend after that?"

"I really wanted to come for the Fourth."

"I don't know what to say, except I'm sorry."

They talked a few minutes longer and then

said goodbye. Eva punched off the call, heavy with disappointment.

Now, unless she wanted to hide out in her apartment or go someplace other than Seattle, she had no excuse for not attending the Willow Beach Fourth of July celebration.

# CHAPTER FIVE

IF THERE WAS ONE THING Eva wasn't going to give up with her move to the coast, it was exercise. At home, she belonged to a health club located in downtown Seattle, not far from the office, so she could stop in before or after work. Sometimes, she even squeezed in a short session during her lunch hour. The club had an indoor track, various exercise machines, a swimming pool and a hot tub. Everything she needed to stay fit.

Such a place was not to be found in Willow Beach. Knowing that, she'd brought a few weights to use in her apartment. For running, there was the outside track at the high school, but it was far enough away to require driving. That left the beach. The hard-packed sand near the water's edge provided a good running track and, best of all, it was only a couple blocks from her apartment.

After her third day at the newspaper, Eva

put on her jogging shorts, an oversize T-shirt and running shoes. She buckled on her waist pouch and tied a scarf around her head, then left her apartment and headed along the access road to the beach. Weaving through grass-topped dunes that rose and dipped like tiny mountains, she made her way to the shoreline. Overhead, seagulls searching for their supper swooped and cawed while shorebirds on stick legs dodged the breaking waves.

She stopped and took in the scene, memories rolling over her. When they were little, the beach had been a playground for her and Brett. Their mother would sit on a blanket and read while they waded in the water and dug in the sand and chased the seagulls. Years after that, Brett would race along the shore in the car their father bought for him. And now they were gone, all three of them. And she was back here in Willow Beach with only her memories.

Pushing away those troubling thoughts, she took a deep breath and started off, relishing the fresh air and cool sea breeze. The sun had dipped low in the sky, and the surrounding clouds promised a spectacular sunset. Other walkers and joggers were out today, and a few cars passed by, but given the beach's considerable breadth, there was room for them all.

A man jogging toward her caught her eye. Mark? She squinted across the expanse separating them. Yep, it was Mark. Oh, great. After spending the workday together, she didn't relish seeing him off-hours. She'd acknowledge him and keep running.

When they were almost abreast, Eva lifted her arm, but Mark skidded to a halt.

"Hey, Eva!"

Reluctantly, she broke her stride. "Mark. Didn't...expect to see you...here."

His sleeveless T-shirt showed off more of his arms than usual and his running shorts revealed legs just as strong as she'd imagined. She tried not to stare.

Mark puffed his cheeks and whooshed out a breath. "That...goes for me, too. Didn't know you were into running." His gaze swept her from head to toe. "Not that you aren't, uh, fit—"

She hid a smile. So he was checking her out, too. "I belong to a health club at home. No such thing here, though."

"There's always the track at the high school.

If I'm not there, I'm out here. Clears my head. And what better setting?" He made a sweeping gesture at their surroundings.

"I've always loved this beach," she admitted.

He propped his hands on his hips. "So, not everything about Willow Beach is a bummer."

"No, not everything."

Conversation died, yet neither made a move to resume running. Eva retied her scarf, wondering what kept her rooted to the spot.

Finally, she said, "Well, see you tomorrow." She took a step forward.

"Eva—"

She stopped and turned. "Yes?" Oh, man, she sounded so…eager. Where had that come from?

"How about I join you for the rest of your run and then we grab a cup of coffee or something? The Beach Café on Seaview Avenue has outdoor tables. It's a nice evening.…"

Spend more time with Mark, when she'd told herself moments ago she didn't even want to stop her jog to speak to him? Still, the prospect of returning to her drab apartment once her run was over held little appeal. Why not accept his invitation?

She tilted her head and adopted a teasing tone. "I don't know…. Think you can keep up with me?"

He lifted his chin. "I'm not worried. Are you?"

"Not in the least. You're on."

"Okay. The café's in the direction you're headed." He pointed down the beach. "My car's at that end, too, and when we're finished, I'll give you a lift home."

She wasn't sure about the lift-home part, but she'd worry about that when the time came. She nodded, and they started off. Despite her bragging, Mark's stride challenged her, but she kept up well enough to earn an admiring glance or two.

After a while, he slowed and pointed toward a pile of driftwood above the tide line. "How about taking a break?"

"Tired already?" she teased.

"Nope. Just thought watching the sun set would be nice."

She glanced toward the horizon, where the sun blazed a brilliant trail of orange and yellow as it slid toward the sea. "Okay. Looks like it's going to be a good show."

She jogged with him to the driftwood. After taking a few minutes to stretch and cool down, they sat side by side on one of the logs. The lowering sun spread its glow through drifting clouds and along the horizon while the outline of a freighter appeared and disappeared with the undulation of the waves.

Mark leaned back and propped his elbows on the log behind them. "How far do you usually run?"

"A couple miles. At home, there's an interurban trail I use or, if it's raining, I run a track at the health club."

"So that's how you keep in such good shape."

She laughed. "Thanks. You're not so bad yourself." She slid a sideways glance down the muscles of his outstretched legs all the way to the heels of his black-and-white running shoes. Nice. "Is running your main exercise?" she asked.

He picked up a stick of driftwood and idly poked the sand. "That and hiking. Ever do any?"

She shook her head. "Unless you call trekking up and down Seattle's hills hiking."

He tossed back his head and laughed. "Hey, I've seen those hills and that qualifies. But around here are some spectacular spots. There's a trail from the beach up to the lighthouse that I like, and another up on the bluff overlooking the town. I've got Sasha started. She's a real little trouper, backpack and all."

"I bet you two have a lot of fun together."

"We do. She's my pal. Hey, there goes the sun."

Eva focused on the horizon as the sun disappeared into the sea. The afterglow spread like liquid gold across the sky. "Beautiful."

"Knew it would be. How about getting that drink now?"

At the Beach Café, they chose an outdoor table shaded with an umbrella, although the protection was not needed now that a soft dusk had settled over the town. A waiter dressed in black shorts and a red T-shirt that said Beach Boy across the front trotted out to take their orders.

"I'll have a tall latte, nonfat," Eva said.

"Plain coffee for me," Mark added.

"You don't like the fancy stuff?" she asked when the waiter moved off.

"Once in a while," he admitted. "But most of the time I'm a plain-black-coffee man." He gestured at their surroundings. "So what do you think of this place? It's new since you've lived here."

"Impressive."

"Willow Beach is catering more and more to tourists."

She nodded at the people strolling by. "I have noticed more summer visitors than I remember. I always thought the town was just a bump in the road where people had to slow down on their way to Oceanside."

He leaned back and propped his ankle on the opposite knee. "Some people would like to make Willow Beach into another Oceanside. But not me. I'm all for promoting tourism, and I know visitors bring in tax dollars, but all those high-rises have ruined Oceanside." He tilted his head. "Since you're from the big city now, tall buildings probably appeal to you. I bet you even live in one."

"Guilty as charged. I live in a fifth-floor condo on Queen Anne Hill. But you can't really compare Oceanside to Seattle. They're two entirely different types of city."

"The idea is the same."

"Some cities don't know where to draw the line."

He nodded. "That's it exactly, where to draw the line."

Mark's voice had an edge that had been missing during their conversation on the beach. She mulled that over while the waiter placed their coffees on the table and they took their first sips.

"Speaking of growth," Mark said, eyeing her, "we've had some interesting city-council meetings on the subject. I usually attend, but why don't you take a shot at it?"

A Willow Beach City Council meeting? That sounded about as exciting as a visit to a slug farm. "I'd hate to encroach on your territory."

He lifted a shoulder. "I just thought you might find it interesting, challenging maybe, to do something different from what you do at *Seattle's Best*."

She leveled him a gaze. "I thought you gave me the Our Town column so that I'd be doing something similar."

"True, the column comes closest to what you were doing in Seattle. But most of what we publish at the *Herald* is news of importance, news that really matters. That was your father's intention and one that I agree with and intend to uphold. Thought you might like to contribute to that—just for a change."

She gave her latte a rapid stir with the straw. "And picking a good restaurant or a movie or a hotel doesn't matter?"

"Depends on your purpose. Like I said, our purpose is news. News that's relevant to our readers."

Eva wished she'd heeded the voice telling her not to accept Mark's invitation for coffee. "I'll skip the city-council meetings," she said. "Unless you're ordering me to go."

He drew back as though insulted.

"Of course not. We're coeditors. I'm only suggesting."

In the silence that followed, Eva focused on the passing scene—cars driving by, their headlights beaming now that darkness had fallen; people drifting in and out of the restaurant; the waiter weaving among the tables, trays of food and drink balanced aloft. After a while, she risked a glance at Mark. He was looking away, but his profile, with furrowed brow and set jaw, left no question about his mood.

She drained her coffee, then pushed away the cup. "I'd better be going ho—" She stopped, then finished, "To my apartment."

He turned and said in a flat tone, "Sure, Eva. Let's go."

She dug into her waist pouch and pulled out a few bills.

Mark reached into his back pocket for his wallet. "Put your money away. This is on me."

"Thanks, but let's split it." Eva placed some bills on the tray the waiter had left with the check.

Mark frowned but said nothing as he added his money to hers.

When they were out on the sidewalk, Mark gestured up the street. "My car's half a block that way."

"You live at the south end of town, right?"

"Yeah, near the high school."

"Then giving me a lift is out of your way."

"A dozen blocks—"

"—on foot would be a good way for me to finish my exercise."

He opened his mouth as though to argue,

then said coolly, "Okay. Then I'll see you at work tomorrow."

"Right. At work."

Eva turned on her heel and headed off down the street. Walking to her apartment took fifteen minutes, and when she arrived she found the first-floor mall closed, with the door locked. Using her key to gain admittance, she passed the dimly lit antiques shops and art galleries and climbed the stairs to the second floor. When she opened her door to the sorry sight of mismatched furniture and dingy walls, a moan escaped her lips.

Then she steeled herself, took a deep breath and crossed the threshold. She went to her wall calendar, picked up a pencil and, with a deep sigh, crossed off another day.

"Can I have another cookie, Daddy?"

Mark looked at Sasha sitting beside him at the kitchen table and then at the plate of oatmeal cookies Eileen had sent home for their evening snack. "You sure have a sweet tooth. How 'bout we split one?"

Diane had liked sweets, too. She always kept the cookie jar full. Not with cookies she made, but with ones she bought from Bon Ton

Bakery. Diane wasn't much of a cook, not for lack of skill but for lack of interest. She had her sights set higher, she'd said. Yeah, and look where that got her. Dead at the bottom of a canyon.

Bitterness welled up inside Mark, followed by the sad, empty feeling he'd had since her death. He pushed the troublesome emotions aside and picked up a cookie. Breaking it in half, he handed one piece to Sasha.

"Be sure to drink your milk." He pointed to her half-full glass.

"I will." Sasha took a bite of the cookie, then dutifully sipped her milk.

"Did you have fun with Grammy Eileen today?"

"Uh-huh. She took me to the library story hour."

"That's nice."

Sasha launched into a retelling of one of the stories. Mark tried to listen, but his attention wandered to his time with Eva. When he'd first spotted her tonight, he'd had trouble not staring. Her curves were in all the right places, her legs long and shapely. He couldn't help being enticed, had been from the moment he set eyes on her that first night she'd come to town.

He didn't want to feel any attraction. He didn't want to get involved again. Not yet. His wounds were still raw, his trust destroyed. Besides, Eva would be here for only the year required by Seb's will. Then she'd head back to the big city.

So why had he asked her to have coffee with him? He'd told himself he could use the opportunity to discuss her job at the newspaper. If he were honest, he'd admit that was only part of the reason. He also just wanted to spend time with her.

Realizing the mistake he'd made hadn't taken long. She hated everything about being in Willow Beach. She hated the newspaper, the town, him.

How there could still be sparks between them, he didn't know.

But there were.

He didn't want to become personally involved. He wanted her gone. He realized that was also wishing away a whole year of his and Sasha's lives, but so be it.

Yet Eva had a fine mind and a talent for journalism. He'd read some of her articles in

*Seattle's Best.* Although he thought what she wrote about was a waste of time, he admired her way with words, her often humorous approach to a subject. Why couldn't she apply her talent to newspaper journalism? He'd bet she could turn out some really good solid *reporting*—if she made the effort.

Sasha tugged on his arm. "Did you ever hear that story when you were a little boy? Miss Jacobs, the librarian, says it's an old, old story."

Mark jolted back to the present. "What? I'm sorry, honey. I was, ah, thinking about work." True enough.

"The story about how the leopard got its spots."

Instead of thinking about Eva, he should pay attention to Sasha. This was supposed to be their quality time together.

"Tell me again, would you?" he said.

This time, he listened, and when she finished, they laughed together. Then he asked, "What would you like to do this evening? We could play a game."

Sasha's blue eyes lighted. "Okay, and then watch TV?"

"I guess," he said reluctantly.

"I know, it has to be ed-u-ca-shun-al."

Mark laughed. "Right. Why don't you pick out one of your games while I clean up the kitchen? How about Go Fish? Remember, Mommy gave you that game for Christmas."

Sasha's brow wrinkled. "She did? No, I don't 'member."

"Well, she did. It's in the cupboard with your other games. Go get it, and later we'll see what's on TV."

"Okay…" Sasha looked thoughtful. "Daddy, do you think Eva's pretty?"

Mark's mouth fell open. "Uh, why are you asking?"

"I don't know. I just thought it."

Mark had to smile. In typical childlike fashion, she often jumped from one topic to another. He just hadn't expected the conversation to bounce from Mommy to Eva.

"Do you think she's pretty?" he countered, not wanting to be put on the spot.

"I really do. And her clothes are pretty, too. She dresses different."

"She's used to dressing up more than we are."

"Do you like her, Daddy?"

Mark picked up Sasha's empty plate and

stacked it on top of his. "Why all these questions about Eva?"

She shrugged her thin shoulders. "I dunno. But I like her. I hope she comes to the picnic."

He added their glasses to the stack of plates. "I think you can forget about that."

Sasha's mouth turned down. "Doesn't she like us?"

He wanted to say, *No, she doesn't*. But he wanted to protect Sasha's feelings.

"Don't you remember that when we were in my office the other day she said she was going to Seattle for the Fourth?"

"Oh, yes, I 'member."

"Everybody you like will be at the picnic. April, Bernard and Maria, and Bella." Bella was Bernard and Maria's daughter and a good friend of Sasha's.

Sasha jumped from her chair. She turned to him and raised her arms. "I love you, Daddy."

Mark leaned over and drew her into an embrace. She meant the world to him. "I love you, too, baby."

They exchanged pecks on the cheek. He let her go and watched her skip off to the living room. He finished clearing the table and put the dishes in the dishwasher. He took the leftover cookies to the clown cookie jar, lifted the polka-dot hat that served as the lid and placed them inside.

The cookie jar had been one of Diane's purchases. He remembered the occasion well. They'd taken Sasha to a circus in a neighboring town. Sasha had loved the clowns, and shortly after that Diane came home with the cookie jar she'd found in a secondhand store.

Those were good times. He'd thought they were anyway. Apparently, Diane hadn't shared his feelings. But he'd kept the cookie jar, as he'd kept so many of her things. Next time he and Sasha had cookies, he'd remind her where the jar had come from, just as he'd reminded her about the Go Fish game. He didn't want her to forget her mommy.

## CHAPTER SIX

Eva stood in front of the *Herald*'s bulletin board gazing at the sign-up sheet for Saturday's Fourth of July picnic at City Park. Should she add her name or not? She'd made no other plans. She could go out of town by herself, but what fun would that be? Or she could hide out in her apartment, but two solid days of confinement would drive her crazy.

Finally she picked up the pencil hanging by a string and added her name to the list. The occasion was a potluck, so she would have to bring something.

The notice said the company supplied the chicken and hot dogs, leaving the side dishes for the staff to bring. Scanning the contributions, she decided on a salad. She had a recipe for a pasta salad Chef Marko had given her when she'd interviewed him for an article. But when she went to the market to buy the ingredients, she couldn't find all of them. Oh, well. What she did find would have to do.

In her apartment, she stared at the array of ingredients with a sinking feeling. She couldn't do this. She didn't want to do this. Nevertheless, she rolled up her sleeves and went to work.

A couple hours later, with trepidation, she dug a fork into the salad. The pasta wasn't as al dente as Chef Marko's, and the absence of capers left it with no zing, but it wasn't bad. She scooped it into a bowl and covered it with plastic wrap.

The following day, she stood in front of her closet. Because it was the Fourth of July, she decided to wear navy slacks, a red-and-white-striped T-shirt and wedge-heeled sandals. Maybe a little fancy for Willow Beach, but looking good would lift her spirits. Instead of pulling her hair back, as she usually did, she let it fall in soft waves around her shoulders.

She packed up her salad and drove to City Park. The lot was nearly full, but she managed to find a spot, then headed down the main path to find the *Herald*'s pavilion.

The park hadn't changed much since she'd

lived in Willow Beach. Asphalt paths wound through grassy expanses where evergreen trees towered over oaks and maples. Smoke from barbecue pits curled into the air, and the sounds of voices and laughter mingled with music from radios and CD players. Many of the shelters were decorated with red, white and blue streamers. American flags planted along the walkway waved in the breeze.

She passed the spots reserved for Bon Ton Bakery, Barnett Drugstore, where she nodded to Hal Barnett, and Macon's Diner. Farther on, she saw a few more familiar faces, including an old friend of her mother's and the Coltons, a couple who lived in her old neighborhood. Her high-school friend Fran Oliver and her family shared a pavilion with several other couples. They called out greetings. As they'd promised at Seb's memorial, Eva and Fran had met for coffee. Eva had enjoyed talking to her friend until they got to reminiscing and Fran told a funny story about Brett. Reminders of her brother were always painful.

At last Eva reached the newspaper's pavilion. She spotted Sasha and a dark-haired girl of about the same age tossing a large red ball. A golden retriever pranced around them, eager to join the game.

Mark and a blonde woman stood over the smoking barbecue pit. The woman turned, and Eva saw that it was April. Of course. The receptionist hovered over Mark as though afraid he were going to disappear.

Dora and two other women stacked paper plates, cups, napkins and utensils on a wooden picnic table. A group of men, talking and laughing, clustered around several ice chests. She recognized Bernie, who was snapping open sodas and handing them around.

Realizing what an outsider she was, Eva stopped in her tracks. Coming today was a mistake. Maybe she could turn around and sneak away before anyone saw her. Clutching her bowl, she took a step backward.

Just then, Mark looked up from the barbecue. He peered at her through the smoke as though she were a ghost. "Eva?"

Eva sighed. Too late to escape now. She straightened her shoulders and stepped forward.

Mark waved a spatula at the others. "Hey, everybody, Eva's here."

Silence fell over the group as all eyes turned

in her direction. Then someone said, "Hi, Eva," and the others chimed in with their greetings.

Sasha threw down the red ball and ran to her. "You came." She grabbed Eva's free hand.

"Yes, I did." Eva curled her fingers around Sasha's and experienced a surge of affection.

"You look pretty," Sasha said.

"Thank you. So do you." Sasha wore pink pedal pushers, a T-shirt decorated with a teddy bear and matching pink tennis shoes. The outfit was just what Eva would have worn at that age.

"Daddy took me to BuySmart yesterday," Sasha said, swinging their hands. "The outfit is for my birthday. It isn't for a couple weeks, but he said I could have this present early for the picnic today."

"I remember hearing about your birthday. You're turning six."

"Yes. Daddy says I'm growing up too fast, but I don't think so."

The dark-haired child Sasha had been playing ball with approached. The dog trailed behind her.

"Who's your friend?" Eva asked.

"This is Bella." Sasha slung her free arm

around the girl's shoulders. "And the dog's Goldie."

"They both belong to Bernie and Maria." Mark gestured to a petite dark-haired woman coming toward them.

Maria had large dark eyes and full red lips, and a halo of black curls framed her face. She held out her arms to Eva. "I'll put your salad in the cooler," she said in a soft, slightly accented voice.

"Thanks." Encouraged by Maria's shy smile, Eva handed over her bowl.

"Come on," Mark said. "I'll take you around, make sure you know everybody. How about Dora's husband, Josh?" He led her to a white-haired man who was unwrapping hot dogs for the grill.

"Sure, I remember Josh," Eva said.

"Good you could come today," Josh said with a smile and a nod.

The Winters had brought Dora's niece and her husband, who lived in a neighboring town. Cody Jarvis had invited his roommate, Mike, who worked for the post office. Cody was busy photographing the event, but stopped long enough to nod at Eva. A couple of the paper's freelance writers were there, as were a woman who had a pet-sitting service and a retired man whose specialty was gardening.

"Hey, Mark." From her post at the grill, April called out, "The coals are ready. Better get the chicken on."

"I'll be right there."

"Anything I can do?" Eva asked.

"Just make yourself comfortable," Mark said as he headed for the barbecue. "And help yourself to a soda."

The rest of the men had moved off to watch a horseshoe game. Eva opened one of the ice chests and took out a bottle of water. She gazed around, trying to decide what to do next. Everyone was busy. A few people glanced her way, but no one invited her to join them. She perched on a picnic bench and pasted a smile on her face. This was going to be a long day.

Just as she was about to get up and walk around the park, Sasha and Bella, accompanied by Goldie, danced over.

Sasha smiled up at Eva. "Come for a walk with us."

"That's just what I was thinking of doing," Eva said. "Where are you going?"

"Over there." Sasha pointed to a bandstand

in the distance, half hidden by evergreens. "My dad said it's okay."

"All right." Anything was better than sitting alone. Besides, she liked Sasha. She was cute and lively. And unlike her father, she didn't pass judgment on Eva about what she did—or didn't do—for the *Herald*.

Sasha grasped one of Eva's hands, and Bella grabbed the other. As they walked along, the girls chattered about kids they knew, games they played and the upcoming fireworks display. The dog stopped here and there to sniff around and then scampered to catch up.

They reached the bandstand. Streamers of red, white and blue decorated the structure, and small flags lined the railing. Three men and a woman dressed in patriotic colors were setting up their instruments.

"There's a dance later," Sasha said. "You can dance with my dad."

The thought of being in Mark's arms brought sudden warmth to Eva's cheeks. "I won't be staying that long."

"You have to stay for the fireworks." Sasha jumped up and down.

"We brought Goldie's carrier," Bella said,

patting the dog. "'Cause she might get scared and run away."

"That was a good idea," Eva said, still dealing with the idea of her and Mark dancing.

"Do you have a dog?" Sasha asked.

"Not now. I used to, though."

Eva thought of Billy, the family's wire-haired fox terrier. She'd begged her parents for a dog. Her mother had said yes, but Seb had said no, and his word was always final. Then Brett decided he wanted a dog, and one day Seb brought Billy home. Although her brother soon lost interest, Eva and Billy had bonded immediately. He followed her everywhere. She taught him to sit and stay and to fetch balls and sticks. They'd had a great relationship until Billy passed away at the age of twelve.

"You could get another one."

Sasha's voice interrupted Eva's musings. She shook her head to clear the memories. Now was not the time to dwell on the past. Yet, here in Willow Beach, the past was sometimes more real than the present.

"We're going to let Goldie have babies," Bella put in. "You could have one."

Eva smiled at the little girl. "Thanks, but

having a pet now is not a good idea. I need to wait until I get settled."

"What does 'get settled' mean?" Sasha's brow wrinkled.

"That I won't be living here always. Next year at this time, I'll be leaving Willow Beach and returning to Seattle."

Sasha put a finger to her lips. "Oh, I 'member. That's what Daddy said."

Eva wondered what else Sasha's daddy might have said about her.

"My auntie Sofie left," Bella said. "And my momma cried."

"Will you cry when you leave?" Sasha asked Eva.

"Uh, maybe." Eva hedged. "Look, they've turned on the lights. Aren't they pretty?" She pointed to the bandstand, where one of the musicians had switched on the red, white and blue lights attached to the railing.

By the time they returned from their walk, the food was ready. Eva spied her pasta salad among the other dishes lined up on one of the tables.

April rushed up to Sasha. "I'll help you with your food."

"I want to do it myself," Sasha said.

April frowned. "You can't reach everything."

"Then Eva can help me. Can't you, Eva?" Sasha's blue eyes were pleading.

Eva was considering how she would respond when Mark appeared.

"I've got your food ready, Sasha." He held out a plate with a hot dog, potato salad and a few carrot sticks.

That settled that. Eva walked over to the buffet. Everything looked appetizing, and her stomach rumbled in anticipation. She dished up barbecued chicken, baked beans and fresh veggies and dip. Now for some of her salad.

Bernie peered into her bowl and wrinkled his nose. "What's this?"

"That's mine," Eva said with a touch of pride. "It's penne pasta."

"Penny pasta? You mean it costs one cent?"

Eva laughed politely. "It's a recipe from a Seattle chef who's a friend of mine."

"Seattle, huh? That explains it—the fancy name anyway." Bernie dug his spoon into the dish and came up with a glob of stuck-together pasta, cheese and bits of lettuce garnish. He tapped the spoon on his plate several times before the mixture fell off.

Eva's spirits hit a new low. Still, when her turn came, she loaded her plate with a generous serving.

Mark waved her over to the table where he and Sasha and April—of course—had claimed seats. When Eva tasted her salad, the strong tang of vinegar almost made her cough. Yuck. She must have misread the recipe.

"You don't have to eat my salad," she whispered to Mark.

"Sure I do." He took a bite—and almost choked.

April smirked.

After dinner, the games resumed. Horseshoes were out for Eva because she'd ruin her sandals in the dirt. The children ran races, and some of the adults headed off to the volleyball court. No one invited her to join them. She offered to help the women clean up, but they had their own system of who did what and waved her away.

She grabbed her salad, now a congealed mass of pasta, lettuce and dressing, marched over to the garbage can and dumped out the mess. So much for her efforts.

Now would be a good time to make her escape. No one would miss her for the rest of the evening. If she wanted to see the fire-works, she could watch from her apartment.

She was about to leave when the strains of "Stars and Stripes Forever" floated on the air, and Sasha and Bella ran to her side.

Sasha grabbed Eva's hand. "The music's started. Come listen."

"I should be getting back to my apartment," Eva said.

"No, no, stay." Sasha's brow puckered. "Please?"

Who could resist those big blue eyes? "Well...all right. Not for long, though. I need to go soon."

"Why?"

"I'm tired. It's been a long day."

"I'm not tired," Bella said. "We could dance all night, huh, Sasha?"

"Yeah, we could." Sasha skipped ahead, tugging Eva along.

Eva had to laugh at the girls' enthusiasm. "Okay, let me get my purse and we'll go."

In the shuffle to grab a seat on the metal

folding chairs, Eva ended up with Mark on one side and Sasha and Bella on the other. April claimed the seat on Mark's other side. For a while they listened to the music and watched couples swirl around the dance floor. Then Sasha jumped up and grabbed Bella's hand. "C'mon, Bella, let's dance."

The two girls raced up the steps to the gazebo. April nudged Mark. "Why don't we dance?"

"Uh, sure, April." Mark turned to Eva. "Will you excuse us?"

"Of course. Go." She flapped her hands at them.

Mark and April soon joined the other dancers and disappeared into the crowd. Eva caught occasional glimpses of Sasha and Bella, holding hands and prancing around the floor.

Her thoughts drifted back to the Fourth of July party she'd attended last year. The event was held in Medina, an exclusive residential area bordering Lake Washington. After an elegant salmon barbecue, the guests boarded their hosts' yacht and cruised out on the lake to witness the fireworks display.

Sadness engulfed Eva. Seattle was her home. She'd worked hard to make a place for herself there, far away from Willow Beach and the painful memories. Tears burned her eyes. Seeing the girls approach, she hastily brushed them away.

While Bella joined her parents, Sasha approached Eva. "Will you dance with me?"

"I, uh, I should be heading to my apartment."

"Oh, not yet. Please." Sasha's eyes sparkled. "It'll be fun."

Eva had to smile. Once again, Sasha's wide blue eyes begged in a way that was impossible to refuse. "Okay, okay."

She followed the little girl onto the dance floor. Over the heads of the crowd, Eva glimpsed Mark dancing with April. Before she could look away, he caught her eye. His smile appeared genuine and made her feel suddenly warm inside. Eva smiled back. Then she clasped Sasha's hands, and they began their dance. Her shoulder purse bounced clumsily against her side, but no way would she leave it unattended or ask someone to watch it while she danced.

When the song ended, Mark, with April close behind, wove his way through the crowd toward them. He gazed down at his daughter. "So, Sasha, is Eva a good dancer?"

Sasha nodded. "She is. You dance with her, Daddy."

Eva took a step backward. "Oh, no, I—" But Sasha—and Bella, who had suddenly appeared—jumped behind Mark and pushed him toward Eva.

"Hey, kids." Mark threw up his hands.

Eva raised her arms, too, intending to create a distance between them. They both miscalculated. His arms flailed, then settled on her waist. Her hands came to rest on his shoulders.

Her purse landed between their chests.

Mark looked down and then back up at Eva. "Do you ever go anywhere without this…this *appendage?*"

"Not many places, no. If you want to dance with me, it's part of the package."

"Let's get it out of the way, at least." He pushed the purse to one side, took her in his arms and swung them into the flow of the other dancers.

Eva gazed at the band, the festive streamers and the lights, bright now in the soft twilight—anywhere but at Mark.

Yet she was all too aware of him. His masculine scent, his muscular shoulders, his hand firmly planted around her waist.

More couples trooped onto the floor, pressing in on them. Mark drew her closer. She should have pulled away, but she didn't. Instead, she thought about laying her head on his shoulder and, if she moved her hand only an inch or so, running her fingers through the fringe of thick hair brushing his collar.

After a while, Mark stopped dancing. Eva looked around and realized they were in a dark corner of the bandstand, in a little pocket of space all their own.

"Eva…"

His voice was low and husky. She looked up, met his gaze. Even in the dim light she could see the gleam in his eyes. Then his eyelids lowered and his lips parted. Again, she knew she should pull away. And again, she didn't. She stayed where she was and let Mark kiss her.

The kiss was warm and sweet. She closed her eyes and gave herself up to it as time and place faded from her awareness. For all she knew—or cared—they could have been spinning in space.

The end of the song jolted Eva to her senses. She opened her eyes and blinked, bringing the world into focus again. Had she really just kissed Mark Townson? Was she out of her mind?

She stepped back and pushed him away. "What do you think you're doing?" she demanded.

He shook his head, as though coming back to awareness. "That shouldn't have happened."

"You're darn right it shouldn't." She ran her fingers over her lips, still tingling from the kiss.

Mark spread his hands. "It won't happen again, I promise you. I'll take you back now." He reached out to grasp her elbow.

She jumped out of his reach. "I don't want to go back with the others. I'm quite ready to leave."

"Then I'll walk you to your car."

"No. I'll go by myself." She had to get away from him.

"Eva, I feel terrible about this—"

"Just forget it ever happened."

Luckily, the gazebo's back stairs were

nearby. Gripping the railing, she hurried down the steps. Glad for the cover of darkness, she sped along the maze of paths, past pavilions lit by lanterns, where the scents of barbecue and roasted corn lingered in the air, past all the talking and the laughter, until she reached the parking lot. She jumped into her car, drove out of the lot and didn't stop until she reached her apartment.

A while later, Eva stood at her front window, watching the fireworks explode with bursts of color into the night sky. Mark was watching the display with Sasha and, of course, April. She pictured him sitting between them, an arm around each of them.

If only she'd gone to Seattle, she and Mark wouldn't have danced tonight, wouldn't have kissed.

Maybe she shouldn't have run away. Mark might take her sudden flight as an indication their kiss had meant something.

Did it?

Of course not. The kiss meant nothing. As fireworks continued to blaze across the sky, Eva kept shaking her head. No, no, no. Nothing.

"EARTH TO MARK."

April's voice penetrated Mark's beleaguered brain as he drove her and Sasha home from the picnic. He'd been thinking about Eva. He took his gaze from the road long enough to shoot April a glance. A passing streetlight revealed a suspicious glint in her eyes. Could she have seen him and Eva sharing that kiss on the dance floor? He didn't think so because they'd been in a dark corner, away from the crowd. Still, April had been his shadow all evening. What he'd said about there being no "us" seemed not to have sunk in.

"Sorry. What did you say?"

April leaned over the console, sending a whiff of her perfume in his direction.

"I asked what you thought of the fireworks display."

"Spectacular. The committee went all-out this year, didn't they?"

If he were to tell April the truth, he'd have to admit the fireworks in the sky tonight paled in comparison to those that exploded inside him when he kissed Eva. Holding her in his arms, hovering only inches away from her sweet mouth, had been more than he could take. He'd had to kiss her.

Even though she'd brought him down to earth with a jolt, he'd climbed right back on that cloud her kiss had put him on. He hoped she'd arrived home okay. Despite her protests, he should have walked her to her car.

"Sasha liked them."

April again. "Huh?"

"The fireworks. Mark, what's wrong with you?"

"Nothing, nothing." Mark peered through the windshield, looking for the turn for April's street.

"You've been kind of goofy ever since Eva left the picnic. What happened between you two?"

"Nothing!"

April jerked back. "Okay, you don't have to jump all over me. Besides, if you keep yelling, you'll wake Sasha." She nodded over her shoulder to where Sasha slept in the backseat.

"Sorry, April. I'm just tired. Been a long day."

"We had a nice time, though, didn't we?" Her voice softened.

"Sure."

"I appreciate your giving me a ride home."

She'd told Mark her housemate, Heather,

had brought her to the party but couldn't take her home. Mark suspected she'd planned to get stuck, hoping he'd offer his services. Sure enough, when they reached the house the two young women shared, Heather's car was parked in the driveway.

April touched her fingers to her lips. "I guess Heather's plans changed. Oh, well, I'd rather have ridden with you anyway." She leaned toward him, her long hair swinging forward to graze his arm.

He flinched, and his foot hit the gas pedal, gunning the motor. "See you Monday."

Her mouth tightened. Then she fluttered her eyelids and, in honeyed tones, said, "Right. I always look forward to work, Mark."

"Good to know, April."

Finally on his way again, Mark sucked in a deep breath, but the back of his neck ached from tension. When Eva had arrived at the picnic, he was glad because her presence would help to bridge the gap between her and the rest of the staff.

But he knew his feelings went deeper than that. He sensed Eva's did, too. She couldn't have responded to his kiss the way she had tonight and not be attracted to him.

What would happen if they followed their feelings?

He huffed a breath. Was he insane? He and Eva had no business messing around with kisses or any other kind of personal interaction. The only business they had together was newspaper business.

There was another, more important reason to not become involved with Eva. Sasha. He glanced in the rearview mirror. She was fast asleep, her chin resting on her chest, blond curls feathering one cheek.

Sasha was taken with Eva, and Eva seemed to like Sasha, too, but a bond between them would be dangerous. Sasha had already lost one important woman in her life. He didn't want to risk her losing another.

# *CHAPTER SEVEN*

EVA SAT AT her desk reviewing an article by one of their freelancers, an elderly woman who chronicled her experiences as a grandmother in a weekly column. Not the kind of thing Eva would read by choice and certainly not what she was used to editing, but the writing had a clever humor that made her smile.

Mark stuck his head in the cubicle doorway. "Do you have Bertha's article ready yet?"

His curt tone grated on her nerves. Since the Fourth of July picnic, they'd avoided each other. When they had to interact, communication on both sides was short and to the point.

"I'm working on it now." She nodded at the computer screen and kept typing.

"I needed it Friday."

"I didn't get it until today."

"A reminder to Bertha might have helped."

She stopped typing and swung around to

face him. "She's been writing this column for years," she snapped. "She didn't need a reminder—she had an excuse. Her husband was in the hospital having emergency surgery."

He straightened and took a step backward. "Oh, I didn't know—" Then his chin shot up. "Okay, get it to me as soon as you can."

"Yes, sir." She gave a little salute.

"And here are some assignments to consider." Instead of entering her cubicle, he leaned in only far enough to slide a paper onto her desk.

She glanced at it. "Assignments?"

"Right. You do work here, don't you?"

"Uh, as an editor."

"We're a small outfit, in case you hadn't noticed."

She sat back and folded her arms. "Oh, I've noticed all right."

"We editors do double duty. And since I know more about what's going on in this town than you do, it falls to me to come up with, for want of a better word, assignments."

"Okay, so what are they?" She picked up the paper and studied it. "'Attending the upcoming city-council meeting.' Hmm, we discussed that, and I said pass. 'New store opening in the mini-mall.' Hmm, that ought to be exciting. 'Groundbreaking ceremony for the new homeless shelter.'" She paused to look up. "Are you sure I can handle all this?"

"Actually, I'm not. I'm afraid you'll be too busy checking out what everyone is wearing to focus on the news part."

She glared. "Cultivating a fashion sense might help the denizens of Willow Beach."

"Just take care of these, will you?"

Before she could reply, he turned and stalked off.

She stared at his retreating back. Their Independence Day kiss at the park must have really unraveled him. Not that she'd been so calm herself since then.

She straightened and swiped a palm over her forehead, as if to chase away the memory. Letting Mark kiss her—and, okay, kissing him back—was a mistake. They had no future. As soon as her year was up, she was out of here.

Eva was putting the finishing touches on Bertha's article when the phone on her desk rang. A deep voice said, "Hey, Eva, Boyd Carlstrom here. Remember me?"

Eva sat up straight. "Dad's old friend and partner? Of course I do!"

"Been a while, hasn't it? Haven't seen you since your dad and I split up. Heard about your glitzy job in Seattle. Good for you."

"Thanks, Boyd, but that's been put on hold." She couldn't help letting a note of regret creep into her voice.

"I know."

His voice dropped as though he understood and sympathized.

"I was sorry to hear about Seb," Boyd went on. "I couldn't make the memorial 'cause I was traveling. Read about it, though. In the *Herald*. Whoever did the write-up did a super job."

"That would be me." His compliment lifted her spirits.

"Always knew you were a fine journalist. So now you're taking over the newspaper."

"No, no. Mark Townson and I are co-editors, and it's only temporarily."

"We need to talk, Eva. Can you get away for lunch?"

His seriousness piqued her interest. "Lunch? Sure. It'd be good to see you again."

"Will today work?"

Eva didn't have to check her calendar to know she had nothing planned. "Today would be fine."

"Good. I'll see you at the Beach Café at twelve-thirty."

A FRESH OCEAN BREEZE ushered Eva into the restaurant at exactly twelve-thirty. She looked around, remembering the night she'd been here with Mark after their jog on the beach.

The hostess, dressed in a red-and-blue print dress that echoed the restaurant's decor, stepped forward. "Eva, welcome to Beach Café."

"Thanks. And you're Margaret, Guy's wife, right? We met at the picnic."

"I am. Guy loves freelancing for the *Herald*. He says it makes his boring day job easier to tolerate."

Eva smiled to herself. Boring day job. That was what she would call working at the *Herald*. But to each his own, as the saying went.

"Are you meeting Mark?" Margaret glanced quickly at the reservation book sitting on the counter.

Why would she ask that? "Uh, no…"

Another gust of wind signaled the opening

of the front door and Boyd Carlstrom strode in, although *lumbered* might have been more accurate. He'd gained quite a bit of weight in the years since Eva had seen him. He wore baggy tan slacks, a dark brown sports jacket and a white shirt open at the collar. His wind-blown white hair swirled around his head like ocean froth.

"Good timing, Eva," he boomed in the deep-as-a-well voice she'd heard over the phone. He carried a black attaché case and extended his free hand. A ruby ring that looked familiar caught her eye.

She took his hand and let him do the pumping. "Boyd. Good to see you."

Boyd turned to Margaret. "I have a reservation."

She nodded. "Got it right here in my book."

Margaret led them to a window table overlooking the sunlit beach and handed them menus.

Boyd set his case on the floor. He opened his menu and peered at Eva over the top. "I'm starved. Order first, then we'll talk."

Eva nodded and studied the selections. A waiter appeared and took Boyd's order for a calamari appetizer, onion rings and a beer.

Eva inwardly cringed at the combination and chose the crab salad and an iced tea.

After the waiter left, Boyd sat back and studied Eva. "Remember when I brought you a teddy bear?"

Eva smiled. "I was just getting over measles. Mom wouldn't let you bring it into my room, though."

A soft smile crossed his lips. "Janice looked after all of us, didn't she?"

"Yes, she was a caring person." Eva looked down and smoothed the napkin on her lap.

"What a shame she went at such a young age. And then losing Brett. What an ordeal that was. I thought Seb would cash it in himself—I really did. That was no picnic for you, either."

Eva grasped her napkin and twisted it hard. "Please, I'd rather not talk about that. The… accident was a long time ago."

Boyd looked uncomfortable. "I'm sorry," he mumbled.

The waiter came with their drinks. Boyd grabbed his glass of beer and took a long swallow, then cleared his throat. "Why doncha tell me about that glitzy job of yours?"

"All right." That was a safe subject, and he looked genuinely interested.

She told him about her work at *Seattle's Best,* including her disappointment at having her rising career interrupted. He listened and nodded and asked an occasional question.

She was still talking when the waiter came with their meals. Eva took a bite of her crab salad, then said, "Now it's your turn. What have you been doing since you left the *Herald?* Did you quit the newspaper business?"

Boyd's laughter boomed into the room, causing several diners to turn their heads. "Quit? No. On the contrary, I'm in the biz more than ever."

"So you work at another newspaper?"

He dipped an onion ring in hot sauce, then popped it into his mouth. He chewed, his cheeks bulging until he swallowed. "I *own* newspapers. Many newspapers." He straightened and puffed out his chest.

"Small-town ones, like the *Herald?*"

"I'll show ya." He reached down, snapped open the attaché case and pulled out a handful of tabloid-size newspapers. He shoved his plate aside and tossed them onto the table. "The *Morganville Messenger.*" He pointed to the logo on the top paper, flipped that aside and pointed to the next one. "The *Drayton Chronicle*."

He went through the stack, reading each logo. There were eight in all.

When he looked up at Eva, pride shone in his eyes. "All weeklies, just like the *Herald*."

"My goodness, how did you acquire all these?"

"One at a time, one at a time."

She wanted to ask where he'd come up with the money, but that was none of her business.

"That's very impressive, Boyd." Eva pulled the *Morganville Messenger* over to her side of the table. "This looks like a, uh, nice paper."

He smiled knowingly. "Oh, I know, not glitzy like *Seattle's Best*. But that's why I especially wanted to meet with you today."

She sat straight, alert, even a little wary. "What's on your mind, Boyd?"

"For starters, I know you're back in Willow Beach because of Seb's will."

She shrugged. "No surprise there. I'm sure everyone in town knows that." She waited for him to continue.

He leaned forward, his brown eyes intense. "Listen, Eva, when your year is up and you're free to go, I want to buy your half of the newspaper."

She should've seen that coming. "You want to buy me out?"

"Right. I know you won't want to stay here. You just told me a few minutes ago about the bad memories. You don't want to live with them in your backyard, do you?"

He was more perceptive than Eva would have guessed. She stared at her plate. "You're right, I won't stay here. The minute my time's up, I'm heading back to Seattle. It's my home now, whether I have a job waiting for me or not."

"I'm sure you can find something to your liking. A talented writer like you."

"Thanks for the confidence. But your offer is a bit premature. I have ten months left to go."

"I learned the hard way it pays to be on top of a situation well in advance."

She wondered if he was talking about his breakup with her father. "What went wrong between you and Seb anyway? I was in college at the time. All I remember is coming home one summer and you were gone. Dad never said what happened."

"All right, I'll tell you. But let me start at the beginning. Seb and I met years ago, at the U, where we were frat brothers." He held up the hand sporting the ruby ring.

"I know. Dad had a ring just like that."

"Yep. Good ole Phi Mu. We had a lotta good times. That's where he met Janice. Her sorority and our fraternity got together for a dance. Actually, I met her first. She and I went out for several months. I was about to give her my ring—that's what we did in those days—but then one day while we were in the student union having coffee, Seb came by." He set his jaw and looked out the window. "And that was the end of me and Janice."

His voice had taken on a flat quality, and he absently twisted his ring.

Eva had never heard that story. "And?"

"And after graduation we went our separate ways. A few years later, we met again. I was writing ad copy for a manufacturing company, and Seb was working for the *Herald*. It went on the block. I was eager for something new. Seb and I pooled our resources, I secured a few loans, and we were in the newspaper business."

"You'd married by then, hadn't you?" Eva

recalled a dour-faced woman with red hair and a sharp voice.

"That's right. I just said goodbye to number three a couple months ago. Six kids altogether. Wonder how things would've turned out if I'd been the one to marry Janice. But then we wouldn't be sitting here having this conversation, would we?"

He drained the last of his beer and set the glass down with more force than necessary. Leaning back, he stretched out his arms. "So what do you say? Do we have a deal?"

"But you'll own only half of the newspaper. Mark will still own the other half. Unless by then he wants to leave, too."

He shrugged. "Not for you to worry about, is it?"

"No, it's not my worry." She tapped her fingers on the table and looked at Boyd. "So, how much are you offering for my half?"

He raised his eyebrows. "So you are interested. Thought you would be."

"I need to know the particulars."

He named a sum that was well above what her research had told her the newspaper was worth. "That's quite generous," she said.

He grinned. "We could seal the deal today.

All it takes is your signature." He reached into the attaché case again, pulled out a sheaf of papers and laid them on top of the stack of newspapers.

"You really think the *Herald* is worth that much?"

"To me it is." He plucked a pen from an inner jacket pocket and held it out. "Are you ready to do business?"

Eva stared at the pen and then at the sheets of slick white legal-size paper. Securing a sale now might be a good idea. Then she wouldn't have to worry about what she'd do with her share come June. She held out her hand, ready to grasp the pen.

But something made her hesitate. A lot could happen in ten months, even though at the moment she couldn't think of anything that would keep her in Willow Beach working for the *Herald*. She shook her head and let her hand drop into her lap. "As tempting as your offer is, I'm not prepared to sign anything today."

His grin faded. He sat back and twirled the pen between his pudgy fingers. "Think you'll change your mind about leaving? I doubt it."

"No, I won't change my mind. But even if

I end up accepting your offer, I'll want my lawyer to look over the deal before I sign it."

Boyd pursed his lips. "You're careful, like your dad, and I respect that. He never would jump into anything on faith, either. Okay, I can wait." He tucked his pen away, pulled out a business card and handed it to her. "If you change your mind, give me a call. My deal will pave your way back to Seattle, maybe not with gold, but with a hefty chunk of silver."

He was right about that.

"So, what's this emergency meeting about?" Bernie asked, settling into a chair in the staff room.

"You'll find out when everybody gets here." Mark paced from the table to the window. On the counter, the coffee urn burbled. Next to it, a couple of tired-looking leftover doughnuts huddled in a Bon Ton box.

Dora entered the room, carrying her yellow knitting tote. "Mark, why are you pacing? Has something bad happened? I don't know how much more I can take."

"Have a seat, Dora." Mark stopped long enough to motion to the empty spot next to Bernie and then took up his pacing again.

April came in, wrinkled her nose at the doughnuts and slumped into a chair. Cody followed, scratching his chin and looking puzzled. He sat next to April, stretching his long legs under the table.

"What's going on?" Cody asked. "This isn't our usual time for a staff meeting."

"I bet it's about Eva," April said in a grumpy tone. "Everything's about her these days."

Cody elbowed her arm. "What's the matter? You jealous?"

"No!"

April glared at him, then slid a covert glance at Mark. He ignored them, pulling out a chair and propping one foot on a rung. "Okay, here's what's going on—"

"Aren't we waiting for Eva?" Bernie asked.

"No," Mark said. "This is about her."

"Told ya." April shot Cody a triumphant look.

"Where is Eva?" Dora asked.

Mark waved a hand. "Probably out buying a new wardrobe."

"Huh!" April said. "Not in this town, she isn't."

"Okay, I don't know where she is. She could

come back anytime, so listen up, please." All eyes focused on him as he cleared his throat. "Boyd Carlstrom is nosing around. Margaret told Guy that he and Eva had lunch yesterday at the Beach Café. He was showing her his newspapers. I'm guessing he wants to buy her half when her time is up."

Dora shook her head. "Seb wouldn't like that."

"I know." Mark propped an elbow on his knee and leaned forward. "But I'm not sure why. I want to talk to Eva about it, warn her, but I need more information. That's why I called this meeting—to see if any of you can help. Dora, you're the best one, but I thought the rest of you might have heard something. You know how closemouthed Seb was about personal stuff—he never told me what happened between him and Boyd."

Dora's needles clicked off another row. "I think their relationship was touchy from the start. They appeared to be friends, but underneath there was a rivalry. First over Janice. Seb took her away from Boyd, back in their college days. They were Phi Mu fraternity brothers at the U. My niece's husband was a

Phi Mu, the one who came to the picnic? One of the best houses…"

Mark cleared his throat. "Please go on, Dora."

"Anyway, they got together and bought the newspaper when the Drakes retired. I think Boyd had most of the money. I figured he came because he wanted to be near Janice, never got over her. None of his marriages lasted very long. For a while, he and Seb got along fine, but then trouble started."

"Didn't their falling-out have something to do with Brett?" Bernie said.

Dora nodded. "Seb wanted Brett to work for the *Herald* after he graduated college and to eventually take over leadership. Boyd wanted his son—Arthur, I think his name was—to be top dog. They fought over whose son was going to be boss."

"What did their sons think?" Mark asked.

Dora shrugged. "I don't know. But when Brett drowned, Seb was devastated. When he recovered enough to put his mind to work again, Boyd and Arthur were running the show. Seb and Boyd's relationship got worse and worse. Seb wanted to buy out Boyd, and finally, he could."

"How could he do that?" Cody asked.

"Boyd had financial problems. I think he made some bad investments. He's an impulsive guy, likes to throw money around. Seb managed to borrow enough to buy him out. Of course, Boyd didn't want to go and vowed that someday he'd end up owning the *Herald* again."

"There's no money owing now," Mark said.

"Under Seb's leadership, circulation and advertising increased. He put the paper in the black again."

"Thanks, Dora," Mark said. "Maybe that doesn't explain everything, but it helps a lot. Seb told me that whatever happened, he didn't want Boyd to own even a piece of the newspaper again."

THE FOLLOWING DAY, as Eva worked on her Our Town column, a shadow fell across her doorway. She looked up to see Mark. His brows were furrowed and his mouth tight. She tensed. She didn't need another confrontation.

"We need to talk," he stated in clipped tones.

"Sounds serious." Eva kept her voice calm.

"But can it wait? I'm in the middle of something." She pointed to the rows of text on her computer screen.

He folded his arms. "No, it can't wait. We'll use my office."

She heaved a sigh. "Give me a minute to finish this sentence."

Eva saved her work and then, nerves tingling, followed Mark down the hall. What could be serious enough to warrant a special meeting?

Once inside his office, she lingered near the door, shifting from one foot to the other. The faint smell of newsprint and fresh ink caught her attention and she noticed a stack of the latest edition of the *Herald* on the worktable.

He stepped behind her and shut the door with a firm hand, then waved at a chair across from his desk. "Have a seat."

She straightened her spine and stood her ground. "If this is a complaint, let's get it over with."

A scowl twisted his features. "It's a complaint, all right—about your meeting with Boyd Carlstrom."

She let his words hang in the air a few seconds. "Wow, the town's grapevine is amazing. But, okay, so he and I had lunch together? Why is that any of your business?"

"If your meeting had to do with the *Herald*—and I'm guessing it did—it is my business."

She lifted her chin. "You don't need to worry about anything."

"Just how much do you know about Boyd Carlstrom?"

Eva refused to be cowed by his intense scrutiny. "I remember him from when I was a little girl. He was always nice to me. I know he and my father went to college together and they bought the newspaper when the Drakes retired."

"But do you know why they had a falling-out?"

"I, uh…" What was the reason? It dawned on her that she'd asked Boyd that very question over lunch, but he'd never answered her. "Let's hear your version."

"Have a seat, then." He gestured again to the chair. "This may take a while."

She would've remained standing, just to defy him, but the flats she was wearing pinched her toes. "All right." She slumped into a chair, but not the one he indicated.

Mark strode to the window. His back was to her as he gazed out, but his firm tone traveled easily across the room. "When your brother was still alive, they argued over which of their sons was going to be the boss here when they weren't around anymore. Might seem to have been a bit premature, but each was set on his son taking over."

Eva clenched her hands into fists. "Do we have to discuss this?"

"Yes, we do. I want to get something straight with you. Anyway, after your brother's death, your father sort of dropped out for a while."

"I don't need to hear what happened then," Eva said through her teeth.

"And by the time he got himself together, Boyd and his son were running the show. Then Boyd got into financial trouble and Seb was able to borrow money to buy him out. But he said he never wanted Boyd to have anything to do with the *Herald* again."

"We don't have that in writing anywhere. It wasn't in the will."

"Okay, but he told me often enough, and you can take my word for it. I'm guessing

that Boyd offered to buy you out when your
year is up."

"It's none of your business what Boyd and
I discussed. He might have asked me to lunch
to say he was sorry about Dad's passing and
because he wanted to renew his relationship
with me."

"For an ulterior motive."

"And you don't have an ulterior motive in
trying to poison me against him?"

He faced her and spread his hands. "No,
my motive is clear and simple. I am honor-
ing your father's wishes. I don't want Boyd
anywhere near the *Herald*."

"Your loyalty is admirable, but I don't
share it."

He crossed the room to stand in front of
her. "Why, Eva? What went wrong between
you two? It's more than your refusal to work
here after you graduated college."

Eva looked down at her hands still clenched
into fists. Straightening her fingers, she laid
her palms flat on her lap and took a deep
breath.

"I have no control over where Boyd goes,
and if he comes here and you want to throw
him out, that's up to you. But I'll associate

with whomever I please. He is an old friend. He hasn't done anything to me, and if I want to have lunch with him, I will."

"Despite what happened between him and your father."

"I'll have to hear his side before I make a judgment call."

Mark propped his hands on his hips. "You're impossible."

"I'm being fair. Which is more than I can say for you!"

Striding to his desk, Mark sank into his swivel chair. He leaned forward and ran a hand through his hair. Several tense moments passed with neither saying a word.

Finally Eva stood. "Is that all?"

He didn't look up. "Yeah, I guess so."

"In that case, I'll get back to work. I have a column to write."

# CHAPTER EIGHT

EVA DROVE ALONG Oak Avenue, her old neighborhood, gazing at the houses as she passed by. She easily recognized the two-story yellow house that belonged to the Halversons. Last time she was here, after her college graduation and just before she left Willow Beach for good, tricycles lined the driveway. Now two-wheelers had taken their place. The Halverson kids were growing up.

The Coltons' house sported a new paint job, bright lavender with navy blue trim. Eva shook her head. That color combination might work for one of the Victorian-style homes up on the bluff, but down here? Uh-uh.

Her stomach tensed as she approached the next house—where she'd grown up and where her father continued to live alone after she moved to Seattle. The house he died in. A modest one-story frame home painted white, with nothing particularly distinctive about it. Unless you'd lived there, as she had, and then the memories stored inside made it special.

She'd been in Willow Beach over a month and she'd yet to begin cleaning out the house. She could hire someone to do it, but she couldn't quite bring herself to involve strangers with something so personal. Yet, she had to get the place ready to put on the market. She'd driven by several times, armed with empty boxes but without the courage to stop and go in. Today being Sunday, and with no other obligations and no trip to Seattle, she decided she couldn't put it off any longer.

She turned into the driveway and cut the engine. For a few minutes she just sat there, absently fingering the keys. Finally, she slipped them into her purse and, with a sigh, pulled out Seb's house key, which Mark had given her the first night she'd come to town.

She stepped from the car and reached into the backseat to grab one of the empty boxes. As she made her way up the stone sidewalk leading to the porch, her gaze slid to the rattan chairs and table, then lingered on one of the chairs. Her father had often sat there in the evening, his feet propped up on the porch railing, the ocean breeze curling the pages of whatever he was reading, a fishing or a golfing magazine or, if it was Wednesday, the current issue of the *Herald*.

A lump rose in her throat and she quickly headed for the door. She slid the key into the lock and let the door swing open. Standing on the threshold, she wished she were someplace, anyplace, else. With a deep sigh, she stepped inside.

Suddenly, she was a child again, living here with her mother and father and Brett. She could hear their voices, her mother's soft and sweet, her father's bold and decisive. And Brett's? Cajoling when he wanted something and laughing when he got it, which he usually did.

Pushing away the memories, she concentrated on the task at hand. Where to start? Not the kitchen. She couldn't go in there. Not yet.

She turned to the living room, which was at the front of the house, and looked around. The furniture she'd either sell to the used-furniture store in Thornton or donate to charity. What needed her attention were the personal items. Her gaze landed on the book-shelf built into one wall. That would be a good place to start.

"Ms. SINCLAIR?"

Eva looked up from her typing to see Luci Jordan, the *Herald*'s high-school intern for the coming school year, standing in the entrance to her cubicle. Mark had introduced Luci to the staff a few days ago. Eva instantly liked the young teen, and seeing her now boosted her spirits.

"Hey, Luci. What's up?"

"Do you have a minute? If not, I can come back later."

"Now's good. Come on in and sit down." She gestured to the straight chair by her desk.

Luci slipped into the chair, pushing her shoulder-length red hair behind both ears to reveal small silver hoop earrings. She met Eva's gaze with a wrinkled brow. "I'm here to ask you for a favor. A big favor."

"I'm listening." Eva sat back and rested her hands in her lap.

"We want to have a fashion show."

"We?"

Luci's brown eyes sparkled with enthusiasm. "Our Home Living class. We want to have a back-to-school show, and we want you to be our announcer."

Eva pressed her palm to her chest. "You want me to be the emcee?"

"Yes, to introduce the models and comment on the clothes."

Eva nodded. "Your teacher is Fran Oliver, right? Is she agreeable?"

"Mrs. Oliver said I could ask you."

"Mrs. Oliver and I went to high school together."

"That's what she said. She was going to call you but then decided I should do the asking." Luci shifted in her chair and crossed her ankles. Her toenails, peeking out of her sandals, were painted a red that matched her hair.

"Anyway, you know a lot about clothes. You always look so nice. And you write such good articles about fashion for *Seattle's Best*." Luci nodded at the framed covers of the magazine that Eva had hung on her cubicle walls.

"You've read my articles?" Eva was amazed. She didn't think anyone in Willow Beach even knew about the publication. "Is the magazine on sale here?"

Luci flipped a lock of hair over her shoulder. "No, but my aunt in Seattle buys it and sends it to me. I plan to go to the U and major in journalism. That's where you went, isn't it?"

Eva nodded. "That's a good choice."

"I figured it was when your father recommended it. He came to our journalism class last year and talked to us about making journalism a career. He was so inspiring."

Eva sighed. Her father popped up in conversations all too often. Yet, why not? This was his territory.

"So, would you help us out?" Luci's brown eyes radiated cautious hope.

An idea popped into Eva's mind. "I will, but there's a catch."

Luci looked down at her hands. "Oh…"

"A fun one. I will be your emcee if you'll write an article about the show for the *Herald*."

Luci pointed her thumb at her chest. "Me? Write an article?"

"Sure. You want to be a journalist, don't you? You're working here, aren't you?"

"Yes, but I'm opening the mail and running errands, not writing anything. Mr. Townson said that would come later."

"This fall will be later."

Luci raised a skeptical eyebrow. "Don't we have to ask him first?"

"Don't worry, I'll take care of that. And Cody can take photos to go along with your article."

"Cody? He's cool. My best friend, Jaycee, has a crush on him."

"Really?" The way Luci's eyes shone, Eva guessed she might be harboring a crush of her own. "I'm sure he'll be a good photographer. Why, the article might even make page one."

Luci clapped her hands. "The front page? Oh, Ms. Sinclair, that'd be awesome!"

Eva reached for the printout on her desk of the *Herald*'s upcoming front page. She pointed to the photo that accompanied the feature article. "Can't you just see, instead of this dull shot of…what?" She leaned closer to read the caption. "Can you imagine, instead of the city-council discussing proposed budget cuts, a big, splashy color shot of the models on the runway? It'd be eye-catching and very dramatic."

"But we don't have a runway. We'll be using the auditorium's stage."

"That's okay. We'll make it look like a runway. You have a drama department, don't you?"

A look of understanding crossed Luci's face. "Yes, and they have stage props. I see what you mean."

They spent a few more minutes discussing the show. Eva promised to call Fran and begin making plans. Luci fairly danced out of Eva's cubicle, and Eva went back to her column with renewed energy. A fashion show. That was something to look forward to. Something that would benefit from her expertise.

Then reality set in and her shoulders slumped. She seriously doubted Mark would approve giving any newspaper space to a high-school event, let alone on page one. He'd consider the article "fluff."

She wouldn't approach him with the idea now, especially in light of the clash they'd had last week over Boyd Carlstrom. The show was a couple months off. There would be time to prepare him later.

THAT EVENING, MARK TOOK the latest issue of the *Herald* into the living room and settled into his recliner. Each Wednesday, he liked to peruse the latest issue as though for the first time. At his feet, Sasha played with her doll family. He watched her for a few moments, smiling at her voice changed as she spoke for the various dolls. Then he settled back and unfolded the newspaper, breathing in the ink scent.

Before he could read the headline, the scene he'd had with Eva last week over Boyd Carlstrom popped into his mind, along with a tension that tightened the back of his neck. Of course, he couldn't force her to keep away from Boyd. By telling her of Seb's wishes, he'd hoped she'd come to that decision on her own. He would bet a month's salary that Boyd had offered to buy Eva's half of the newspaper once the year of coeditorship was up. Well, he wouldn't allow that to happen. Seb hadn't wanted Boyd to have anything more to do with the *Herald,* and somehow, Mark would see that Seb got his wish.

He rubbed his forehead in an attempt to banish the negative emotions his thoughts churned up. Why was he worrying about the future now? This was his time to enjoy the fruits of his labor.

The article he'd written about the city's proposed budget cuts, featured on the front page, presented both sides of the controversy, and Cody's photo of the lively discussion at the council meeting captured the intense feelings of the debate.

He finished reading the paper and felt a surge of pride and satisfaction. Yes, sir, news, *important* community news, that was what the *Herald* was all about. He wished Seb were here to see the issue. He'd be pleased, too. A wave of sadness rolled through Mark. He missed his mentor every day. He'd never forget the man or the lessons he had taught him.

His chest tight, he put the newspaper aside and leaned forward to gaze down at Sasha. "How are the dolls tonight?"

She looked up from poking a flat-heeled shoe on a child doll's bare foot. "Janie is sad."

"Really? Why?"

"Well, she has a daddy—" she picked up a male doll dressed in a business suit and waved it at Mark "—but she doesn't have a mommy."

"Then who is that?" He pointed to the female doll dressed in a skirt and blouse lying nearby.

"She's just a friend. Not a mommy."

"Ah, does Janie want a mommy?" He held his breath, waiting for her answer.

Sasha poked out her lower lip. "'Course she does. I do, too."

Mark's heart wrenched. He slipped from the chair and sat beside her, laying a hand on her thin shoulder. "Sweetheart, you do have a mommy. She's not here with us, but she's still your mommy. We have a lot to remember her by. She even bought the chair I was sitting in."

"But it's hard to 'member her."

"Her picture is over there on the mantel. And you have another one on the table by your bed."

Sasha looked up at the photo. "That's only a picture, not a real mommy."

Mark straightened the collar of her pink blouse. "And you've got a daddy—me. I'll be the best one I can be."

She relaxed her pout into a smile. "I know. I love you, Daddy."

He struggled to control his voice. "Love you, too, baby." He put his arm around her and gave her a hug. Then, pulling away, he picked up the male doll. "So this dude is Janie's daddy, huh? What kind of job does he have?"

"A job in an office, like you, 'cept he dresses up more."

"I see that. Must be a banker or a stockbroker. So, where's his office?"

"Over there, by the big chair."

"Okay." Mark hopped the doll across the carpet and propped him against the chair's leg and then turned back to Sasha. "Hey, I know a little girl who's having a birthday soon."

Sasha giggled as she picked up the female doll. "Me."

"Right. Have you decided who to invite to your party?"

Sasha hung a plastic purse over the doll's arm. "Um, Bella, and Suzette, and Colleen. And Mary Lou…"

"All girls, huh?" He grinned.

She wrinkled her nose. "I don't like boys."

"Uh-huh. For now, you don't."

"What do you mean, Daddy?"

She slanted him a quizzical look, and he couldn't hold back a laugh. "Never mind. That sounds like a good group."

Sasha walked the female doll over to join the male. "Oh, wait. Eva, too."

"Eva?" Mark frowned. "I didn't know you had a friend named Eva. Is she new in town?"

"Don't be silly, Daddy. Eva at your office."

Of course, he'd known which Eva she meant. But he didn't want her to come to his daughter's party.

"Inviting Eva isn't a good idea, honey." He brushed a lock of hair from her forehead.

"Why?"

"She's an adult. Your party is for kids your age."

"April's coming, and Grammy Eileen. They're big people."

"Yes, but they're helping to give you the party. They're hostesses."

"Eva could be a hostess."

What could he say without revealing his personal reasons for not inviting Eva? He couldn't tell his daughter that outside the office, he and Eva needed to keep their distance. He couldn't tell her he didn't want to risk her getting attached to Eva because within the year she'd up and leave them, just like Diane had done three years ago.

And so he took a deep breath and said, "All right, we'll invite her. But don't be disappointed if she can't come. She might be going to Seattle that weekend."

"I bet she comes to my party," Sasha said.

EVA SLIPPED HER TAPE RECORDER into her purse, turned off her computer and stepped from her cubicle. She checked her wristwatch. One-thirty. She had half an hour, plenty of time to get to her interview with Trevor Milan, the Rotary Club president. As she headed down the hallway to the front door, she spotted Eileen Dugan and Sasha coming toward her.

"Hello there. Your daddy's in his office, Sasha." She gestured over her shoulder toward Mark's office.

"I came to see you." The little girl, dressed in a pink sundress with a ruffled hem, opened her pink purse and took out a small square envelope. She handed it to Eva.

Eva took the envelope. "What's this?" She looked down at Sasha and then over her head to meet Eileen's gaze.

Eileen lifted her chin and rolled her eyes. "You'll see."

"Open it, open it." Sasha jumped up and down.

Eva lifted the flap and pulled out a card showing a little girl dressed in pink and wearing a gold crown. Underneath were the words "You're invited…" She opened the card and read the words inside. She raised her eyebrows at Sasha. "Wow, I'm invited to your birthday party?"

"Uh-huh." Sasha's eyes shone. "Can you come?"

"Why, I—" Eva looked at Eileen again. "The party's for adults and children?"

Eileen's brow wrinkled. "Not exactly. April and I are helping out, and of course Mark will be there, but the rest of the guests are Sasha's little friends."

"Oh." Eva felt uncomfortable around both women, especially April. Eileen was aloof, but she'd never been rude. April, however, openly expressed her disdain in sneers and smirks.

"Please come," Sasha said.

Her wide eyes and clasped hands tugged at Eva's heartstrings. What was important here? Sasha, of course.

"I'd love to come. In fact, I wouldn't miss it."

"Oh, goody!" Sasha opened her arms.

Eva bent down and gave the child a hug. As Sasha hugged her back, warmth filled Eva. Suddenly she wished she had a child of her own to love and care for.

"I'VE SURE MISSED this view." Sitting on her beige sofa, balancing a plate holding a teacup and a raspberry scone, Eva nodded toward the balcony overlooking downtown Seattle. Amid all the skyscrapers, the Space Needle poked its familiar head as puffy white clouds drifted across a cobalt-blue sky.

Susan Jensen smiled and sipped her tea. "I've missed you, Eva. I'm glad you could make it this weekend."

Eva picked up her scone and took a bite. She closed her eyes as she chewed, savoring the sweet, fruity flavor. "Ah, de-li-cious. I've missed Avery's Bakery. And I've missed you, too."

Susan raised one eyebrow. "Don't tell me Willow Beach doesn't even have a bakery."

"Yes, the Bon Ton, and it's a good one, but the scones from Avery's are special. I'm glad you've discovered them."

"How could I not when I pass the store whenever I enter the building? And that might not be a good thing." She patted her stomach. "I've already gained a couple pounds. But like you, I love their stuff."

Eva's gaze drifted over Susan's mauve shirt

and the silver beads that decorated the neckline. "Nice top, Suse. Is it new?"

Susan beamed and sat up straighter. "It is. I bought it at Zeno's show."

Eva frowned. "I hated missing that—especially after writing the article about him for the magazine."

"Your article got a lot of praise. Even Margo Janovich said you did a good job."

Eva wrinkled her nose. "Margo Janovich. The new assistant editor. The job *I* was supposed to get. But that was nice of her to throw me a compliment."

"She's okay to work with, but I'd rather be working with you. Hey, we can check out Zeno's line at Macy's when we go shopping today."

"Good idea. You can't imagine how much I've missed shopping. Willow Beach has one clothing store. Only one. Can you imagine?"

Susan widened her eyes. "No, I can't. You said on the phone you're looking for a birthday gift."

Eva finished another bite of scone. "Right. For Mark's daughter, Sasha. She's turning six and has invited me to her party. I want to get her something special. Something I wouldn't be able to find in Willow Beach."

"Your coeditor?" Susan raised her eyebrows. "Is there a Mrs. Mark?"

Eva shook her head. "She died three years ago in a bus accident. I don't know much else. Mark doesn't like to talk about her, and I sense he's still hurting."

Susan leaned back against the sofa cushions. "Ah. So tell me about Mark."

Eva smiled. "He's quite handsome and very athletic. We jogged together on the beach."

"Like a date?"

"No, we saw each other out one evening and joined up to finish our run and have coffee afterward."

"What's a guy like him doing in Willow Beach?"

"He actually likes living there. He's dedicated to the *Herald,* and the staff loves him. I can see why my father valued him."

Susan frowned. "I'm getting mixed messages. You hate being there, but you don't exactly hate *him*."

Eva looked away. "No, I don't hate him. We argue a lot, but there's…an attraction." Eva thought of the dance and the kiss she and Mark shared on the Fourth. "You can tell when a person's attracted, no matter how much they might act as though they don't like you."

Susan grinned and waggled a forefinger. "Aha! Could he be the one?"

Eva shook her head. "No, he can't be. I'm still determined to move back home as soon as my year is up. I can't live in Willow Beach again. I just can't."

"I'm hearing you, Eva, but why not? I know you like living in Seattle and working for the magazine, but I sense there's something else about the town that bothers you."

Eva nodded and fingered the silver chain that held Brett's medal. "You're right, Suse. A lot of bad memories are there that are hard enough to live with when I'm away—they'd be impossible to deal with if I had to move back permanently. Being there for a year is difficult enough."

Susan's brow wrinkled. "Okay, I get it. I didn't mean to pry."

"You weren't. You're being a good friend, and I appreciate that."

A sly grin curved Susan's lips. "I have to

say, though, that I think your heart's on an entirely different wavelength."

"And since when did you become the expert?" Eva teased.

Susan's eyes took on a dreamy look. "Since I met Greg."

Eva sat upright. "What? You've met someone?"

Susan nodded. "Greg Martin. And I think he's the one."

Eva propped her hand on her hip. "And here I've been going on about my situation, and you're sitting there with big news of your own. Tell me about him."

Susan finished her tea and placed her cup and saucer on the coffee table. "He recently moved here from Chicago to work at Micro-Tech. My cousin, Kayla, works there. She introduced us, and we hit it off. We have a lot in common. He likes to travel and to ski, and he loves it here."

"He sounds perfect for you."

"He is." Susan's eyes sparkled. "I really feel this is it."

"I'm so happy for you, Susan. I hope everything works out."

They chatted for a few more minutes, then

Susan glanced at her watch. "It's almost ten. We'd better get going if we want to do some shopping before we meet Janette and Rochelle for lunch."

"Right. Let's clean up the dishes."

As Eva carried their teacups and plates into the kitchen, she thought about Susan's news. Although she was happy for her friend, she couldn't help envying her, too.

# *CHAPTER NINE*

ON MONDAY MORNING, after stowing away her purse in a desk drawer and turning on her computer, Eva headed to the staff lounge for a cup of coffee. The only person there was Mark. He stood at the counter filling his mug from the coffee urn. He wore his usual form-fitting jeans and short-sleeved cotton shirt, his muscular arms in full view.

Holding his mug in one hand, he turned and spotted her. Ready to start the day on good terms, she smiled, but the cheery "Good morning" died on her lips when he frowned and said, "So, how was Seattle?"

The disapproval in his voice puzzled Eva. She'd made clear from the beginning that she'd spend some of her weekends at home—her real home. She calmly plucked a mug from the stand and held it under the spigot, breathing in the aroma of the fresh brew. "How'd you know I went to Seattle?"

"I ran into your landlady, Mrs. Halsey, at Charlie's on Friday night—Sasha and I went there for fish-and-chips. She said she saw you earlier heading out to your car with your overnight bag. I figured you went to Seattle. Where else would you go?"

Eva shrugged. "Oh, I might make a quick getaway to Mexico or California. You never know. But, yes, I went home."

Mark grabbed a napkin and wiped away a drip of coffee on the counter. "So how's everything back *home?*"

Eva sipped her coffee. "I had a great time visiting with Susan—she's the one who's renting my condo. We went shopping—"

Mark tossed the napkin into the wastebasket. "Of course, shopping."

She sighed, but ignored his sarcasm. "Then we met some friends for lunch."

He put down his mug and crossed his arms over his chest. "That so? Well, good for you. We had a great time here, too. At Foster's Shoe Store opening."

The real reason for this conversation finally dawned. She groaned and slapped her forehead. "Oh, no. I forgot I was supposed to cover the opening."

"Right. I thought the assignment was something you were interested in and wanted to do."

"I'm sorry." She dipped her head and pressed her lips together. "Why didn't you text or call me?"

"Would you have turned around and come back?"

Eva thought of the birthday present she'd bought for Sasha in Seattle. If she'd returned to Willow Beach, when would she have had another chance to purchase it? The party was this coming weekend.

"Thanks for covering for me," she said, sidestepping his question.

"You agreed to report on the opening. If you didn't want to, you should have said so."

"I did want to. Look, I said I was sorry, okay?" Eva's shoulders tensed. How much apologizing did she have to do?

He stuck out his jaw. "Okay. Give me the interviews and notes you did earlier and I'll put something together."

"Why don't you give me *your* notes, and I'll write the article?"

Impatience flickered across his face. "Because I went to the actual opening."

"And my interviews take a backseat to that? Why don't we sit down together?"

Mark put his mug on the counter and propped his hands on his hips. "Yeah, I can see that working. I'm quoting the effect the store will have on our economy and you'll be describing what people were wearing."

She gave him a stony look.

Bernie entered carrying his personalized coffee mug. He stopped and glanced from one to the other. "Oh. Am I interrupting something?"

"Not at all," Mark said in a smooth tone. "We're just discussing the Foster's store opening."

Bernie strode to the coffeemaker. "That was fun. Maria and Bella and I went. Free coffee and doughnuts and balloons for the kids." He turned to Eva. "Didn't see you there, though."

"She went to Seattle," Mark said.

"Oh, yeah, Seattle," Bernie said flatly. "Well, you missed a good time. We're going to have a feature on it, aren't we, boss?"

"You bet we are, which I will be writing."

Eva gritted her teeth. "I'll bring my notes to your office, Mark."

"You do that, Eva."

MARK WATCHED EVA stalk from the staff
lounge, then carried his mug to one of the
tables and sank into a chair. He put down his
coffee and ran a hand through his hair.

Bernie came over and peered at him.
"What's got you so riled up? 'Cause she
missed the store's opening? You can write a
better feature than she can any day."

"She gets on my nerves."

"Humph." Bernie pulled out a chair beside
Mark and sat. "I'd say there's more going on
between you two than arguing over a missed
assignment."

Mark raised his head to meet Bernie's
twinkling eyes. "I know what you're thinking, but you can forget it. She's not my type."

"So, what *is* your type? You don't like any
of the ladies Maria and I bring around."

"I'm just not ready," Mark insisted.

"It's been three years... Everyone's on their
own time schedule, but you've got a little girl
who's ready for a new mommy."

Mark frowned. "What makes you say that?
Sasha still thinks of Diane as her mother."

"Does she? I hear her talking to Bella about
a real mommy, not just one in a photograph."

"So I keep a lot of pictures around, and so

I haven't changed anything in the house since Diane's been gone? It's important for Sasha to remember her mother." Aware his voice had risen, Mark clamped his jaw shut.

Bernie raised both hands. "Hey, forget I said anything. Not my business."

Mark forced a grin and gave Bernie a soft punch on the shoulder. "Sorry. I didn't mean to jump all over you when you're trying to help. How does all this relate to Eva? You don't even like her."

Bernie nodded. "Glad you reminded me. But I still say there's some sparky stuff between you two."

"Maybe there is. But that doesn't mean I have to do anything about it."

"No, I guess not." Bernie drained his mug and stood. "I gotta get back to work."

"Glad you're on the job, buddy. Check with you later."

After Bernie left, Mark sat there rubbing the back of his neck, hoping to ease his tension. He was upset with himself for the way he'd treated Eva. Sure, forgetting her obligation about the store opening was annoying, but he'd been able to step in and cover for her. She went to Seattle and spent time with friends. So what?

He knew the answer. He'd missed her. He'd secretly hoped they would meet up at the opening and spend the day together. Maybe the evening, too. Corralling his feelings about Eva was driving him crazy. He'd lectured himself over and over that there could be nothing between them. Yet whenever she came near, his reasoning was forgotten, and all he wanted to do was take her in his arms and kiss her.

A little less than ten months to go? Might as well be ten years.

"HAPPY BIRTHDAY, SASHA!"

Eva joined the chorus of voices that filled the living room. The birthday girl, a gold paper crown atop her blond curls, sat on the floor surrounded by her guests. The birthday cake, with *Happy Birthday, Sasha!* written in pink icing across the top, sat on the coffee table next to a stack of paper plates and plastic forks.

They'd played Pin the Tail on the Donkey, an alphabet game and a rhyming game, and now it was time for eating cake and opening the gifts. Cheeks puffed, Sasha leaned forward and blew out the six candles. Before the smoke cleared, April pulled them off and picked up a knife to cut the cake. Eileen added a scoop of ice cream and delivered the plates to the guests. Eva had offered to help earlier, but not surprisingly, the two women waved her off, saying they had their own system. As she ate her cake and ice cream with the younger guests, Eva looked around. She hadn't had much chance earlier, and she'd admittedly been curious about Mark's house. All she'd known was that he lived in the south end of town near the high school.

His home turned out to be a modest frame home, similar to Seb's but smaller. The furniture in the living room was mostly royal-blue, with yellow and lime-green cushions and an afghan for accents. Not colors Eva would pick but apparently chosen with some thought.

A flower arrangement that was obviously fake sat on an end table. It looked as if it could use a good dusting. A blue crocheted doily peeked out from under the silver pot. Who used doilies anymore?

The house, although outdated, obviously had a woman's touch. In fact, had she not known Mark's wife had died, she'd think a woman lived there still.

Her gaze caught a row of framed photos on the mantel. Looking around to make sure everyone else was busy eating and talking, she got up and, still holding her cake plate, casually made her way to them. The most prominent photo, in the center of the group, was of a woman with short blond hair and wide-set blue eyes. Her lips looked overpainted, as though she were trying to make them appear fuller than they were.

The eyes, as well as the dainty nose and the bow-shaped mouth, confirmed this was Sasha's mother, Diane.

Eva studied the other photos. One showed Mark and Diane on their wedding day; another had them with baby Sasha in Diane's arms; and still another captured them digging clams at the beach.

To her surprise, Eva felt her throat tighten. They appeared to be such a happy family. What a tragedy for both Mark and Sasha to have lost Diane. But as she gazed around the room again, she got an eerie feeling that, somehow, Diane was still here.

"Time to open your gifts, birthday girl!"

April's strident voice broke into Eva's thoughts. She gobbled the last bite of cake and returned to her seat.

Sasha perched on the sofa, the children clustered at her feet. April gathered the presents from the dining-room table and brought them to Sasha. With its glittery paper and huge bow, Eva's gift was easy for her to spot.

April sat beside Sasha and handed her a bulky package. "Open mine first."

Sasha tore off the paper to reveal a backpack decorated with the picture of a cartoon rabbit. "Ohhhh."

"Look inside," April said.

Sasha opened the pack and pulled out two children's books.

"You'll soon be able to read them," April said.

"I already know my ABC's and some words." Sasha gazed at the books' covers then put them down and reached to give April a hug. "Thank you, April."

"You're welcome, honey." April hugged her back.

Sasha continued opening her gifts, accompanied by oohs and aahs from her audience. A board game, a jump rope, a mechanical dog that sat up and begged for a plastic bone. Finally, April handed over Eva's gift.

Sasha tore off the wrapping paper and opened the box. A navy blue patent leather purse was on top. She held up the purse, her eyes shining. "It's bea-u-ti-ful!" She put it down and pulled out a long-sleeved navy-blue-and-white striped top, blue leggings, a navy blue skirt and, finally, a matching jacket. Her eyes rounded to saucers. "Wow."

"I thought you might like something new for school," Eva said, pleased with Sasha's reaction to her gift.

April wrinkled her nose. "Too fancy for school."

Eva didn't know from experience what girls Sasha's age were wearing to school, but she felt compelled to defend her choice. "The outfit was part of a back-to-school display at Macy's in Seattle."

"Oh, of course, Seattle." April's voice was cold.

Sasha looked up at Mark, who watched from the doorway. "Can I wear it to school, Daddy?"

Mark cleared his throat. "Why, sure," he finally said. "If that's what you want."

"I want to put on the jacket now."

Eva sat on Sasha's other side and helped her to slip into the jacket. As she'd hoped, it fit perfectly.

Sasha smoothed the fabric with one hand. "It feels soft," she said, then leaned to Eva. "Thank you."

Eva put her arms around Sasha. "You're welcome, sweetie."

Tears suddenly misted Eva's eyes. What was that all about? She kept her gaze lowered until she'd blinked them away.

Mark stepped farther into the room and beckoned to the group. "Come on outside, everyone, and see my gift to Sasha."

Eva helped Sasha out of the jacket, then she folded it and returned it to the box. With the children chattering excitedly, they all trooped through the kitchen and out the back door. The fenced backyard was a child's dream, with a large playhouse, a swing and slide set, and a sandbox. In one corner sat a trampoline with a big red bow tied around one post.

"Daddy, you got it!" Sasha ran to give him a hug, and then, with the other children close on her heels, she scampered to the trampoline.

Mark cupped his hands around his mouth.

"Only three on the trampoline at one time," he called after them. He hurried over to make sure the children followed his directions. While April dogged his heels, Eva watched from the kitchen doorway.

Sasha and two other children began jumping. The remainder of the guests watched for a while, then headed for the swings and slide. Two of the children's mothers and one father arrived. Along with Eileen, who'd finished tidying up the gifts and discarded wrappings, they joined Mark and April. Laughter and chatter filled the backyard.

Something akin to envy crept over Eva. She always felt out of place in a group of parents and children. They all had something in common, whereas she was the outsider. April wasn't an official parent, but she might as well be. Why didn't Mark marry her? Her feelings for him were obvious. Eva decided to leave but not without thanking her hosts. She managed to catch Mark's eye. She waved, and he broke from the group and trotted over.

"I need to leave," Eva said, "but I wanted to say thanks for inviting me. Tell Sasha goodbye for me, will you?"

"Okay, but we're all going to the Pizza Palace. You want to come along?" He slanted her a dubious look.

Eva stepped back. "I, uh, no!" That sounded sharper than she intended. "I mean, no, thank you," she said in a softer tone. "I really need to get back to my apartment."

In truth, pizza sounded good, but tagging along with the group would just make her feel more uncomfortable and out of place.

Propping an arm against the doorjamb, he leaned toward her, his face close enough to send a wave of his aftershave in her direction.

"Sure I can't talk you into coming? What's the matter? Don't you like pizza?"

She sucked in a breath, knowing she should move away, but her feet were rooted to the spot. The voices and laughter coming from the backyard faded into the distance.

"Sure, I like pizza. But I need to leave. I'll see you on Monday."

He frowned and then said, "Right. Monday."

That should have settled the matter, yet neither made a move. The air thickened. Eva swallowed and licked her dry lips. He leaned closer.

"Mark," a voice called. "Oh, there you are."

April ran up and pushed between Eva and Mark, forcing them to step back.

Eva jolted to her senses. Mark shook his head, as though to clear it.

"Yeah, April?" Mark's voice was impatient.

"I took a head count, like you asked me to. There are twelve of us." She turned to Eva. "Unless you're coming, too."

"No, I'm on my way out. Just saying good-bye." Eva brushed past them and hurried across the kitchen.

"I'll see you out," Mark called after her.

"Never mind. I can find my way."

As she headed for the front door, April's petulant voice drifted behind her.

"We need to get ready to go, Mark. The Pizza Palace will only hold our tables for fifteen minutes."

# CHAPTER TEN

Eva STARED AT the single sentence at the top of her computer screen. Her total output in the past hour. Needing something to do in the evening after work, she'd begun writing a novel. So far, she had twenty-eight pages. She'd always wanted to write fiction. She'd thought it would be as easy as turning out one of her articles for *Seattle's Best* and certainly as easy as writing a piece for the *Herald*.

"Write what you know" was the accepted wisdom, so she started a story about a woman who'd been forced to take a job she didn't want. She had no idea where the story was going. So far, it was a very familiar-sounding mishmash of the woman's complaints.

She rose, made herself another cup of tea and strolled to the window. Outside, twilight dusted the sky a lovely shade of peach. Lovely? When had she used such a word to describe anything in Willow Beach? Yet that was the word that came to mind and the one that fit.

She was still contemplating the sky when she heard a knock on the door. She jumped. Who could that be? Probably her neighbor across the hall, wanting to borrow something. She put down her cup, went to the door and peered through the peephole.

Mark.

She pressed her lips together in exasperation. What was he doing here? He was supposed to be at the Pizza Palace with the others. Furthermore, he'd never come to her apartment before, not once in the two months she'd been here.

She smoothed her hair and straightened her blouse and then realized what she was doing and stopped. She didn't need to look good for Mark Townson.

When she unbolted and opened the door, he stood there looking uncertain and cautious.

"Mark. What brings you here?"

"Pizza." He dipped his head toward the flat box he carried.

She looked at the box and then back up at him. "You didn't have to do this."

"I wanted to."

When he made no move to hand her the box, she realized he was waiting to be invited in. She wasn't sure she wanted to be alone with him. There was that startling kiss at the picnic to consider, and today, before April interrupted them, they'd come awfully close to *something* at the birthday party.

But she didn't want to be rude.

"Want to come in? Or do you need to get home?" *Please say you need to go home.*

"I can hang out for a while," he said, stepping over the threshold with no hesitation. "The pizza party's still going strong, and Eileen's taking care of Sasha."

The aroma of melted cheese made her realize how hungry she was. She hadn't bothered to fix anything to eat since she'd been home, and the cake and ice cream from the party had long worn off.

He crossed the room and set the box on the kitchen counter. "It's cold now, but you can warm it up."

"I will. I'm hungry." Eva opened the box and sniffed the air. "It smells yummy. What all's on it?"

He looked over her shoulder. "Sausage and mushrooms and olives and lots of other stuff.

I wasn't sure what you'd like, so I ordered the one they call Kitchen Sink."

"Do you want to join me?"

He patted his stomach. "I saved room for a piece or two."

Opening a cupboard, she took out her one glass oven dish. It had a chip in one side, but perhaps he wouldn't notice. "I'll make some coffee. Or would you rather have a soda?"

"Coffee's fine."

While she cut slices of pizza and slid them into the dish, he strolled to the window. "Great view."

"It is. I really enjoy the sunsets."

He turned and raised one eyebrow. "Does that mean you're beginning to like living here?"

Eva covered the dish with plastic wrap, tucked it into the microwave and set the timer. "No, it's only a view—it doesn't work miracles. Besides, I have a view at home. Not of the ocean, of course, but of the city's skyline and a bit of Elliott Bay."

She thought he looked disappointed at her answer, but he turned back to the window before she could be sure.

She took out plates and set them on the

table, then stepped to the computer, preparing to shut it down. Mark came up behind her, looking over her shoulder at the screen-saver and its photo of the Seattle skyline, the Space Needle front and center.

"You're not bringing work home, are you?" Mark asked.

"No, just checking my email." That was true. She had checked her email—earlier. But she didn't want to tell him about her novel. The project was too new, too personal to share with anyone.

When they finally settled at the table, the pizza fairly melted in Eva's mouth. "This is wonderful."

Mark nodded. "The Pizza Palace is the best."

They ate in silence for a couple minutes, then she cast him a sideways glance. "It was thoughtful of you to feed me tonight, but I can't help feeling something else is on your mind."

He put down his coffee cup and sat back, his eyes troubled. "You're right. There is something. It's about your gift to Sasha...."

The gift. She might have known. "The outfit is too dressy and you want me to take it back."

He raised a hand and, his tone harsh, said, "No, of course not." Then, in a softer voice, he added, "Okay, I admit it's not something I would have picked out."

"But she would have."

"Yeah, she would have. She loves it. When you mentioned seeing the clothes at Macy's, I realized you must've bought them when you were in Seattle last weekend. And I felt like a jerk because I gave you such a hard time for missing the store opening."

Eva helped herself to another slice of pizza. "Yeah, you were a jerk, but that was my assignment and I shouldn't have forgotten about it."

He drew back. "A jerk, huh?"

She shrugged. "You said it first."

"Okay, I won't argue—this time. Tonight I want to be Mr. Good Guy and thank you for thinking of Sasha and for helping to make her birthday special."

Mark's words sent a curious warmth spiraling through Eva. "You're welcome. I knew that would be the only weekend I had to shop for her present. Susan and I had fun picking out the clothes, and I'm glad Sasha likes them." Remembering April's comment, she frowned. "But maybe April's right and they are too fancy for school."

"Why don't we let Sasha decide?"

"Good idea."

They ate in silence for a couple minutes, and then Mark said, "I thought the feature about the shoe store turned out well. Your interviews were a good contribution."

She raised an eyebrow. "Are you paying me a compliment?"

He held up a hand. "Hey, I never said I thought you were a bad writer. I just don't have much use for what you write about. You do have a knack for interviewing people. You know how to get them to talk."

"Interviews are what I do for *Seattle's Best*. Did," she corrected, lowering her gaze.

"Well, we turned out a worthy feature."

"Yes, we did," she replied, noticing they'd both said *we*. The word sounded strange and alien, yet kind of nice, too.

"Just a fluke," Mark said.

"Right. Won't happen again."

Mark looked away. "No, of course not."

After that, conversation died, and they finished their pizza in silence. "More coffee?" she finally asked.

"No, thanks. I'm good."

"Well, then, I guess that's it." She stacked the plates and carried them to the sink.

He pushed back his chair and stood. "Anything I can do?"

"I don't think so. This is an easy cleanup." She set the dishes in the sink, intending to rinse and load them in the dishwasher after he left. Which she hoped would be soon.

She turned to find him standing directly behind her.

"Eva…"

Mark's voice was low and husky. He reached out as though to draw her to him. She wanted to let him. Oh, yes, she did.

But before he could touch her, she stepped back and folded her arms. "Don't you have to pick up Sasha now?"

For a moment he looked puzzled, as though he didn't know what she was talking about. Then he blinked and shook his head. "Sasha… yeah." He checked his wristwatch. "Time to pick up my little girl."

"Thanks again for the pizza."

"You're welcome."

He made no move to leave. Eva felt his gaze on her but was afraid to meet his eyes. Afraid she'd fall into his arms and let him kiss her. And then what would happen? Where would it end?

Finally she made her feet move across the room toward the front door. He followed. She opened the door, they said a couple of polite goodbyes and then he was gone.

Eva shut the door, leaned her back against it and whooshed out a breath. She listened to Mark's footsteps fade away. He was gone at last. What a relief. She rested against the door a few more moments and then wandered back to the kitchen table, where her computer waited. She reached out to open the cover and switch on the machine, but then dropped her hand to her side. No energy left for writing tonight. The encounter with Mark had drained her.

Eva sighed. How had life become so complicated?

MARK COULDN'T GET AWAY from Eva's apartment fast enough; he pushed the speed limit all the way to Eileen's. Still, he decided he'd made the right decision to leave the pizza party and drive to her apartment. Clearing the air over her gift to Sasha relieved the distress he'd felt since the party.

But if he'd expected to ease all the tension between them, he'd been wrong. Their attraction to each other was as strong as ever. He ached to touch her, even as simple a gesture as placing a hand on her arm.

And then, just before he left this evening, the desire to kiss her almost undid him. He wondered what would have happened if she hadn't broken the spell.

Later, after he and Sasha had arrived home and they'd stepped inside the house, he looked around at the blue upholstered sofa and chairs, the yellow and green cushions, the artificial plants and the photographs and felt Diane's presence more than ever. Yes, she had hurt him deeply, but he needed her to be here. For Sasha's sake, he always told himself. But tonight, he had to admit he needed her for himself, too.

Resisting his attraction to Eva was the right course of action. He didn't want to risk giving away his heart again, especially not to Eva. Why put him and Sasha through the misery of another ill-fated relationship?

EVA PULLED HER CAR into the parking lot at Willow Beach High School. She stepped out and hurried toward the building's entrance. Today was the back-to-school fashion show she'd agreed to emcee. Together she and Fran Oliver had chosen the clothing from the town's one shop and from a store in nearby Langston. The outfits weren't as stylish as those they might have found in Seattle—in Eva's opinion anyway—but overall, she was pleased with the results.

Once inside the building, she headed for the auditorium's backstage, where the teenage models had assembled. Chatter and laughter charged the air as the girls spilled in and out of the dressing rooms.

Fran emerged from one of the rooms. She hurried over to Eva, her blond curls bouncing as she walked. Her eyes had a frantic look. "Thank goodness you're here. Trilly can't find her wedge heels, and Marla's having a bad hair day. Help!"

Eva laid a calming hand on Fran's arm. "Not to worry. Tell Trilly the shoes are on the shelf in dressing room C, and reassure Marla that the ladies from the hair salon should be here any moment."

An hour later, the models were all dressed in their initial outfits and ready to appear on the stage's makeshift runway. Eva peeked out the curtains. The auditorium, full of students and teachers, hummed with anticipation. In the orchestra pit, a band from the Music Department tuned their instruments. Off to one side, Cody bent over his camera and tripod. Along with some of her friends, Luci sat in the front row, hands poised over her laptop, ready to take notes for her article.

Eva took a deep breath and stepped onto the stage. The band's lively music escorted her to the microphone. "Good afternoon," she began, "and welcome to Willow Beach High's Back to School Fashion Show…"

With only a couple minor emergencies—a skirt's hem had to be mended and a loose button secured—the show went smoothly. Afterward, the teens crowded around Eva, full of appreciation. "We've never done anything like this before," one of them said. "It was so fun," another chimed in.

"Glad you liked it," Eva said. "You all did a wonderful job."

As the girls drifted off, Fran bustled over. "Eva, that was wonderful." She clapped her hands but then in the next instant sobered and ducked her head. "I have a favor to ask."

"Need some help cleaning up? I'd be glad to stay—"

Fran shook her head. "No, that's all taken care of. I want to know if you'll talk to my Home Living class. About managing money. Especially tips on budgeting."

Eva pressed a hand to her chest. "Me? Talk to a class? I have written articles on the subject, but I'm not a teacher."

Fran waved her hand in a gesture of apology. "Oh. I just thought—I mean, you worked so well with the kids on the show—"

"It's okay, Fran. You just took me by surprise." She considered a moment. "And you're right. This was fun. I'll speak to your class."

"Great." Fran gave Eva a hug.

They made plans to discuss the details soon over coffee.

As Eva headed for the door, the owner of the local clothing store stopped to ask about a new ad in the *Herald*. Eva promised to have Bernie Sanchez give her a call.

Eva left the school with a spring in her step. She'd had *fun*. The show wasn't as glamorous as those she'd attended for *Seattle's Best,* but working with the teens was challenging and rewarding, and emceeing the show had been a special treat.

The following day, Luci emailed Eva the article she'd written. Eva read the piece and had it displayed on her computer screen when Luci came to her cubicle later that day.

Eva waved the intern into the chair by her desk. "You did a good job, Luci. You've included all the essentials and made it interesting." In a gentle tone, she added, "Let's make the lead a bit stronger." She offered a few suggestions but told Luci she could make the final decision.

After Luci reworked the lead, they selected one of Cody's photos to accompany the article.

When they were finished, Luci sat back and smiled at Eva. "I've learned so much. I can't wait to see my words in print."

"This is exciting for me, too," Eva said.

Now all she had to do was convince Mark to give the article top billing. Considering his preference for hard news, she knew she'd be facing a tough challenge.

THAT EVENING, dressed in sweats now that the weather was cooler, Eva jogged along the beach. She hadn't gone far when she glimpsed Mark heading toward her. Since the night they'd shared pizza at her house after Sasha's birthday, he'd joined her for these early-evening runs once or twice a week.

She was especially glad to see him today because she needed to talk to him about Luci's article. She'd sent him the piece earlier that day with the recommendation that it be given page-one status and had expected him to get back to her. He hadn't. Did he find the idea so ridiculous he couldn't even respond?

Maybe discussing the article on neutral ground would be a good way to handle the matter.

She waved at him. "Hey, Mark!"

He stopped. "Eva. Thought you might be out here tonight."

"I need to talk to you."

He hesitated, then shrugged. "Okay, Beach Café?"

"Perfect."

They ran beside each other without speaking again until they reached the café. The weather was too cold to sit outside and they weren't there for dinner, so Mark led them into the bar. They wound their way around the potted palm trees and underneath hanging ferns to an empty corner booth. The waitress ambled over and took their order. A few minutes later, she returned bearing a tray with Eva's latte and Mark's plain coffee.

Eva sat back against the padded booth and sipped her coffee. On another occasion, she might enjoy having a leisurely drink after an invigorating run. But tonight, worry about Luci's article kept her nerves on edge.

"So how's Sasha doing in first grade?" she asked. Talking about his daughter would be a safe way to start a conversation.

"Good, good. She and Bella are in the same class, and they like their teacher."

"And since you read to her a lot, she probably has a head start there."

"Probably." He raised an eyebrow. "I appreciate your interest in my daughter, Eva, but I don't think that's what you really want to talk about. What's on your mind?"

"Okay, I sent you Luci's article today. Did you not see it?

Avoiding her eyes, Mark carefully set his cup on the paper coaster. "I did. I read it."

"So, what do you think? Or is that a stupid question?"

He looked up and met her gaze. "Aw, Eva, you can't expect me to all of a sudden like fluff pieces. I'm like the leopard—I don't change my spots."

Eva gripped the cup so hard the warmth of the porcelain made her skin tingle. "Fluff. I hate that word. Besides, the article is not fluff. You must have missed the part about Fran Oliver using the show to teach lessons in budgeting and comparison shopping."

"I got that. Still—"

Eva made a fist and pounded the table. "If you kill this piece, I'm walking out of here right now. And I swear you'll never see me again, will or no will."

He held up a hand. "Hold it. I never said we wouldn't run it. But you can't expect it to be page one."

"Why not? A school levy is up for a vote in November. Seems to me Luci's article ought to be a boost for its passage. You are in favor of funding education, aren't you?"

"Of course I am. And you've got a point. But we also need to run the piece I wrote about the new highway construction. That's big news. How about a couple of paragraphs

at the bottom of page one for Luci's article
and the rest inside?"

Eva narrowed her eyes. "I'll go for that if
we use one of Cody's photos of the show as
the page's feature photo."

"Hmm." Mark rubbed his chin.

"Mark…" How could he be so stubborn?

Finally, he said, "Okay, three columns and
the feature photo."

Eva sagged back against the seat and let
the tension seep from her stiff shoulders. Her
face felt warm. As she ran a hand over her
forehead, she caught Mark's grin.

"What?" she snapped, irked that he seemed
to find their argument amusing.

"I've never seen you so *passionate* about
anything to do with the *Herald*. You enjoyed
working with Luci and being out in the community. Didn't you? Just a little?"

Eva flattened her palms on the table. "So
that's what this is all about. You've been giving me a hard time so I'll admit I *enjoyed*
what I was doing?"

He lifted a shoulder. "Maybe. Sort of."

"Okay, I did like working with Luci and
the other teens. But it had nothing to do with
the *Herald*. Luci reminds me of myself at

that age, when I was thinking about becoming a writer."

"When your dad mentored you."

Eva lifted her chin. "We need to get something straight. Seb never mentored me. My brother was the one he wanted to follow him at the newspaper."

"Why not both of you?"

She shrugged. "Brett was always Dad's favorite."

"But then when your brother died— Yes, don't look so surprised. I know about his... accident at Pine Lake."

Accident. She put down her cup and hugged her arms against the pain that spiraled through her.

"After that, your father did want you in the business. He sent you to school, didn't he?"

She snapped back to the present. "Why are we talking about this? What does it have to do with Luci's article?"

"Because I want to know more about your father. He was like a father to me sometimes."

Realizing how little she knew about him, she asked, "What about your own dad?"

Mark set his jaw. "He walked out on my mother and me when I was a baby. He went to work one day and never came home. Mom tried to find him, but she never could. She raised me on her own."

"Where's your mother now?"

"She remarried but not until I was grown and out of the house. She and her new husband moved to Florida." He waved his hand. "He's an okay guy. He has a big family there, so she has lots of step-relatives. Mom saw Sasha once when they came for a visit. She sends gifts and letters, though, and phones occasionally."

"Well, good that Seb found you, then, isn't it?"

"I found him. I'm the one who came looking for a job." He leaned forward. "But I also want to know more about what happened between you and him because I want to understand you better."

She widened her eyes. "Me? Why?"

"Well, ah, because now you're here, and we have a business to run. I want it to run as smoothly as possible."

"Oh. The newspaper. Of course."

"Maybe the newspaper isn't the only reason…"

He reached across the table and grasped

her hand. She welcomed his touch. The kiss they'd shared on the Fourth of July seemed aeons ago.

Mark looked about to say more, but just then a deep voice said, "Well, look who's here."

Eva turned around to see Boyd Carlstrom lumbering toward them. *Oh, no, not* him. *Not now.*

Maybe his interruption was a good thing, though. She and Mark were venturing into dangerous territory. She withdrew her hand from his and sat up straight.

Boyd reached their booth. Instead of the suit jacket and trousers he wore when he and Eva met for lunch, tonight he was more casual in jeans and a blue windbreaker. The jacket hung open to reveal a white sweatshirt tightly stretched across his prominent stomach.

Eva smiled up at him. "Hello, Boyd. You're in town again."

"Yep. Lookin' at property. Thinkin' about moving back." Turning to Mark, he stuck out his hand. The ruby fraternity ring gleamed under the overhead lights. "You must be Eva's other half."

Mark scowled but reached out for a handshake. "I'm the other editor at the *Herald*," he said in a tight voice.

"Right. I've been meaning to stop in and introduce myself. See if the place has changed any since I was there. I know Dora's still there. She's been there since the Drakes were the owners. Saw her in town the other day, putting those scarves she makes in Betty's Boutique."

Withdrawing his hand, Mark crossed his arms over his chest. "If you want to talk about buying the newspaper, don't waste your time on me. My share isn't for sale. Never has been, never will be."

Boyd's eyelids flickered. "Good thing that isn't the case with Eva here."

"This really isn't a good time to discuss business." Eva flashed Boyd what she hoped was a back-off look.

Boyd's slight nod indicated he got the message.

"Just wanted to say hello. When Helen and I came in, I told her, 'Hey, there's someone I need to say hi to.' I got her settled and came on over." He nodded across the sea of tables to the bar along the far wall.

Peering around him, Eva saw a slim blonde

sitting on one of the stools, facing their direction. She grinned and fluttered her fingers. Eva waved back.

Boyd pulled a brown leather wallet from a back pocket of his jeans and dug into it. He fished out a business card and slid it across the table to Mark. "In my business, I've learned never to say never. So, in case you change your mind, you'll know where to reach me."

Mark made no move to pick up the card. He clamped his jaw shut and regarded Boyd with cold eyes.

Boyd stuffed his wallet away. "Alrighty, then. Be seeing you. Especially you." He pointed a pudgy finger at Eva. "Nice meetin' you, Mark."

Mark barely nodded before Boyd turned away and shuffled back to his companion.

Eva sagged against the back of the booth. She let a moment go by, waiting for Mark to speak first. When he didn't, she said, "That was…awkward."

Mark shook his head and narrowed his eyes. "You're not really considering doing business with that slimeball, are you?"

His criticism of her judgment stung. She set

her jaw. "Okay, so he could use a little polish. I told you how kind he was to me when I was a child. He must have some smarts to own so many newspapers."

"Do you think they're as good as the *Herald?*"

"I don't know. I didn't read any of the ones he showed me. They looked the same, though."

"So are you going to sell to him?"

"I can't do anything until next summer. That's nine months away." She closed her eyes and sighed. "A *looong* way away."

"I'm sorry being here is such an *ordeal* for you."

She curled her fingers into fists. "I hate this bickering."

"So do I. We'll call it a night."

"Fine by me."

As she rose from the booth to follow Mark, she glanced back at the table and saw Boyd's business card still lying there. Mark's insult to someone she considered a friend irked her and, even though she already had one from their lunch together, she picked up the card and tucked it into her pocket.

## CHAPTER ELEVEN

THE FOLLOWING FRIDAY, Mark strode into Bernie's cubicle. "Emergency staff meeting, four o'clock this afternoon."

Bernie looked up from the notes scattered across his desk. A frown knit his dark brows. "Staff meeting? Didn't Eva take off at noon for Seattle?"

"Yeah, she did. That's why we're having a meeting."

A look of understanding swept across Bernie's face. "We need to discuss our future. Again."

"You got it."

Mark spread the word to the rest of the employees and at four o'clock they assembled in the staff room. Mark waited until they'd settled down with coffee and the pastry left over from April's morning run to the Bon Ton, then he plunged in.

"Boyd Carlstrom is in town again." He told

them what had occurred at the Beach Café. "He's thinking about moving back to Willow Beach. He's been looking at property."

"Because he plans to own the *Herald* again?" Bernie said.

"Looks that way. He and Eva are pretty thick."

Dora's knitting needles flew. "I thought she was settling in. At the Country Store the other day, she had a basket load of dishes, towels and throw rugs, stuff like that."

"She's the consummate shopper," Mark said. "I don't think her buying stuff for her apartment means much."

"She was nice to me when we worked on the high-school fashion show." Cody leaned back in his chair. "Told me what she wanted and then let me do my thing."

Mark cradled his coffee cup and nodded. "And I let her talk me into putting Luci's article on page one. No offense to your fine photography, Cody. It's always good enough for page one."

"None taken," Cody said. "But Luci ran her draft by me before she showed it to Eva. I thought her take on the show was pretty good."

"It was good. But not page one. Fashion shows are not the kind of news we feature. We have letters to the editor that back me up on that. Our readers have expectations— expectations that Seb established and that I aim to uphold."

"So what's the bottom line here, boss?" Bernie asked, tapping his foot.

Mark ran a hand through his hair. "We can't allow Boyd to buy Eva's share of the newspaper. We don't want him here. Seb didn't want him here, either."

"Boyd sounds like bad news, all right," Bernie said. "Pun intended. But I don't see how we can keep Eva from selling out to him if she wants to. Unless you can buy her out."

Mark snorted. "Huh! Not likely."

"Could you get a loan?"

"I don't know. I could look into it. Trouble is, we don't know how much he's offered her, and I doubt either one of them would tell us."

"Maybe if we all pooled our money…" Bernie said.

"Yeah, we could be like a co-op," Cody said.

"I don't want to take your money." Mark shook his head.

"But we want to help." Dora put down her

knitting and straightened her shoulders. "Let us try."

"I can give you fifty next paycheck," Bernie said.

"Josh and I have a CD coming due," Dora said. "I'll chip in a hundred."

"Put me down for twenty, but not till next week," Cody said.

April shrugged. "My landlord just raised our rent, but count me in for ten this week and ten more after payday."

Even if he could get a loan, Mark had his doubts about them ever raising enough money to match Boyd's offer, but they were all looking at him with such enthusiasm that he couldn't say no.

"If that's what you want to do, okay," he said. "In the meantime, let's do everything we can to make the *Herald* a publication Seb would be proud of."

"What do you think of this outfit?" Susan Jensen held out her arms and twirled around as though she were a runway model.

Eva turned from the rack at Belle Boutique where she was sorting through tops and gave her friend's periwinkle-blue skirt and tunic top a sweeping gaze. "Very nice. Good color for you."

Susan patted her stomach. "Does the longer top make me look slimmer?"

Eva tilted her head. "Um …"

Susan pouted. "I know what you really want to say—that the only thing that will make me look slimmer is fewer raspberry scones. All your fault." She pointed a finger. "If I hadn't moved into your condo with that bakery on the street level, I would never have become addicted to those scones."

Eva tossed back her head and laughed. "Okay, blame me if you insist. The outfit is gorgeous. Have the clerk wrap it up and let's go eat lunch."

"Okay. But aren't you buying anything?"

"A couple tops is all." Eva held out the clothing draped over her arm.

"You're not even looking at the dresses?"

"I haven't worn a dress or a skirt in months. All my work clothes are going to be out of style by the time I come back to Seattle."

Twenty minutes later they pushed through the door at Clay's Waterfront Restaurant. "I'm so glad to be home again, even for a couple days," Eva said and then stopped short as she almost ran into someone. "Whoa, what's this? A line for tables? Do we want to wait?" She stood on tiptoes. "There must be two dozen people ahead of us."

Susan shifted her shopping bag from one hand to the other. "There's always a wait here. It's never stopped us before."

"Right. Of course we'll wait. I wish I hadn't worn these shoes, though. My feet aren't used to high heels anymore."

When they finally were seated and had placed their orders, Susan said, "How are things between you and Mark?"

Eva sipped her iced tea and then frowned. "We've gone from bad to worse." She told Susan about Boyd Carlstrom and his offer to buy her half of the *Herald*.

"That would be a good out for you, wouldn't it?"

Eva nodded. "But Mark would have a fit. He says my father didn't want Boyd to have anything to do with the *Herald* again. What happens to the newspaper is not my concern. And I can accept Boyd's offer if I want to."

"Too bad you feel that way."

Eva looked down at her plate. "Yes, isn't it? Maybe if things had been different…"

"What do you mean?"

"If my brother had lived…"

"I remember you mentioning a brother, but you've never said much about him."

"No, I don't talk about him a lot. But since I've been back in Willow Beach, he's been on my mind. And that's the main reason I don't want to live there again. It harbors too many painful memories."

"I hear you. I've never lost anyone close to me—yet—but my sorority sister's brother committed suicide while we were in college. I don't think Jilly and her family are over it to this day. What happened to your brother?"

"He, uh, drowned in a boating accident. Right after he graduated high school. He was supposed to go to the U and then work for my father's newspaper, but he…"

Susan leaned forward. "Yes?"

Eva closed her eyes and put down her fork. "I can't talk about it, Suse. I'm sorry."

Susan laid a hand on Eva's arm. "You don't have to, hon."

Eva forced a smile. "I want to hear something happy, which is you and Greg…I hope. Tell me, how are you two getting along?"

Susan's eyes brightened. "Our relationship is moving along quite nicely, thank you."

"You're still sure he's the one?"

"Oh, absolutely. And he's hinting at a permanent relationship."

"As in marriage?"

"That's the only permanent I'll accept. You know I've been dreaming about being a bride since I was a little girl. Well, Greg hasn't actually proposed yet, but he's danced all around the subject, asking me what kind of house I'd like to live in, how many children I want and whether I favor a large or a small wedding."

"That does sound serious."

Susan held up a hand. "I haven't picked out my china pattern yet, Eva. But I am excited about this relationship."

"I'm happy for you, Susan. I really am."

EVA SAT AT the dining-room table, her fingers flying over the computer's keyboard. Her novel was going full speed. When she'd scrapped the self-pitying story she'd started with and used her imagination to come up with something else, the story rolled along. Even if she never got it published, at least she was filling her time with something that interested her.

She took a break to make a cup of tea. While she waited for the water to heat, she glanced at her wall calendar and her enthusiasm drained away. Filling the time or not, more than half a year of her exile remained. Nothing she could do about that. Time moved at its own pace.

October's fall colors had faded into November's gray, with fewer sunny days and a windstorm or two. And with November came Thanksgiving. How would she spend the holiday? Last Thanksgiving she'd invited a dozen of her friends to a dinner at her condo. She hadn't actually cooked the dinner—her favorite caterer had supplied the food—but no one seemed to mind.

An idea brought a smile to her lips. Maybe this year she and Susan could collaborate on a similar party. Greg would be included, of course. The occasion would be a good chance to meet the man who had so captivated her friend. She picked up her cell phone and punched in Susan's number.

"How about you and I hosting Thanksgiving at the condo for all our friends?" she suggested when Susan came on the line.

"That's a great idea, Eva, but I've already planned to ski Whistler over the holiday."

"Oh, is there a group going?" Maybe she could tag along. She wasn't particularly fond of skiing, but she could always hang out in the lodge.

"Actually, no," Susan said. "I'm going with Greg and his parents. They have a vacation condo there."

"You're meeting his parents?" Eva teased. "Sounds serious."

"I'm excited, but a little nervous, too."

Clutching the phone, Eva stood and wandered to the window. She gazed idly into the distance, where the ocean sparkled under a moonlit sky. "I can have my own party, like I did last year."

"I'm sorry." Susan's voice was heavy with apology. "I've already promised my cousins they can have the condo then. Wish I'd known earlier that you wanted to come. I'm sure you could be included in their party."

"No, no, I don't want to intrude on their celebration. It's just that I miss Seattle sooo much."

"I know," Susan said in a softer tone. "I'd feel the same way if I were away from home.

But hang in there. You're almost halfway through. Did you ever think of that?"

"Always, but the holidays are a difficult time."

"They are, and don't think I'm not having my own little meltdown. Meeting Greg's folks has me tied in knots."

"You'll do fine, Suse. They'll love you."

After they hung up, Eva thought about calling a few of her other Seattle friends to see what they were up to for the holiday. Or maybe some of the friends she had here. Or used to have here. She hadn't kept in touch with anyone, save for an occasional email exchange with Fran. No, she wouldn't call anyone, either here or in Seattle. She didn't want them to think she was begging for an invitation.

The following day at the newspaper office, when she went to the staff room to refill her coffee mug, Mark was there. He sat at the table, looking over some notes. He glanced up and they nodded to each other.

As she stood at the coffee urn, he said, "I suppose you're going home for Thanksgiving."

"I'm not sure yet. My plans are, uh, fluid at the moment."

"Fluid, huh? Okay, here's a thought. If you happen to be stuck here and need something to do—" He paused to sip his coffee, gazing at her over the rim of the mug.

Was he going to suggest they spend the holiday together? She poured hazelnut creamer into her coffee, picked up a spoon and gave the brew a vigorous stir.

"The community center cooks dinner for people who have no place to go," he finally finished.

Oh. So he wasn't asking her to spend the day with him and Sasha, after all. She brushed away a niggle of disappointment.

"No, I don't think I want to eat there."

"I wasn't suggesting you eat there. I was suggesting you help out. You would get your dinner, too, if you wanted."

"Help out. You know I'm not much of a cook."

He smiled. "Yeah, we had a sample of your cooking at the picnic, didn't we? There are other ways to help. I happen to know they particularly need servers. I don't think you'd have any trouble dishing up food."

"Thanks, but I don't think that's where I want to be, even if I do stay in town—which I probably won't."

"Of course. But if you change your mind, just give the center a call and have Thelma put you on the list."

That evening, Eileen Dugan phoned Eva. "You're welcome to join us for Thanksgiving dinner," she said. "It's later in the day, after the community center's dinner is over."

"You're volunteering at the center and cooking dinner for your family, too?"

Eileen laughed. "George and I are in charge of decorations for the center's dinner, and we're decorating on Wednesday. Plus, our son and his family will be here to help with our family meal. Anyway, you're welcome to come."

"Thanks, Eileen. My plans aren't set yet, but I'll let you know soon, one way or the other."

Eva hung up, touched by Eileen's invitation. When Eva had moved back to Willow Beach, she sensed Eileen disapproved of her and figured that she, like so many other townspeople, couldn't understand why she'd refused to join her father at the *Herald*. Of course, Eileen knew about Brett's accident, but not the whole story. No one knew. Not even Eva's father.

But today Eileen sounded as though she really wanted Eva to join her family for Thanksgiving dinner.

Eva was reluctant to accept. She'd still rather spend the holiday someplace other than Willow Beach.

Yet, a few days later, still with no other plans, Eva found herself calling the community center and volunteering to help with their dinner.

"We'd love to have you join us, Eva," Thelma, the center's secretary, said in her soft, melodious voice. "We can always use an extra hand. What hours are you available?"

"Early in the day would be best. I'm going out for dinner later."

Next, Eva called Eileen and accepted her invitation. She hung up, wondering if she'd made the right decision. One thing was for certain—this would be a Thanksgiving like no other.

## CHAPTER TWELVE

THANKSGIVING MORNING DAWNED gray and cloudy. Eva went for her jog on the beach as usual. When she'd finished and returned to her apartment, she was so cold not even a cup of coffee warmed her. She took a hot shower and dressed in jeans and a pullover sweater. When time came to report to the community center, she put on a blue windbreaker with a hood in case it rained, grabbed her leather purse and headed out the door.

A six-block walk brought her to the center, a two-story brick building on a side street near City Park. One of the oldest buildings in town, it had character, Eva noticed as she paused to take in the ornate cornices on the roof and above the windows. The signs advertising the dinner pointed to the basement door. Delicious smells of roasting turkey, sweet potatoes and pumpkin pie floated up the stairs, along with the sounds of talking and laughter. Eva stopped on the top step and took a deep breath. Did she really want to do this?

Never mind—backing out now was not an option.

Gripping the railing, she started down the stairs. The steps opened out to a large room, at the end of which she glimpsed a kitchen. Long tables covered with butcher paper filled the room. Eileen and George's wall decorations of cardboard turkeys, pilgrims and pumpkins gave the place a festive air.

Eva joined the group in the kitchen, where steam rose from pots on the stove and the worktables held huge bowls of cranberry sauce and green salads and cloth-covered baskets of rolls. Several urns burbled with brewing coffee and hot water for tea.

A middle-aged woman with an air of authority stepped forward. "You must be Eva." At Eva's nod, she continued, "I'm Betty Foster." She turned to the six or seven other people occupied with various tasks. "Hey, everybody, this is Eva Sinclair. Seb's daughter."

Everyone stopped to wave or nod, and Eva greeted them in turn. She recognized Hal

Barnett from the drugstore and a couple of others.

Betty picked up a spoon and stirred a pot of green beans. "I moved here after you left, but of course I knew your father. Everyone did. What a great guy."

"Yes, he was, wasn't he?" Eva mumbled as she took off her windbreaker.

"Hang up your coat and purse over there." Betty pointed with her spoon to a row of pegs nailed to the wall, where other coats and jackets hung. "And grab an apron while you're at it." She nodded at a stack of denim on a nearby table.

After hanging up her coat and securing her purse on top of it, Eva picked up an apron and slipped it on. It reached nearly to her ankles.

"How about makin' the gravy?" Betty said.

Eva frowned. "Mark said there wouldn't be any cooking involved." She spread her hands. "Not that I don't want to. It's just that I'm not very good at it."

"Not to worry. I have a recipe right here." Betty picked up a small card covered in plastic and handed it to Eva.

Eva glanced at the card. "Okay, this looks simple enough."

As she was measuring the flour into a bowl, the back door opened with a blast of cold air. She turned to see who had entered. Mark.

Eva dropped her measuring spoon into the bowl. She hadn't expected to see him here. She figured he and Sasha would have their own dinner or one with friends.

"Hey, everyone." Mark grinned and waved to the group. His gaze landed on Eva.

"You didn't tell me you were going to be here," she said.

He grinned. "You didn't ask." He shrugged out of his windbreaker and hung it on a peg next to hers.

He rolled up the sleeves of his plaid shirt and grabbed an apron. "Eva cooking?" he said to Betty with a grin. "That's risky."

Eva stuck her fingers in the flour and flicked some at him. "Enough out of you, buddy."

Betty looked as though she wasn't sure whether or not to take them seriously. "Now, now, let's all get along," she soothed.

She put Mark to work mashing the potatoes. Soon it was time for dinner. Someone opened the door to let in the people who'd lined up

outside. They streamed in and quickly filled
the tables. For the next couple of hours, Eva,
Mark and the others served up food nonstop.
The tables remained filled. As soon as one
diner left, someone else would come in and
sit down in the empty seat. There were singles
and couples, families with children, people
of all ages.

During a lull, Eva peered out at the crowded
dining area. "Where do all these people come
from? Willow Beach can't possibly have so
many homeless people."

"They're not all homeless." Mark scooped
more potatoes onto his serving tray. "Anyone who can't afford a Thanksgiving meal is
welcome. The word has spread, and some of
these folks are from nearby towns. We don't
turn anyone away."

Betty came up behind them. "The time you
signed for is up, Eva. Only thing is, your replacement just called in sick."

"I can stay," Eva said without hesitation.
"Until around four-thirty. I'm going to a
friend's for dinner then."

"That's when my time's over, too," Mark
said. "I guess you're going to Eileen and
George's. I'll give you a lift."

"I didn't know you were going there, too," Eva said.

His eyes sparkled with teasing. "You didn't ask."

Betty offered a wide grin. "Super, Eva. That will really help us out."

When she'd moved off, Eva narrowed her eyes at Mark. "Is this whole thing a conspiracy?"

"No. I didn't tell Eileen to invite you, and I didn't tell your replacement to call in sick. But as long as you're going to stay, you might as well ride with me over to Eileen's."

Eva shrugged. "Might as well."

At four-thirty, Mark put down his serving spoon and took off his apron. "All the turkey and trimmings around here have made me mighty hungry. Grab your suitcase, Eva, and let's go."

"My suitcase, huh?" Eva took her purse from the hook and swung it at him.

"Hey, watch out!" He ducked and raised his hands over his head.

"You watch it, mister. My purse and I don't take insults lightly."

Their sparring drew a round of laughter from the others.

Eva and Mark left the center and drove in Mark's SUV to the Dugans' house. The place buzzed with activity. Eileen's son, daughter-in-law and their three children had already arrived, plus some of the neighbors. Sasha was deep into a board game with the other children but took time to run over and give Eva and Mark a hug.

Eileen insisted Mark and Eva relax with glasses of cider while final preparations were put to the dinner. Grateful for a chance to sit, Eva sank onto a comfortable sofa by the blazing fire.

Eileen's daughter-in-law, Rilla, came to sit beside her. She told Eva about her home-based business designing and making hand-bags. "I just love working with fabrics," she said.

"I'd like to see some of your work," Eva said. "If you're looking for sales outlets, I can give you some Seattle contacts."

Rilla's eyes lit up. "That'd be great. I'm selling mostly on the internet, but I'd like to branch out into stores."

Eileen called them to dinner. Eva sat next to Sasha, with Mark on his daughter's other side. Everything tasted wonderful, and Eva accepted second helpings when the plates of food came around again.

Halfway through the meal, the doorbell rang. "Who could that be?" Eileen wondered aloud as she rose and hurried from the room.

A few moments later, she returned with April in tow. "Look who's here," she said.

"I got back to town from my uncle's earlier than I thought." April shed her navy blue parka into Eileen's outstretched hands. Her gaze roved the table, lips curved in a smile—until she saw Eva. George brought a chair to the table for her.

"I'll sit by Mark," April said.

Everyone shifted as George slid the chair beside Mark. April leaned across him to talk to Sasha, pointedly ignoring Eva, who pretended to not notice. By now, she was used to April's hostility. Still, her rudeness grated.

When everyone had their fill of food, they moved to the living room for coffee and pumpkin pie. The children built houses with Lego while the adults chatted. Eva purposely chose a seat away from Mark, who sat on the sofa. April plopped down beside him, and Sasha climbed up to cling to his other side.

Half an hour later, Mark said, "We'd better hit the road, Eileen. Our little gal here appears to have had enough Thanksgiving." He pointed to Sasha, who had fallen asleep with her head against his shoulder. "What about you, Eva?"

Eva nodded. "It's been fun, but I'm ready to go."

"Me, too," April said. "My roommate dropped me off…" She cast a sideways look at Mark.

"We can give you a ride," Mark said and then slanted Eva a questioning look.

Eva shrugged. Why did he think he needed her approval? They weren't on a date.

"That would be great." April beamed.

When they reached Mark's SUV, Eva immediately said, "I'll sit in back with Sasha."

Eva hoped her gesture would send a signal to both Mark and April that she had no designs on breaking up their relationship, even though she still didn't know exactly what that relationship was.

No one spoke during the drive home as Sasha slept. Eva stared out the window at the dark streets, wishing more than ever that she'd spent the day in Seattle, even if it meant being alone.

THE FOLLOWING MONDAY, Mark waited in his office for Eva to arrive for their weekly planning meeting. At exactly nine-thirty, she appeared in his open doorway.

"Come on in." He motioned to her.

Today she had on black slacks and a black-and-tan knitted sweater, and her hair was loose rather than in the twist she wore when she first came to town. He liked her casual look.

Her "Good morning" was as cool as the breeze drifting in from his open window. Was she in a bad mood? "Have a seat." He motioned to the chair near his desk, which he'd positioned especially for her.

She crossed the room and took another chair farther away. Opening her iPad, she fiddled with the attached keyboard.

He cleared his throat and studied the notes he'd made in preparation for their discussion. "So, you'll edit the mayor's column and the letters to the editor this week."

She raised her head and smoothed a lock of hair from her forehead. "Right. Then I have a lunch appointment with the owners of the new gallery on Main Street."

"You ought to enjoy that." He pumped enthusiasm into his voice. "I hear they've contracted some really fine artists."

"That would be nice. This town could use a little culture."

Ouch. "What about those antiques shops on the first floor of your apartment building?"

"Yeah, but the souvenir shops outnumber them three to one."

"Visitors like them. Haven't you ever visited a place and brought home a souvenir?"

"Not that I can remember."

"Well, maybe you should."

She pressed her lips together. "Could we get back to the agenda, please?"

"Yeah, sure." He shuffled his notes.

They discussed the rest of the week's schedule and then she scooted to the edge of her chair. "Are we done here? I have a couple of phone calls to make."

He spread his hands. "That's all I have."

She rose and headed for the door.

"Eva…"

She stopped and turned, giving him raised eyebrows.

"I, uh, how'd you like our Thanksgiving?"

"Dinner at Eileen's was nice."

He tried again. "What did you think of

working at the community center? You seemed to enjoy yourself."

"I did. I was glad I could help out."

"We were glad to have you."

She tapped her pen against her notebook. "Are we done now?"

"Sure. Sure. See you later." He gave her a dismissive wave.

After she left, Mark sat there shaking his head. While working side by side with Eva at the center and sharing Thanksgiving at Eileen and George's, he'd sensed something different about their relationship. A camaraderie of sorts. Today, the ocean might as well have separated them. Why?

He figured April was part of the problem. After she'd arrived at Eileen's, Eva had withdrawn and kept her distance. Darn April. He'd told her time and again there was no personal relationship between them, but whenever given the chance, she acted as though they were a couple. He needed to be more forceful. But that wasn't his style. He had no trouble establishing leadership on the job, but personal relationships were another matter.

EVA SAT ON THE BENCH at the edge of the dunes watching the waves break on the sand and, farther out, the whitecaps rising and falling with the rhythm of the tide. The ocean was her favorite part about being back in Willow Beach.

She'd walked here today, a Saturday, because she'd hit a block in her writing and hoped to find inspiration. Maybe it was the holiday blues that had her stuck. True, she'd enjoyed herself on Thanksgiving, but with that over, and everyone revving up for Christmas, her spirits had hit a new low.

She pulled her jacket tighter against the wind and watched a pair of gulls swoop down and land on the sand. They hopped about, pecking at the earth, and then took off again. She traced their path across the sky until they disappeared from sight. If only she could be as free as they were. She was like a caged bird. Her father had made this cage for her and made sure she'd have to stay in it.

What was the point? Had he thought being here and working for the newspaper for a year would change her mind and she'd want to stay in Willow Beach forever? How could he have been so deluded? Had he thought she'd forget all about their argument or what had happened to Brett at Pine Lake? If he had, he was very much mistaken. Being here for the past six months had only made her more eager to leave.

She longed for her condo, for her friends, for her old job. Here she felt as out of place as one of those seagulls would on a mountaintop.

Making it to Seattle for Thanksgiving hadn't worked, but maybe, just maybe, she could be home for Christmas. As soon as she returned to her apartment, she'd give Susan a call.

MARK FINISHED TIGHTENING the screws in the tree stand and then stood back and surveyed his work. The evergreen reached almost to the ceiling with just enough room left for the gold star. He turned to Sasha, who was busy opening boxes of ornaments. "What do you think, honey? Is it straight?"

Sasha studied the tree, tilting her head. "I think so, Daddy."

"I think so, too." He put down his screwdriver and opened the box of lights.

Earlier that day, they'd picked out the tree at the local lot. It was so early in the season that the trees were still being unloaded from the truck. Mark would've waited until closer to Christmas, but Diane always wanted the tree up shortly after Thanksgiving, so he had carried on the tradition.

He pulled out a string of lights and began winding them around the branches. "Soon as I get these done, you can start hanging up the ornaments," he told Sasha.

She nodded and continued lining up the ornaments, purple in one row, blue in another.

He finished with the lights and plugged them in. Their purple glow always gave him a start. He'd have preferred traditional red and green, but Diane had wanted purple, and so that was what they bought. The ornaments were not traditional balls, either, but triangles and squares.

While they hung the ornaments, Sasha told him about the holiday party they were planning at school. "Santa Claus will be there," she said, "but I know who he really is."

"You do?" Mark hung a blue ornament near the top of the tree, filling in a place Sasha couldn't reach.

"Yes, he's Bella's daddy."

"You sure about that?" he teased. Yet he

knew she spoke the truth. Bernie always did
the Santa Claus gig for the grade school.

"I am." Sasha danced around to the back
of the tree to fasten an ornament. "But that's
okay. I'll pretend I don't know."

After a couple minutes, she said, "Do you
think Eva could come for Christmas?"

He jolted. "You mean for Christmas Day?"

"Uh-huh."

"But we usually go to Eileen and George's."

"I know, but I just thought it."

"I'm sure Eva already has plans of her
own."

"She came to my birthday party."

"That's right, she did." And she helped out
at the community center and then joined them
for dinner at Eileen and George's. Maybe she
would be hanging around for Christmas, too.
Not because she wanted to, of course. Bad
weather might keep her from traveling to Seattle. Or, just like at Thanksgiving, her condo
might not be available.

He tried to picture her here, with just him
and Sasha. Scary thought. Maybe he should
have a party and invite her. Having other people around would be a good idea. He really
wasn't much of a party host, though. Sasha's

birthday party had been a success thanks to
Eileen—and, okay, to April, too.

Still…

"I'll think about it," he told Sasha. "Mean-
while, let's finish Mommy's decorations." He
gestured to the remaining boxes sitting on the
floor. Garlands for the mantel and underneath
the window sashes spilled from one, and the
candle from a table centerpiece poked from
another. He blew out a breath. They'd be busy
for the rest of the morning.

FOR THE NEXT FEW DAYS, Mark stewed over
the idea of inviting Eva to his and Sasha's
house for Christmas. He reminded himself
that he didn't want Sasha to get attached to
Eva, since she'd eventually be leaving, but he
didn't want to deny his daughter something
she wanted, either.

He'd ask her at this morning's meeting.
They'd be in his office, just the two of them.
That way, if she flatly turned him down, no
one would know. Breaking the news to Sasha
would be a problem, but he'd worry about that
when and if the time came.

Eva appeared at his office door promptly at
nine-thirty for their weekly meeting. Carry-

ing her tablet computer, she swept across the room with an unusual energy and settled into the chair next to his desk. A smile lit up her face. That was unusual, too—and certainly a change from their last meeting, when she was in a grumpy mood.

Mark swallowed and gripped his pen. Should he wait until after their meeting was over or begin with his invitation?

*Do it now.*

He leaned toward her. "Eva, Christmas will be here in a few weeks, and I—"

She looked up at him, her brown eyes dancing. "I know, and I have great news."

He drew back, alert and puzzled. "Really? What?"

"I'm going home for Christmas."

Her words hit him like a bucket of cold water thrown on a blazing fire. "Oh, that's, er, nice…"

"Nice? It's fantastic. Susan phoned last night. She's spending the holiday in Hawaii with her boyfriend, Greg, and his parents."

"Well, uh, good for her." He twirled the pen between his fingers.

Her eyes took on a faraway look. "I'll have a Christmas Eve party, like I used to. I've al-

ready called some of my old friends and invited them. Oh, I can hardly wait. And if I
leave on Wednesday, I'll be able to attend the
party at *Seattle's Best* on Thursday."

He cleared his throat and shuffled some
papers on his desk. "Don't forget our tree-
lighting ceremony. That's an important town
event and one that belongs in your Our Town
column."

"I know. I'm not taking off that early. Susan
won't be gone until the week before Christmas anyway." She peered at him. "Mark, are
you okay?"

"Of course I'm okay," he said, infusing
gruffness into his tone. "Let's move on to
our agenda. I have a ten-thirty appointment
at city hall."

Mark forced himself to focus and somehow
made it through their meeting. After she left,
he could've kicked himself all the way to his
appointment. What was he thinking to even
consider inviting her to spend Christmas with
him and Sasha?

# CHAPTER THIRTEEN

EVA SAT AT her apartment's kitchen table making a list of things she needed to do for her Christmas Eve party. Planning an event from a distance presented problems. Good thing she had firm connections in Seattle for everything that needed to be done.

She was composing an email to the caterer when the strains of "Jingle Bells" drifted into her consciousness. She jumped up and ran to the window, gazing down into the street. Two blocks to the south, a crowd had gathered at the turnaround. The Christmas-tree-lighting ceremony. She'd forgotten about it and she'd promised Mark she'd be there.

She shut down her computer, shrugged into a wool jacket, set a matching wool hat on her head and hurried out the door.

Mark had been correct when he'd told her the ceremony was a big event. Quite a throng had gathered around the towering evergreen in the middle of the turnaround. Strings of lights encircled the tree, waiting to spring to life. At the top perched a huge star, poised to send its golden glow into the night. A five-piece combo and a chorus of high-school students, looking like something out of a Dickens novel in their Victorian garb, entertained the crowd with Christmas carols. Their voices rang with the joy and celebration of the season.

Standing on tiptoe, Eva scanned the crowd for Mark. She finally spotted him and Sasha on the other side of the chorus. She worked her way over to them.

"Sorry I'm late." She bent to say hello to Sasha, who held her father's hand. "Hey, Sasha."

Sasha's eyes danced. "Eva, you're here. Daddy said you'd forget to come, but I knew you'd be here."

Eva's gaze slid to Mark.

He shrugged. "I figured you were busy getting ready to go to Seattle."

"I am. But I said I'd be here, and I do try to keep my word."

"I appreciate that. So does Sasha." He smiled at Sasha and squeezed her hand.

The leader of the chorus invited the crowd to sing along with them, and Eva turned her attention to the program. After a few songs, Mayor Fitzsimmons gave a short speech and then gave the signal for the tree to be lit. To an accompanying drumroll, the evergreen blazed with hundreds of colorful bulbs. The star on top winked on, its light a beacon against the black sky.

"Oh, wow!" Sasha jumped up and down and clapped her hands.

Eva caught her breath at the stunning sight. The ceremony was new since she'd lived here nine years ago, and she'd had no idea it was such an important—and impressive—occasion.

After a couple more songs, the crowd dispersed to the nearby establishments, where shop owners were serving hot cocoa and cookies. Sasha looked up at Eva. "Come with us, Eva."

Eva was about to refuse. She still had her list to finish. Then she caught Mark's gaze over the top of Sasha's head.

"If you have time," he said.

"I'd love to come," she said and grasped Sasha's free hand.

They fell into step and headed for the nearest store, which was Cooper's Hardware. As they waited in line for refreshments, Eva spotted Fran. Since the fashion show, Eva and Fran had met several times for coffee, and Eva had spoken to Fran's class. Her husband, Jason, and Mark knew each other and played on the same basketball team. The couple's eight-year-old twin boys, Tyler and Kyle, were with them.

Once everyone had their cocoa and cookies in hand, they found a table where they all could sit together. Another couple appeared. The man tapped Mark on the shoulder.

Mark looked up. "Hey, Joe." He gave the tall, bearded man a playful punch on the shoulder.

Fran's husband stepped in to make the introductions. "Eva, meet Joe and Rene Helman. Joe's the best center we've ever had, and Rene is Mayor Fitzsimmons's number-one assistant."

Rene and Eva pointed fingers at each other and said in unison, "University of Washington, News Writing 101," and then they both laughed.

"I thought you were headed for New York

after graduation," Eva said to Rene, a petite blonde with a wide, friendly smile.

Rene tossed back her head and laughed. "That train got derailed." She gave her husband an affectionate look. "I love my job at city hall."

"I'm glad to hear that," Eva said, not knowing how else to comment on something she couldn't understand. Give up the glamour of New York for Willow Beach?

"I've been meaning to call you," Rene said. "I belong to a group of university women that meets once a month. Would you like to join?"

"Why, uh, you probably know I'll only be here until next June."

"So I've heard. But you could come to a few meetings. We have fun as well as do some charity work. Here are the particulars." She dug into her black tote, pulled out a business card and handed it to Eva.

Eva took the card, glanced at it and stuck it in her pocket. "I'll see if I can make a meeting. Thanks for thinking of me."

"You and Mark have done a great job taking over the *Herald*," Joe put in. "Your dad would be proud of both of you."

Eva didn't dare to look at Mark. She merely nodded. Had she really been trying? Or just coasting?

ON CHRISTMAS EVE, in her Seattle condo, Eva finished setting the dining-room table with her best china and flatware and then stood back and smiled with satisfaction. Everything was ready for her party. The caterer had delivered the food, and the florist had brought several lovely potted poinsettias and a centerpiece of holly and candles for the table. The spicy scent from a cut-glass bowl filled with potpourri added a festive touch, and Christmas songs rang out from the CD player.

Yesterday, Eva had attended *Seattle's Best*'s Christmas party, where she was welcomed and fussed over. Even the new assistant editor was gracious and forthcoming with compliments she'd heard about Eva. Seeing her old colleagues was fun but also sad. Eva couldn't help wishing she were back on her career track instead of fulfilling her obligation to her father in Willow Beach.

The doorbell rang. Her guests had arrived. Eva hurried to let them in.

For the next three hours, talk and laughter

filled the condo. Eva busily played hostess, making sure everyone had enough to eat and drink. How exciting to see her old friends and catch up on their news.

When she finally closed the door on the last departing guest, she took a moment to catch her breath, and then, humming along to "Deck the Halls," she cleaned up the kitchen. That finished, she made herself a cup of mint tea and settled on the sofa. Outside the window, a bright silver moon glowed in the cloudless sky, while inside the lights from her miniature Christmas tree, sitting on a table in the corner, sent a glow over the room.

Warm satisfaction filled Eva. The evening had been a success. But as she continued to sit there, some of her good feeling drained away. Yes, she'd had a wonderful time with her friends. Yet...yet what? She shrugged. Nothing. Nothing at all.

The following day, she went alone to her church's Christmas services and then ate leftovers for lunch. After that, she took down her decorations and put them away. When Susan came home after New Year's, she wouldn't need reminders of Christmas.

With everything back to normal, she stood

in the center of the living room gazing around. The holiday was over already. And now she had to leave. Sadness and regret filled her. This was where she belonged, not back in Willow Beach.

On Sunday, it started to rain as she left Seattle. The bad weather followed her all the way to the coast. Her apartment was cold and clammy because the heat had been off while she was gone. She turned on her computer and brought up her novel, but instead of feeling inspired after being away, she faced a blank wall that no amount of concentration could overcome.

After half an hour, she shut down the computer and paced to the window. The dark and stormy sky and the foam-capped waves crashing on the shore mirrored the restlessness she felt inside.

She put on her hooded parka, left the apartment and drove around aimlessly in the rain. Suddenly she found herself passing the *Herald*'s front door. Only the night-lights shone from the reception area. Still, without knowing why, she drove down the alley to the back of the building. Mark's black SUV sat in its usual place in the parking lot, rivulets of rain streaming down the windshield. Why was he here today? Well, no surprise, really, given his dedication to the newspaper.

On impulse, she parked beside his car and jumped out. Pulling her hood over her head, she sprinted across the lot. The building's spotlight shone down on the basketball hoop, where the net hung rain-drenched and limp. She pulled out her key and opened the back door. The hallway was dark except for a square of light spilling from the open doorway of Mark's office. She stopped for a moment and then headed toward it.

He sat at his desk, brow furrowed, studying his computer screen. The sleeves of his blue shirt were rolled up, exposing his sturdy forearms. A faint tapping floated from the keyboard as his fingers worked the keys.

She swallowed and took a step forward. "Mark…"

His head shot up, and his eyes widened. "Eva! I didn't expect you until tomorrow."

She pushed back her hood and ran a hand through her damp hair. "I got back a couple hours ago. Miserable drive, pouring rain, wind…"

He stood and walked around his desk. "I bet. So, how was your party?"

She shoved her hands into her coat pockets. "Connecting with my friends again was wonderful. And I went to a party at *Seattle's Best*."

He arched one eyebrow and took a step toward her. "Are they saving a place for you?"

"Not that anyone said. But at least I'm keeping up my contacts."

"Right."

A beat of silence went by, and then he said, "Sasha's crazy about the art kit you gave her for Christmas. She's already drawn several pictures. You'll be getting her thank-you note soon."

"I'm glad she likes it."

He lifted his shoulders in a questioning gesture. "Do you have some work to do here? I thought you were all caught up when you left." Another step brought him closer.

A little voice told her she should move away, but her feet remained rooted to the spot. "I, uh, right. Work to do… My column."

"You turned that in before you left."

"Oh. How could I forget?" She knotted her hands, still buried in her pockets.

"How indeed?" His voice dropped a couple notches. He took another step, now only inches away. If she wanted to, she could reach out and touch his arm, his shoulder, his face. She stared at her feet, willing them to move. They might as well have been glued to the tile floor.

She looked up and their gazes collided. Time skidded to a halt, and she could barely breathe. Then, before she knew what was happening or exactly how, she was in his arms, pressed against his chest, his warmth surrounding her. She pulled her hands free and returned his embrace, resting her palms on his back, feeling his muscles flex as he drew her even tighter.

"You feel good," he said, his mouth against her ear.

"You do, too," she whispered before she realized what she was saying.

He held her awhile longer and then drew back. His eyelids lowered, his gaze focused on her mouth. Knowing instinctively what was coming next, Eva stepped back. "No, no, I'm…I'm all wet. My jacket, my hair…"

"I don't care." He reached for her again. She sidestepped his grasp and held up her hands. "Mark, no. Remember, you said at the picnic that what happened then wouldn't happen again."

He seemed to come to his senses and gave her a wry smile.

"I've been known to say some stupid things."

"That was the right thing to say. This is wrong. Wrong for *us*. We don't belong together."

"Then why does holding you and kissing you feel so good?"

She folded her arms and looked away. "Two people can be *attracted* but still be wrong for each other." She darted him a glance. "Don't you agree?"

"I suppose. So, what do you suggest we do about our, ah, *attraction,* as you call it?"

"Nothing. Just make sure our association is strictly business." Before he could reply, she turned and hurried from the office.

AFTER EVA LEFT, Mark returned to his desk and sank into his chair. He stared blankly at the words on the computer screen. He hadn't planned to work over the weekend, but Sasha was spending the night at Bella's and he'd had nothing to do at home. Work was the only other place for him, and so he'd come to the office intending to write his From the Editor's Desk column.

Now Eva's sudden appearance had destroyed all his concentration. He'd thought about her a lot over Christmas, wondering how her party had turned out and wishing instead that she'd chosen to spend the holiday here with him and Sasha.

Sasha, too, had been disappointed when she learned Eva would not be joining them for Christmas. He'd tried to compensate with inviting Bella and some of her other friends for a sleepover. Still, Sasha frequently mentioned Eva and how much she missed her.

Then, when Eva suddenly appeared tonight, he hadn't been able to resist taking her in his arms. They'd clung to each other like long-lost lovers.

Which of course they weren't. Far from it. She'd soon made that clear. He'd do well to heed her warning and keep their relationship strictly business.

"OH, EVA, PLEASE COME."

"A house party? I don't think so." Eva sipped her latte and then met Fran's gaze across the table. They were having a holiday lunch at the Beach Café. Eva had returned to work at the *Herald,* while Fran, being a teacher, was still on vacation.

"Like I told you, it's at the old Fenton mansion, up on the bluff."

"Yes, I know the house. Lovely old Victorian, complete with gingerbread trim and widow's walk. It's been turned into one of those rental places for tourists, where all the dishes and linens and such are provided."

"Right. A bunch of us rent it every year for New Year's. We have a blast. I would have invited you earlier, but I thought you'd be in Seattle for the entire holiday."

"I didn't want to push for so much time off work, or I would have. But isn't your party for families?" Family gatherings weren't her thing. In Seattle, there were enough singles to balance get-togethers. But Willow Beach was definitely family country.

Fran poked her fork at her chicken salad. "Yes, but there will be singles, too. Most of us stay overnight. There are rooms for the kids, rooms for the couples, and singles sleep dorm-style. It's a huge house. The Fentons had, what, twelve kids? Good thing old man

Fenton made a bundle on real estate. But you wouldn't have to stay over. It's close enough that you could drive to your apartment." She grinned. "Unless you've had one champagne cocktail too many. Then I wouldn't let you."

"So who all will be there? Anyone else I know?"

"Oh, my, yes. Will Greer and Robbie Romero from our class are two of the single guys. Oh, and Kathleen Young. She's divorced now."

Eva nodded. "I remember her. She always sat at our table in the lunchroom."

"Uh-huh. And she had such a crush on your brother. Remember the time she waited for him after school, faking a sprained ankle, hoping he would give her a ride home?"

"Oh…yeah." Eva looked down at her plate, where the remaining half of her ham sandwich had suddenly lost its appeal.

Fran leaned across the table and touched Eva's arm. "I'm sorry, Eva. I know you don't like to be reminded. It just slipped out."

Eva made a dismissive wave. "It's okay, Fran." She heaved a sigh. "I'll never get over what happened to Brett out there at Pine Lake."

"It happened to you, too, Eva."

Eva shook her head. "We definitely don't talk about that. Dad never could, either."

"Your dad loved Brett, but he loved you, too."

"Whatever. We got off track here. The party. What about food? I'm not much of a cook, you know."

A teasing smile crossed Fran's lips. "Hmm, yes, I seem to remember a lot of burned pans when it was your turn to cook in our Home Living class. But don't worry about food. Pick up some cookies or a cake at Bon Ton."

"You're making it very easy, aren't you?"

"I want you to come!"

Eva sipped her coffee and, focusing on the beach outside, asked in a low voice, "Will... Mark be there?" Since their talk Sunday evening, their association at work had been polite and businesslike—just as she'd requested. Which should have eased her concerns. Curiously, though, whenever their paths crossed, she felt more on edge than ever.

"Mark? Yes, he will."

"He's not from the old high-school gang." Eva set down her cup and ran her forefinger around the saucer's rim.

"No, but he and Jason are on the same basketball team. Bernie's on the team, too. He
and his wife and Bella are coming. Why?
Does that make a difference?"

"It's just that, well, Mark and I don't always get along."

"So, you can keep your distance. There will
be plenty of other people there to talk to."

Fran had a good point, but would Mark
take her appearance at a party he was also
attending as a sign she wanted to relax their
"strictly business" relationship? She couldn't
afford for that to happen.

"I'll admit I'm tempted," Eva said. "But I
feel so…so in limbo. As though I don't belong anywhere."

Fran sobered. "I wish you felt you belonged
here again. But I understand, really I do."

AT 2:00 P.M. ON New Year's Eve, Eva pulled
her car into the parking lot at the side of the
Fenton mansion. After much deliberation,
she'd decided to put aside her worries about
Mark and accept Fran's invitation.

Half a dozen other cars were already in
the lot. Mark's black SUV was one of them.
The sight of his car almost made her turn

around and drive back to her apartment, as dull and drab as it was. Then she straightened her shoulders and lifted her chin. She would not let his presence ruin her New Year's Eve or her chance to spend time with people she considered friends.

She got out of the car, walked around it and reached into the passenger's side for the box resting on the seat. She'd taken Fran's advice and visited Bon Ton Bakery. There would be no food disasters like the one at the Fourth of July picnic.

She studied the house as she headed up the walk to the front door. Painted a soft yellow with the gingerbread a rusty brown and the widow's walk poking up from the roof, it truly was magnificent. She imagined what the place was like when the Fentons lived there. With twelve children, the house would be teeming with noise and activity.

Just then, the front door opened and three children, two boys and a girl, ran out—Sasha and Fran and Jason's twins, Tyler and Kyle. They clattered down the front steps. Sasha rushed to Eva and flung her arms around her waist. "Oh, Eva, I didn't know you were coming."

Eva laughed and returned Sasha's hug. "I wasn't sure, either, until a couple hours ago."

"I bet my dad doesn't know you're here. He will be surprised."

"I'm sure he will," Eva murmured.

The boys stood a few feet away, looking on with unabashed interest.

Eva pointed to the one nearest. "You're Tyler, right?"

"No, I'm Kyle."

"I'm Ty," the other twin said, grabbing his ankle and hopping on one foot.

"Sorry, I'll never be able to tell you apart."

"No one can," Kyle said.

"Not even Dad," Tyler echoed. "Mom can… usually."

Kyle laughed. "'Cept for the time I snitched the cookies and she thought you did it 'cause I had on your baseball cap."

Tyler stood on both feet again and balled his hands into fists. "You'd better not try that again. I was grounded for two days."

Sasha grabbed Eva's hand and led her up the stairs and into the house. The place was full of people, with music blaring and enticing smells coming from the back of the house. "I need to find Fran," Eva told Sasha.

"Okay, but I want to show you the picture I made with the art set you gave me. Did you get my thank-you note?"

"I did. I found it on my desk yesterday. And I'd love to see your picture."

Sasha and the boys ran off, and Eva continued on to the kitchen. She looked around surreptitiously—she hoped—expecting to see Mark, but he was not in sight. She reached the kitchen. Fran and a few other women were grouped around a butcher's block, stuffing several whole salmon with a rice mixture.

Fran's eyes lit up. "You came!" She stepped away to give Eva a hug. "You can put your whatever over there." She pointed to a counter full of covered dishes.

Eva squeezed her cake box onto the counter. She turned to greet Kathleen Young, a tall woman with a single braid and no makeup, except a light lipstick. Fran introduced Eva to those she didn't know.

"So where are the guys?" Eva asked, looking around and seeing only women.

Kathleen frowned. "You're not trying to fix us up, are you, Fran? 'Cause I'm free now and aim to stay that way."

Fran shook her head emphatically. "No, no, not at all."

"I just wondered if the men were hiding out so they didn't have to do kitchen duty," Eva said.

"They're outside." Fran tipped her head toward a window at the back of the kitchen.

Eva walked over and looked out. Directly behind the house was a patch of pavement with a basketball hoop. Several of the men were shooting baskets, while others stood around talking and sipping from bottles of soda. Her gaze landed on Mark just as he jumped and stretched out his long arms to shoot the ball. It hovered on the rim and then fell in the basket. The onlookers whistled and clapped. Mark grinned and took a bow. As he straightened, he looked up at the window. His eyes widened. Eva pasted a smile onto her face and fluttered her fingers.

When the men trooped in later, Mark stepped up beside her and said, "Hello, Eva," but then moved off before she could do much more than return his greeting. Not that she would have started up a conversation. What did they have to say to each other? Still, it soon became clear that being at the same party with Mark, no matter how big the Fenton mansion, would prove uncomfortable and distracting. In the narrow hallway they ran into each other going in opposite directions, and both did an awkward little dance before Mark flattened himself to the wall and made a sweeping motion for her to pass by.

Later, Eva was sitting on a sofa in the parlor, where kindling and logs were ready to light in the huge fireplace, and card tables had been set up for games. Sasha danced in carrying a sheet of drawing paper in both hands.

"Here's the picture I made." She laid the paper in Eva's lap.

Eva set down her glass of soda and studied the picture. The drawing showed three people, two adults and one child, walking on the beach. They were all holding hands. Several birds flew overhead and dramatic waves rose from the water's surface. The figures Sasha had drawn were more than the stick figures usually created by young children. These were fleshed out, even wearing hats and coats.

"That's us," Sasha explained. "You, me and Daddy."

Eva placed a hand to her chest. "You're quite an artist, Sasha, but—"

From the corner of her eye, she glimpsed someone standing behind the sofa. She turned to see Mark, arms folded across his chest, gazing down at the drawing.

Sasha looked up at Mark. "What do you think, Daddy?"

"I think you're a very good artist, too, sweetheart." He cut Eva a swift glance and then stalked away.

After a while, the guys disappeared again to cook the stuffed salmon on several outdoor barbecues, while the women set up the rest of the food on the dining-room table. When it was time to eat and Eva had filled her plate, she sat at a table where only one seat was left—and where none of her tablemates was Mark. The children were off by themselves, so she didn't have to worry about Sasha wanting the three of them to sit together.

Jay Hatcher produced his tub of homemade ice cream, which would accompany the cake Eva brought.

"Jay's an expert at making ice cream," his wife, Celia, said as she accepted a dish from her husband. "The recipes and the maker have been passed down in his family for generations."

Jay nodded and pushed his eyeglasses up the narrow bridge of his nose. "My grandfather was the real pro. His chocolate was, as my lovely wife would say, 'to die for.'" He laughed and put an arm around Celia's shoulder.

"Aw, honey." She kissed his cheek, at the same time resting a hand on her obviously pregnant stomach.

Witnessing the couple's affection warmed Eva's heart, yet she couldn't ignore a touch of envy. They seemed so happy and so in love. What would it be like, she wondered, to be happily married and expecting a baby? Would she ever know?

They sat around for a while after dinner, drinking coffee and talking, and then Jay looked at his wristwatch. "Only two hours to go. Time for the next event. Come on, guys, pitch in."

"What's happening now?" Eva asked Kathleen, who sat next to her on a sofa.

"I'm guessing dancing." She wrinkled her nose. "Like I want to do any of that. My ex always said I have two left feet."

Eva scooted to the edge of the sofa. "I'd better be going."

Kathleen gave her a curious look. "You're not staying overnight?"

"No. I have a lot to do tomorrow."

Eva headed for the kitchen, where Fran had disappeared a few minutes ago. But before she could walk through the swinging door, a voice behind her said, "Where ya goin', pretty lady?"

Not Mark's voice. Besides, he would never call her "pretty lady." She turned to see Will Greer.

"I have to leave now, Will."

"What? Before the New Year blows in? Come on, you can spare one dance." He reached out and took Eva's hand.

"All right…one dance."

But one turned into two, and then three, and then Robbie Romero tapped Will on the shoulder and claimed Eva. Before she realized how much time had passed, it was eleven forty-five. She sighed. She might as well stay for fifteen more minutes. She hadn't seen Mark dancing and figured he must be putting Sasha to bed. When Robbie went off to help Jason get the champagne ready, Eva stood in the parlor doorway, idly watching the couples swaying to the music. She smiled to herself. For all her complaining, Kathleen sure looked contented as she rested her head on Will's shoulder.

And then, from the shadows behind her, someone placed both hands on her shoulders. She knew it was Mark before he spoke.

"I haven't had my turn yet," he said close to her ear.

A shiver rippled along her spine. "Who says you get a turn?"

"I say." He moved his hands down her arms. Gripping her elbows, he turned her around and said, "How can I pass up an opportunity to dance with you without competing with your purse?"

She had to smile at the memory of their Fourth of July dance and how her straw purse had slammed him in the chest. But that night seemed aeons ago.

"Where is your ever-faithful companion anyway?"

"Faithfully waiting for me in the car."

"Good place for it." He grasped her around the waist and clasped her hand.

She held herself rigid. "Wait a minute.

What about our strictly business relationship?"

He grinned. "No business being conducted here tonight. Just partying."

"All right, but one dance is all you get."

He shook his head. "Oh, no. You're not pulling that I-must-go-before-my-coach-turns-into-a-pumpkin bit again."

"I don't know what you're talking about."

"You ran on the Fourth. You ran the other night from my office. Now you want to run again."

"Maybe it's safer that way."

"You're probably right."

"Then why are you insisting I stay?"

"Just shut up and dance."

Eva clamped her jaw shut and concentrated on following Mark's lead. The song was slow and dreamy, the kind of music that made you want to melt into your partner's arms—if your partner was the right person. Which of course Mark wasn't.

He guided them into the living room to join the other couples. Before the dance was over, midnight arrived and down on the beach the town-sponsored fireworks began to explode.

Everyone grabbed their whistles and noise-makers and ran to the windows to watch.

Instead of joining the others, Mark drew them back into the shadows. He held her close and whispered, "Happy New Year, Eva."

She hardly had time to whisper back before he cupped her chin and closed his lips over hers.

## CHAPTER FOURTEEN

BACK AT WORK on Monday, Eva didn't know what to expect as she prepared for her and Mark's weekly planning meeting. Had things between them changed since New Year's? Absently, she touched her fingertips to her lips, recalling the kiss they'd shared at midnight. Despite her resolve to keep her distance, she'd given in and kissed him. Okay, a kiss at midnight was traditional, but theirs was anything but the casual kiss one might exchange with an acquaintance or a stranger. Their kiss was deep and lasting and…and full of feeling. Feelings Eva didn't want to admit she had for him.

When they'd finally come to their senses and pulled apart, they joined the others in a champagne toast. Half an hour and several dances later, Eva finally convinced Mark she needed to leave. He was reluctant to let her go, insisting she call him as soon as she was safely inside her apartment.

Now, after all that, would their working relationship have changed, too? Whatever, they had to work together for six more months. She'd finished only half of her exile. With a sigh, she picked up her tablet computer, left her cubicle and headed for his office.

Mark sat at his desk, as usual. She lightly tapped the doorjamb. He looked up. Recognition and then a smile lit his face. Eva's tension eased a little.

"Come in, Eva."

She crossed the room and sat in the chair by his desk.

"Have you recovered from our big night out?"

She laughed. "I don't know. That group sure knows how to throw a party."

"They do. You were probably smart to cut out early."

"Yeah. I missed all the cleanup, didn't I?"

"Hey, I'll have to remember that for next time."

Their gazes held for a moment. Then he broke eye contact and cleared his throat. "So, ah, we'd better get down to business."

"Yes…business."

He studied his computer screen. "Here's what I've got for our next issue."

They were no more than five minutes into their discussion when his desk phone rang. He picked up the receiver. "Yes? Is that so?" His gaze slid toward Eva. "Sure. I'll send her out." He hung up and turned to her. "We'll put our meeting on hold. Someone is out front to see you."

Eva pressed a hand to her chest. "Me? Who could that be? I don't have an appointment with anyone."

"I expect you'll recognize the person."

She turned off her tablet and rose. "Why are you being so mysterious?"

He waved at her. "Just go."

Eva dropped off her tablet in her cubicle and then continued on to the reception area. A heavy-set white-haired man stood with his hands clasped behind his back, perusing the current edition of the *Herald* on the counter. April sat at her desk, casting surreptitious glances in the visitor's direction.

"Boyd!" Eva approached him with her hand outstretched. "This is a surprise."

Boyd turned and shook her hand. "Happy New Year."

"And to you."

"I brought you a little present." He dug into his jacket pocket, pulled out something small and fuzzy and handed it to her.

"Oh, what a cute little bear," she said, setting it in her palm. The bear wore a red plaid jacket and a matching tam.

"For your collection. Do you still collect them?"

"I do, but I left my stash at home—in Seattle."

He nodded knowingly.

"This little guy will be all alone here." *Like I am,* she wanted to add.

"Won't be too long now, you'll be back where you belong."

"So, what can I do for you today?"

He stuck his hands in his pockets and gazed around. "I just came from making a down payment on a house in Willow Beach Heights."

"The new development up on the bluff? Near the lighthouse?"

"Yep. So, I thought I'd drop in and take a look around. And see you, of course."

"I doubt the place has changed much since you've been here. But would you like to come back to the staff room for a cup of coffee?"

Boyd gave her a wide grin. "Sure."

April popped up from her chair, a scowl on her face. "We don't usually let visitors into the back."

Boyd turned to her. "I'm hardly a visitor, Miss—" he squinted at her nameplate sitting on the counter "—Miss Hensen. I used to be an owner here. Plan to be again."

"Now, Boyd," Eva began, "that is a bit premature, don't you think?"

"No, I think I know you pretty well, Eva. And I don't blame you one bit for not wanting to stay here any longer than necessary. I was here when all that bad stuff happened to you."

Eva looked down at the bear, absently straightening its jacket. "Yes, well, let's get on to that cup of coffee, shall we?"

Eva led Boyd down the hallway, dropping off the bear in her cubicle. She hoped Mark would stay in his office. She didn't relish a confrontation between the two men. But he was filling his coffee mug when they entered.

She was about to say in a cheerful voice,

*Look who's here, Mark,* but he already knew Boyd was her visitor.

He turned and scowled, first at Boyd, then at her.

"Here's Mark, your other half," Boyd boomed, striding into the room.

His mouth a tight line, Mark brushed past them and out the door.

Boyd stared after him and shrugged.

"How do you take your coffee?" Eva asked.

"Is that hazelnut creamer I see? Dump in some of that."

When they were settled at the table with their coffee, Eva said, "You must know Mark's against you having anything to do with the *Herald.* He knows you and Dad had a falling-out and he takes Dad's side. He's very loyal."

"Maybe so, but he only knows Seb's version of events." He sipped his coffee. "And do you share his loyalty?"

She shook her head. "No."

He sat back, a satisfied smile on his face. "Didn't think so."

"I'm just trying to get through this year as quickly and as painlessly as possible." Painlessly. Bad choice of words. As if that were possible. "But with Mark's attitude, do you really want to work with him?"

"I've never let anything like a bad attitude stop me yet. But does Mark's, uh, reluctance to deal with me bother you?"

She shook her head vigorously. "No. Not at all."

After they finished their coffee, Boyd pushed back his chair. "How 'bout showing me around? I need to get some ideas going."

"Well..." Boyd's poking around was sure to annoy Mark. But the *Herald* was half hers, for now anyway, and if she wanted to show a friend around the offices, she would. "Sure. Let's do it."

They went down the hallway toward the back of the building. Mark's door was open, and she risked a glance inside. Not seeing him, she exhaled a relieved breath. Maybe he'd left the office and would not know about this tour she was giving Boyd.

"Isn't that Seb's office?" Boyd pointed to the closed door next to Mark's office.

"Yes. Now it's available for our freelancers to use. I'd rather not go in, though, if you don't mind."

"Sure, I understand."

At the end of the hallway, Boyd stopped to look out the little window at the top of the door leading outside. "Plenty of room for expansion." As he placed a hand on the wall beside the door, his ruby ring caught the light. "If we knock out this wall, we can enlarge Seb's office, which will be mine. Or Arthur's. Haven't decided where he's going to land yet."

They went back down the hallway to the front of the building, Boyd commenting half to himself, half to Eva about the changes he would make. When they reached the reception area, he pointed at the counter. "We'll get rid of that. Takes up too much room. Miss Hensen, is it? She can barely see over the top when she's sitting at her desk."

April glared at Boyd. "I saw you come in, didn't I?"

"And those." He pointed to the chairs with their molded plastic seats. "Did you ever sit in one of 'em? Gives you a pain in your butt."

"Some people do that, too," Eva heard April mutter.

"I have to agree with you, Boyd," Eva said, "but what you're proposing will—"

"Be a great improvement, doncha think?"

"Cost a lot of money."

Boyd turned to her with a big grin on his face. "Well, now, that's not your worry, is it?"

"No, I guess not."

"I DON'T EVER want to see that man in this building again," Mark said that afternoon.

Sitting in her cubicle, her back to him, Eva kept on tapping the keyboard. So much for their pleasant beginning this morning.

"I can't keep him out of the building," she said in an even voice, "because we're open to the public. If you want to toss him out, that's your choice. You had an opportunity this morning. Why didn't you take it?"

"Because I don't want to go to jail for assault. I have a newspaper to run."

She finally stopped typing—she'd lost her concentration anyway—and wheeled around to face him. "If you'd give him a chance, you might find you like him."

He rolled his eyes. "I'm trusting Seb's judgment on Boyd."

"Maybe you won't have to work with him. He might send his son, Arthur, in his place. Boyd has a lot of newspapers to manage."

Mark widened his eyes. "You're really going to sell to him, then?"

"I didn't say that."

"You might as well have. If that's the case, we have nothing more to say to each other." He turned on his heel and stalked off.

"We never did have much to say!" she called after him, but he kept walking. She did hear some muttering, though.

A COUPLE WEEKS LATER, on a Monday morning, Eva had just taken her last bite of toast when her cell phone rang. Frowning, she stared at the phone. Who could be calling her at this early hour?

Caller ID showed Mark's number. What did he want? After their blowup over Boyd, they'd managed to be civil to each other and to keep their association focused on the newspaper. And thankfully, Eva had heard no more from Boyd. True, she was leaning toward selling to him, but had decided when he first made the proposal that she would wait until June before doing anything definite.

"Good morning, Mark," she said into the phone, keeping her tone impersonal yet pleasant.

"Eva," he croaked and then coughed.

Eva sat up straight. "Mark? You sound terrible."

"Got a bad sore throat."

"Oh, I'm sorry." She picked up her empty plate with her free hand and carried it to the sink. She meant it, too.

"Listen…I need you to cover for me…" His voice trailed off into another fit of coughing.

"Cover for you where? Doing what?" She turned on the water and rinsed the plate.

"City-council meeting…tonight…seven."

"The city-council meeting?" she repeated dumbly. "No, no. Not my thing. I told you early on I wouldn't do that. Get someone else. What about Guy?"

"Don't want Guy…want you to…be there." Another bout of coughing drowned out the rest of his words.

"But—"

*Click.*

"Mark!"

The line was dead.

Eva twisted off the faucet and tossed her phone down on the table. What was he thinking? Why would he want her to attend the city-council meeting when he knew that wasn't her kind of assignment?

She folded her arms and tapped one foot, thinking. Okay, he'd refused to contact Guy or any of their other contributors. But that didn't mean she couldn't make some calls on her own.

When she reached the office, she took out her list of freelancers and, one by one, phoned them. Two were out of town, one had to attend a daughter's musical recital and the fourth flat-out refused.

"Sorry, Eva," the woman said, "but anything to do with government makes my eyes glaze over."

Eva wanted to say, *Mine, too,* but wisely refrained. She hung up and crossed the woman's name off her list. Now what should she do? She considered her options. She could let the meeting go without anyone from the newspaper attending.

Then she recalled that tonight's meeting was especially important. The mayor had resigned, and the city council was going to announce his successor. Although the townspeople would certainly know the outcome before the paper was published, they would expect to read commentary. The appointment of a new mayor was news that should be reported, whether or not the subject appealed to Eva.

Yet attending the meeting and writing the article was definitely not something she wanted to do.

Her indecision kept her on edge all day and right through dinner. Finally, at twenty minutes to seven, she stuffed her tablet computer into her leather purse, grabbed her jacket and flew out the door.

She arrived at the meeting room just as the council's president banged his gavel to call the session to order. She took a seat at the end of one of the back rows and, after setting up her tablet, directed her attention to the eight men and women sitting behind a semicircular table at the front of the room. The meeting began, and soon her fingers were flying over the keyboard.

When the president announced a short break, she tucked her tablet away and headed for the coffee urns. Two council members, a man and a woman, approached her.

"Aren't you Eva Sinclair?" the woman asked.

Eva reached for a porcelain cup. "Yes, I'm

taking Mark's place tonight. He has a nasty virus."

"Sorry to hear that." The man picked up a carton of creamer and poured some into his cup. "But we're glad to have you in his place. Your father used to attend, too. He was a crackerjack journalist."

"We were lucky to have him at the *Herald*'s helm," the woman said. "And we feel lucky to have his daughter following in his footsteps." She gave Eva a wide smile.

"But I'm not— I'm only—"

Another man joined them. "Oh, Wayne, this is Seb's daughter," the woman said.

Soon others had clustered around them, expressing appreciation for her being there. Eva listened to the praise heaped on her father, praise she'd heard at every turn since her arrival in Willow Beach. One would think he was a saint.

A newcomer joined the group. Eva looked up to see Boyd Carlstrom. Her stomach jolted. She hadn't noticed he was in the audience. When he said he was settling back in town, he wasn't kidding.

"Didja tell 'em you're leaving soon?" Boyd bellowed in his deep voice.

"Leaving?" the man named Wayne asked.

Boyd nodded. "Sure. Soon as June rolls around, she's gonna go back to Seattle."

All eyes turned to Eva.

"I, uh—"

Boyd held up both hands. "But don't worry, folks, because I'll be back at the *Herald*'s helm, and your weekly will survive."

"What about Mark Townson?" Wayne asked.

Just then the council's president banged his gavel. "Time to get back to business, people."

As the group scattered, Eva leaned toward Boyd and whispered, "Boyd, please. Let's keep our business private." She doubted he heard her, though, because he was busy talking to one of the council members.

Eva managed to concentrate enough to take notes on the rest of the meeting, which featured the announcement of the new mayor. As soon as the session was over, she leaped up and headed for the door.

Mark had told her how much the townspeople valued the *Herald,* but she hadn't believed him. Tonight had shown her the truth of his words. Did Boyd really have the newspaper's best interests at heart? Or, as Mark claimed, was her father's former partner only interested in his own ego?

MARK STAYED HOME sick for another week, and Eva found herself in charge of the newspaper. Since everyone on staff knew their job well, being the boss made little change in her own routine. A few matters did require her expertise, such as choosing which of Cody's photos would grace the pages of the upcoming issue and editing the copy of a new advertiser Bernie had signed on.

On a couple of matters, April had insisted she needed to talk to Mark directly and called him at home. His voice was still little more than a croak, however, and April had ended up coming to Eva for direction. Not without a sulk, though.

On Wednesday, Cody brought the fresh copies of the newspaper from the printer.

"Here it is," he announced as he lugged the first of several boxes through the back door. He carried the box into the workroom and set it on the table.

Eva had been hovering near the door, watching for his red truck. She'd told herself she just wanted to make sure the edition arrived, but as soon as Cody left to retrieve another box, she ran to the one on the table and snatched up the top copy. The smell of fresh ink drifted off the newsprint, bringing a flood of memories. Memories of being a little girl and standing beside her brother and watching her father do the very thing she was doing now—taking that first copy from the stack of newly printed papers.

She'd never forget the look on Seb's face—a mixture of joy, pride and excitement. *Look what we got here, kids,* he'd say, waving the paper under their noses. *Nothing beats the* news.

Eva took the latest issue of the *Herald* to her cubicle. She sat at her desk and read it, just like her father used to do. When she was finished, she leaned back and let a deep breath expand her chest. A slow smile curved her lips. She'd done a good job. She should be proud of herself.

Then her gaze fell on the framed covers of *Seattle's Best* hanging on the walls. Glossy, colorful covers and all featuring her byline.

She looked at the *Herald,* and full of news or not, the newspaper seemed dull and drab in comparison. The excitement charging through her dissolved into despair.

"THANKS FOR RUNNING the show while I was out," Mark told Eva when he returned to work the following Monday. They were having an informal meeting in the staff room.

Eva shrugged. "You're welcome…I guess."

"You guess? You should be proud of this issue." He picked up a copy from the table. "Everything looks great."

His praise pleased her but made her uncomfortable, too. She cast him a sideways glance. "Even the front-page feature on the dog show?"

He grinned. "Well…I probably would've moved that inside, but your lead article on the city-council meeting and the announcement of the new mayor is right on target."

"Glad you approve."

He put down the paper and studied her. "How'd you like attending the meeting?"

She lowered her gaze. "It was okay."

"I heard Boyd Carlstrom was there."

Noticing the disapproval in Mark's voice, Eva tensed. She met his gaze. "He was. He spoke to me during the break."

Mark shook his head. "And bragged to everyone about taking over the paper. He's worming his way into our town every chance he can get. I wish he'd move on."

Eva picked up a pen lying next to a scrap of paper and idly doodled a few circles. She still didn't know what to think about Boyd. He was pushy and rude and obnoxious, but she couldn't forget how kind he'd been to her when she was a child. He couldn't be all bad, could he?

AT THE HIGH-SCHOOL gymnasium, Mark dribbled the basketball down the court, then tossed the ball to Bernie. Tonight their team, the Bombers, was playing the Jets. He and Bernie had arrived early to warm up while they waited for the others. He flexed his arms as he waited for Bernie to take a shot.

Bernie bounced the ball a few times, the sound echoing around the empty gym. He paused to take aim, then sent the ball flying. It balanced for a second on the basket's rim before it slipped inside.

"How do you do that?" Mark shook his head in wonder. "That's your third in a row."

Bernie grinned. "Just talented, I guess.

Maybe I shoulda played basketball for a living instead of selling ads." He ran after the ball, caught it and tossed it to Mark.

Mark leaped ahead and grabbed the ball in both hands. "You'd probably be a rich man by now."

"Yeah, right. Maria wouldn't go for me being on the road so much, though. Gotta keep the wife happy. Let's take five, okay?"

Mark nodded and trotted after Bernie to the bleachers. They plopped down on the bottom bench. Bernie picked up a towel and wiped his forehead. "Glad you're back. We missed you."

"That goes both ways. I'm not used to being laid up. Spending all that time alone and away from work was no fun. I really missed Sasha, too. But I sure appreciate Eileen keeping her until I got well. I didn't want her sick."

"I hear you."

"Things seemed to perk along at the paper. You all get along with Eva okay?" He shot Bernie a sideways glance.

Bernie shrugged and tossed down the towel. "I guess. Except April—she spent the entire time in a funk."

"Yeah, well, April's in her own space."

"A space she wishes *you* were in, too. But I'm thinking your interests lie in another direction. Am I right?"

Mark gave a start. "You mean Eva? Is it that obvious?"

Bernie nodded. "Judging by how you two rang in the New Year at the party, I'd say, yeah, it is."

Mark leaned back and propped his elbows on the bench behind them. "But you don't like her, do you?"

"I'm mellowing on that. Maria likes her. So does Bella."

"So do a lot of other people around town. She made a big hit at the city-council meeting. And we've received letters praising her article."

Bernie leaned over to retie a shoelace. "They can't all be wrong."

"She's still leaving in June. Why can't I just give up on her?"

"Only you can answer that, my man."

"I keep thinking there's got to be more to her reluctance to be here than just an argument with Seb because he wanted her to stay and she wanted to work for *Seattle's Best*. Something to do with her brother…"

"The one who drowned in the boating accident."

"Yeah. Seb never talked much about it. And I never asked."

"So, the brother was first choice. When he died, Seb wanted Eva to take his place. She didn't want to be second choice."

"But I think there's even more. I just don't know what."

"Why don't you ask her?"

"Whenever the subject comes up, or is even hinted at, she shuts up tighter than a clam. Nobody else ever talks about that time, either. I figured it was out of respect for Seb, since he was silent on the subject."

"There might be other ways to find out. Why don't you do a Google search?"

"Yeah, maybe I will." He gave Bernie a playful punch on the shoulder. "I knew there was a reason I keep a smart guy like you around."

"Watch out, though," Bernie cautioned. "You might wish you'd left it alone."

The double doors to the gym swung open, and the guys on the opposing team burst in. "Well, look who's here," one said. "A couple of Bombers. Practicing?"

"Yeah, we want to make sure you guys lose big tonight," Bernie said.

"That'll be the day" came the reply.

Mark joined in the banter, glad to have a diversion from his dilemma over Eva. Still, as he played the game and helped his team to win, a part of his mind stayed anchored to her. He vowed to do all he could to find out what had happened on that fateful day eleven years ago at Pine Lake.

## CHAPTER FIFTEEN

LATER THAT EVENING, after putting Sasha to bed, Mark sat in front of his computer, typing search words into Google. Several newspaper articles had been written about Brett Sinclair's death. He clicked on the first one that came up. It was from the *Seaview Sentinel*. The headline read Boy Drowns at Pine Lake. The date was June 10, eleven years ago. Brett Sinclair, eighteen, had been with a group of Willow Beach High School students who were celebrating their upcoming graduation with a party at Pine Lake.

Mark had been to the lake and liked to hike the trail that followed the shoreline. He'd never hiked completely around the lake, though, because it was quite large. On one side was a popular resort, with cabins, boating and fishing and a couple of restaurants. On the opposite shore were private homes. An island sat in the lake's center. Uninhabited, it was a popular destination by boat for a picnic or a short walk.

Mark read the article and then sat back, stunned. As he'd suspected, there was more to the story than he'd been told. What he hadn't realized was how that missing piece involved Eva.

MARK STEWED FOR several weeks about his newfound knowledge and what to do about it. What he wanted most was to talk to Eva and tell her what he'd uncovered, but given her reluctance to discuss the incident—which he now understood far better than before—he feared upsetting her. He wanted to respect her wishes, but he also wanted to talk about it. He needed to make the connection between them—he wasn't sure why. With four months still remaining before her year was up, he risked destroying even the shaky relationship they had managed to develop so far.

He didn't want to bring up the subject at the office, yet that was about the only place they saw each other. He had no excuse for inviting her to his house, and she never invited him to her apartment. The holidays had provided opportunities for getting together outside of work, but those were over. He considered inviting her to have dinner with him and Sasha on Valentine's Day, but that holiday was for lovers, wasn't it? And they were hardly that.

Then, one Saturday when he was on his way to the high-school gym to run the indoor track, he passed by Seb's old house and saw her blue car parked in the driveway. He knew she'd been cleaning out the house but hadn't asked about her progress. It seemed to be a slow process.

On impulse, he pulled into the driveway and parked behind her car. He hadn't been here since the day Seb died, and now that day and its sad events rushed back to him. Worried because Seb hadn't shown up for work by ten o'clock, he'd come to his house and discovered his lifeless body. That discovery had changed so much for Mark.

He stepped up to the door and rang the bell, as he had that day. No one had answered, and he'd used the key Seb had given him. Today, the door inched open and Eva peeked out. She frowned. "Mark. What brings you here?"

"I was passing by on my way to run at the high school and saw your car. You're still cleaning the place, right?" He craned his neck to peer over her shoulder. A stack of cardboard boxes sat at the end of the hallway.

She sighed. "Right. I need to get it on the market."

He nodded. "Do you want a hand with anything? I've got time."

She shook her head. "No, thanks. I'm just packing up some stuff for Goodwill." She nodded over her shoulder toward the boxes.

"You can't cart those in your car."

"They're sending over one of their trucks on Monday. I'll have to take a few minutes from work to let them in."

"Why don't you let me drop off the boxes today? Their store is just a little ways past the high school."

"Well…all right. Come in, then."

She opened the door wider and he stepped inside.

The house smelled musty, but that was to be expected, having been closed up for, what, nine months? Most of the curtains were closed, too, which gave the place a dim, shadowy appearance.

"I haven't quite filled up all the boxes," she said, leading him down the hallway.

"I can wait. And give you a hand in the meantime."

She stopped at the end of the hallway. "Right now I'm doing the kitchen. I saved it for last. Not saved it, exactly, I just couldn't…"

"I know what you mean. But like I said, I'll help."

"Well…okay. You can empty the drawers."

He bypassed the boxes and stepped into the kitchen. Cupboard doors and drawers hung open, and most of the shelves were empty, the dishes and glasses stacked on the counters. His gaze strayed to the round table in one corner, the table where Seb had been slumped over his plate of eggs and toast. Mark swallowed and looked away. If that one memory affected him so much, what must the memories of all the years Eva had spent in this house be doing to her?

She was packing a box with dishes, wrapping each piece in butcher paper. "This must be tough on you," he said gently.

"It's not easy, but someone has to do it, and there's no one but me."

He thought of his own house. After Diane died, the only things he had removed were her clothes, which he, too, had donated to charity. But his situation was different, wasn't it? He and Sasha still lived in the house and he wanted to keep Diane's presence alive for their daughter.

He pulled open a drawer. It was full of towels and dishcloths. He grabbed a handful. "Where do you want these?"

She looked up. "Just put them on the counter. I'll sort through them, although they'll all probably be donated."

He resumed his task. As he was emptying the third drawer, he noticed a mug sitting on the counter with some other cups and glasses. It read *Brett* in bold black letters. The one next to it had *Eva* in black script.

He picked up the mugs, one in each hand. "Hey, these look familiar. Aren't they from the county fair? I got one like them a couple years ago." He looked at the other side, and sure enough, small print near the bottom said *Clallam County Fair*.

She glanced up and then quickly away. "Yeah, the fair. The booth where they had mugs with every name you could think of."

"Right. There were hundreds. I didn't think there'd be one with Sasha's name, but there was."

"I don't know why Seb hung on to these."
She set her mouth and grabbed another piece
of butcher paper from the pile on the table.

He put down the mugs. "Wish I'd had the
chance to know your brother," he said, realizing he was venturing into dangerous territory but determined to forge on.

She said nothing.

He cleared his throat. "Eva…I, uh, I know
you were with Brett that day at Pine Lake."

He expected surprise, or shock, but her
voice was deadly calm as she said, "Is that
what this is about?"

"What do you mean?"

"Your stopping by today. You want me to
talk about Brett, about the past."

"I do want to help you today, but I have to
admit, since I've found out, the accident has
been on my mind a lot."

"So who told you?" She slid a stack of
plates along the counter so she could better
reach them, then lifted one off the top.

"No one. I did some research."

She nodded. "Of course. Nothing's private
now that we have the internet."

Mark took another handful of towels from

a drawer. "Anyway, I know you were in the boat with Brett when it capsized."

"And that I was rescued. Obviously. So, end of story."

"No, that's just it. That's not the end of the story. There's so much more."

She stopped with half the plate wrapped, her eyes challenging him. "And you expect me to tell you."

"Eva, I want to understand you better."

"Why?"

"Because I care about…the *newspaper,* and I want it to be the best it can be. And if I understand you better, then we can work together better. Does that make sense?" He'd almost slipped and said, *Because I care about you.* Close call.

She tilted her head and resumed her wrapping. "I get it about the newspaper. But we've managed so far on the information you've had. I can't see what difference my telling you more will make."

He set his jaw. "Let's give it a try and find out. According to what I read, the occasion was a party for graduating seniors."

She shook her head. "You are something else, Mark Townson. Like the proverbial dog with a bone. Okay—" she leveled him a stern gaze "—but what I say goes no farther than this room."

He held up both hands. "Of course not. You can trust me."

She folded her arms and leaned against the counter. "Yes, it was a party for graduating seniors. Not a school-sponsored event, just some seniors getting together. A few of my friends and I tagged along. During the course of the party, Brett took me sailing in one of the rental boats. It was a really small boat, barely big enough for two people."

His task forgotten, Mark focused on Eva. "Brett knew how to sail, of course."

She waved a hand. "Brett knew how to do everything, or so he made people think. But, yes, he'd had a couple lessons. Anyway, we started off and by the time we got around to the other side of the island, out of sight of the resort, the wind had picked up, and then it started to rain. You know how fast storms blow in from the ocean."

He nodded. "And I know that lake is big. You can barely make out what's on the opposite shore, and with the island in the middle,

302                    EVA'S DEADLINE

seeing across the lake is practically impossible."

She shifted her weight and turned slightly to look out the window. "Brett tried to get us to the island, but before he could, a huge wave swamped us and we tipped over."

Mark could imagine the scene, the cold water, the wind, the waves. "But someone saw what happened."

Eva nodded. "Two men who'd been working on their dock. They jumped in a motorboat and headed out. One of them pulled me into their boat. But Brett had disappeared." She snapped her fingers. "Just like that, he was gone."

"Weren't you wearing life jackets? I thought that was mandatory when you rented a boat."

She gave a cynical laugh. "Brett wear a life jacket? We had them on when we left the dock, but as soon as we were out of sight, he took his off."

"Did you take yours off?"

She looked down. "No."

"And after the accident—"

She folded her arms again and walked to the window. He followed but kept his distance. Over her shoulder, he glimpsed the backyard, the grass overgrown and Seb's to-mato vines hanging limply on their string fence.

"Dad was a wreck. We all were. I felt hor-rible."

"Because you survived and Brett didn't."

She nodded. "And Brett was Dad's favor-ite. But not only because of that…"

He waited, and finally she said in a low voice, "Because the accident was my fault."

His jaw dropped. "Why do you say that? Brett was the one who took off his life jacket."

She turned, eyes flashing. "Because I kept begging him to take me out in the boat. He didn't want to go sailing. He wanted to stay on shore and party with his friends. But I kept nagging him, and finally, to shut me up, he went and got the boat." She stopped, sucked in a breath and then went on, her voice drop-ping to a whisper. "If I hadn't kept at him, we wouldn't have gone out, and, and…"

Oh, man, this was more than he'd bar-gained for.

"Dad didn't know that part of it," she con-tinued, her voice still whispery. "I never told him."

Seconds went by as Eva ran her fingers

along a silver chain peeking out the neckline of her blouse. He'd noticed her fingering the chain at other times, too. He wondered if the necklace had something to do with Brett but didn't dare ask.

Finally, she dropped her hand and continued, "Years later, after I'd graduated from college and Dad had decided he wanted me to work for him, to take Brett's place, all I wanted to do was stay away. I didn't want to come back here and, okay, I didn't want to be second choice, either. But mostly I didn't want to come back because then I'd be constantly reminded of what happened.

"But Dad wouldn't take no for an answer. He kept at me until I told him something else, something I knew would hurt him."

"And that was?" He held his breath. What more could there possibly be to this sad story?

"Right before we capsized in the storm, Brett told me that he wasn't going to work at the *Herald* like Dad wanted him to. He wasn't going to the U, either."

"What was he going to do?"

"Enlist in the army. He'd been talking to recruiters who'd come to the high school. 'No way am I staying in Willow Beach and working for Dad,' he'd told me. 'Not when I can see the world.'" A sad smile crossed her lips. "He was so excited about his future."

"He wasn't worried about your father objecting to his decision?"

"He didn't care. He said he'd 'take on the old man any day.' When I told Dad that Brett had said those words to me that day in the boat, he didn't believe me. We argued some more, and then I left Willow Beach. We didn't talk much after that. And now he's gone."

She gazed at the table, as though she, too, were remembering that was where Seb had spent his final moments. Then she turned to him. "You satisfied now?"

Mark slowly shook his head. "I wish I'd known all this at the beginning."

Her eyes flashed again. "Why? What difference would knowing have made? I still would have accepted the terms of the will, and we'd be doing just what we are doing, running the newspaper. But when my time is up, I'm going home. I could never live here again. It's been bad enough all these months. The memories pop up constantly, sometimes when I least expect them."

Mark nodded and paced a few steps to

the counter and back. "I know about painful memories."

"What do you mean?" A note of wariness crept into her voice.

"Oh, not to do with Seb. With my wife, Diane."

"You said she died in a bus accident."

"Yes, but there's more to that story, too."

"You don't have to tell me."

Here was an out, if he wanted it. Yet, she'd finally confided in him. Didn't he owe her as much? "I want to tell you. Unless you don't want to hear it."

She shrugged, then nodded. "You listened to me."

"Yes, but I wanted to know about you."

"Well…maybe I want to know about you, too." She went back to the counter and picked up another plate and a piece of butcher paper. "Go ahead."

Now it was Mark's turn to stare out the window. That seemed safer than looking at Eva. "I'll start back when we first came to Willow Beach. Diane wasn't as enthusiastic about living here as I was. I knew I wanted to work for a newspaper, but I wanted the job to be in a small town where I could enjoy the out-of-doors. Diane would rather have lived in a larger city." He stopped and smiled over his shoulder. "Kind of like you."

Eva nodded. "I can relate."

"She was interested in acting and said a big city would offer her more opportunities."

"She was right about that."

"I know. But we do have the Little Theater. And she joined their troupe. I thought that would be enough. We were happy. At least, I thought we were."

"Until—"

"Until some dude from Hollywood came to town."

"A talent scout?"

Mark snorted. "So he said. Actually, he was visiting his son, who lives here. And while he was here, he went to a play at the theater. A play Diane was in. He sought her out afterward and told her what a good actress she was. He said if she came to Hollywood, he would see that she got a screen test."

"And you didn't want her to go?"

He walked back to where she stood and faced her, propping his hands on his hips. "Of course not. If she passed the test, we couldn't up and move to California. Our life was here.

We argued about it, and she backed off, and I thought she'd given up on the idea.

"Then one day I came home and found a note saying she was leaving me and Sasha and going to Hollywood."

Eva stopped wrapping and set down the plate, eyeing him in disbelief. "Leaving you for good? Or just long enough to take the test?"

"For good. That's what the note said."

"But she never got there."

"Nope. She didn't get any farther than Grant's Pass, Oregon. That's where the bus went over a cliff."

Eva closed her eyes and shook her head. "Does Sasha know why her mother left?" She looked up at Mark sadly.

"Not the Hollywood reason. I told her Diane was going to visit her brother. And that was true. Her brother lives in L.A. But that was all I told her. Anyway, I just wanted you to know you aren't the only one dealing with a painful past."

"I guess we're both hurting," she said, not meeting his eyes.

"I guess we are."

Neither said anything more. He studied her,

wondering what she was thinking. He ached to take her in his arms. Only a few feet separated them, and he could easily reach out, but in spirit, they were oceans apart.

She confirmed that when she looked up and said, "Well, now that we're done with true confessions, do you still want to help me with these boxes?"

"WHAT DO YOU think of those shoes?" Susan pointed to a pair of tan-and-white athletic shoes in the store window and then turned to Eva.

Eva tore her gaze away from the black-and-white high heels she'd been considering and focused on Susan's question. They'd been shopping in downtown Seattle for a couple hours, and each had made several purchases. After her and Mark's intense discussion at Seb's house, Eva desperately needed space and had escaped to Seattle the next weekend. Greg was out of town on a business trip, and she and Susan had taken the opportunity to do what they both loved—shop.

"Kinda fancy for casual wear," Eva said.

Susan laughed. "I've gone beyond casual. Greg's got me jogging, of all things. And since you're a jogger, I thought you could help me pick out a good pair of shoes."

"Those look more like walking shoes than jogging, although sometimes you can use the same pair for both. Generally, though, a running shoe needs more cushioning, especially in the heel."

Susan pressed a palm to her forehead. "Uh-oh, my head's starting to hurt already. But I knew you were an expert."

"Let's go in the store and find someone to help us. Choosing will be easy, I promise you."

Half an hour later, they emerged from the store. "You were right, Eva." Susan nodded to the shoe box tucked into her tote. "Between you and the salesman, I managed to avoid having a nervous breakdown."

"You made a good choice."

"Greg will be so impressed." Susan pushed back the sleeve of her jacket and glanced at her wristwatch. "Lunchtime. What's your pleasure?"

"How about The Sandwich Shoppe on Third?"

Susan's eyes grew big. "I'm tasting their Monte Carlo Special already." Then her mouth turned down. "But that's loaded with calories."

"They have a diet special, don't they?"

Susan wrinkled her nose. "Everybody has a diet special. Turkey burger or chicken breast and a side salad. Bor-ing."

Once they were settled in a high-backed booth at the restaurant and had given their orders—both opting for the Monte Carlo—Susan said, "Okay, Eva, enough about me and Greg. What's happening with you and Mark?"

Eva leaned back against the seat and gazed at the ceiling fans lazily stirring circles of air. "Bad, bad, bad."

Susan raised her eyebrows. "What does that mean?"

Eva sighed. "Oh, we got into the past the other day and spilled our guts to each other."

"Why is that bad?"

"I don't know. Now I feel funny around him. Self-conscious. I told him stuff I've never told anyone. How could I be so stupid?" She straightened and looked at Susan. "Do you and Greg share things from your past?"

"A little. But when I think about it, there's a lot I don't know about Greg's past. I've never thought too much about that part of his life. I just know I love him and I trust him."

"Aren't you scared sometimes about being in love with him?"

Susan tilted her head. "I was at first. But the more time we spend together, the more sure I am that he's right for me. Maybe what you need is more time with Mark."

Eva shook her head. "Time is definitely something we don't have."

## CHAPTER SIXTEEN

"So you'll do the interview with the colonel?" Mark asked Eva.

Eva leaned back in her chair and considered his question. It was Monday morning and they were in his office having their usual planning meeting. They sat at a small table near the window, papers and notes spread out around them. Outside the window, the maple tree had sprouted tiny green leaves, a sure sign that spring had arrived.

Eva picked up her tablet computer, brought up her calendar and studied it. "I suppose I could. Wednesday's open." She looked up. "But wouldn't you rather? You said you knew him."

"True, but you're good with personal stories."

Eva narrowed her eyes. "Trying to flatter me into taking the assignment?"

One of Mark's eyebrows arched. "No, I'm

paying you a compliment. A sincere compliment. I'll say it again—you're good with personal stories. You like interviewing."

Eva had to agree. Her favorite assignments for *Seattle's Best* had been interviews with interesting people.

"I'm also saying that we make a good team," Mark added.

"Don't say that. You know I—"

Mark leaned forward. "Come on, Eva, you can't tell me you haven't enjoyed at least some of your work here. Look at all the positive feedback on your coverage of the city-council meeting, for one thing. That's gotta make you feel good."

"Okay, I'll admit appreciation is nice." Eva briefly closed her eyes. "Are we done here?"

Mark glanced at his notes. "I guess. Why the hurry?"

"I have work to do." She gathered the papers and photos on the table. In truth, she needed to get away from him. His nearness had kept her senses humming the entire time, and this sudden turn of the conversation threatened her somehow. She grabbed her tablet and pen, pushed back her chair and stood.

Mark rose , too, and as she turned to leave, he stepped forward and blocked her way. "Eva…"

His voice had dropped a couple notches. Eva's pulse spiked.

He reached out and gently laid his palm against her cheek. Ran his hand along her jaw and down to the back of her neck, pulling her closer.

"Mark, we…"

"Shh." He placed his other forefinger over her lips. "I wanted so badly to touch you that day."

"What day?" she asked, although she knew very well what he meant. But if she kept him talking, then what she feared—or maybe what she *wanted*—wouldn't happen.

"That day at Seb's house—"

"Should never have happened. I never should have let you in."

"But you did—and we did."

"And nothing's changed."

"And *everything's* changed. For me, for you—for us."

He leaned closer and slid his arm around her waist. His warm breath spread over her cheek. "Maybe we should dance. That always seems to work. If I can get you to put down your tablet." He shook his head. "Always something between us."

"There's more than just a tablet or a purse between us, Mark." Eva gripped her tablet even tighter to her chest.

"There's a lot between us, Eva. In a good way. It's time you realized that."

He came closer, and by the gleam in his eyes, she knew he intended to kiss her. She put out her arms to stop him, but his lips brushed hers before her hands connected with his shoulders. Even the slight touch electrified her, as it always did. She leaned into him. The kiss deepened. The last time they'd kissed seemed ages ago. Too long ago.

"Ahem!"

Eva pulled away from Mark and turned toward the doorway.

April stood there, her face as red as her scarlet blouse.

Eva felt her own face flame. She put some more distance between her and Mark.

"What can we do for you, April?" he asked in a calm tone.

April flipped her hair over one shoulder. Her gold hoop earring sparkled in the light from the window. "I wanted to talk to you about my Police Beat column," she said in clipped tones. "But I see you're busy. I'll come back later."

"You can discuss your work with Eva here. What's on your mind?"

April scowled. "I'd rather come back."

Mark stepped to his desk and glanced at his calendar. "How about one-thirty? That work for you, Eva?"

Before Eva could answer, April turned and stalked out.

Neither Mark nor Eva said anything for a few moments. Then Mark raised his hands and said, "There is nothing between April and me, I swear."

"Maybe you know that, but I don't think she does."

"I've tried to set her straight many times. When she comes back, I will have a very serious talk with her."

"Don't do that on my account, Mark, because it won't change anything between us as far as I'm concerned."

PROMPTLY AT ONE-THIRTY, April appeared in the doorway to Mark's office. He did a double take at the sight of her red-rimmed, teary eyes and slumped shoulders. Quite a different picture from the angry young woman of a couple hours ago. Still, he wouldn't let sympathy get in the way of what needed to be done. He squared his shoulders and steeled himself for what he figured would be an ordeal.

"Come in, April, and sit down." He gestured to the chair by his desk.

April shuffled over and perched on the edge of the seat.

Mark closed the door and sat in his chair. Although he had his speech all planned, he decided to let her speak first.

"I'm sorry I interrupted you this morning," she said in a voice that sounded sincere.

"Not your fault, April. I'm glad we made this appointment, though, because we need to talk."

Her brow wrinkled. "You don't want me to do the Police Beat anymore?"

He picked up the newspaper's current issue from his desk and opened it to the Police Beat column, which took up the top half of a page. "Of course I do. You're doing a fine job with the column. Good writing, good organization…" He put down the paper and cleared his throat. "April, we've talked before about our relationship—yours and mine—and that it's strictly professional."

Defiance lit her eyes. "No. We went out on a date. To dinner."

Mark took a deep breath, summoning all his patience. "Yes, we had dinner together, once. That was after we'd met—by chance, let me remind you—at the concert on the beach, and I invited you to join me at Charlie's."

"We stayed a long time talking."

"Yes, we did. Mostly about the newspaper, as I recall."

"I thought you liked me."

"I do like you, April. You are a valued employee and a good friend to my daughter."

April leaned forward. "You liked me in a personal way—until *she* came."

"My feelings for you are exactly the same as they've been from the beginning. We are colleagues. That's all."

April's lips twisted as though she'd tasted something sour. "No, that isn't all. Everything was fine until she came. I thought we were going to buy her out. We started that fund."

Mark waved a hand. "I don't see that happening. We have only a few hundred dollars so far. Eva's share is worth much, much more than that."

"Have you tried to get a loan yet?"

"I'll let you all know if and when that comes about."

"I bet you haven't even tried. I bet you're hoping that you and she—"

"April, have you ever thought you might be happier working someplace else?"

"Are you trying to fire me?" Her nostrils flared.

He rubbed the back of his neck. "No, I'm trying to find a solution to your unhappiness. I'm thinking that as long as you work here, you'll be unhappy."

April stuck out her chin. "I'll be fine as soon as she leaves."

"GREAT SHOW," EVA TOLD the girls gathered around her. They'd just finished the high school's Spring Fashion Show and were assembled backstage. "And I have a surprise for you." Eva exchanged a wink with Fran Oliver, who looked up from checking off items on her clipboard. "The participating stores are donating one outfit for each of you to keep. How about that?"

A cheer went up. "Thank you, Ms. Sinclair! You're the best!"

Melanie danced around her. "Can we do it again next year, Ms. Sinclair?"

"What do you think, Fran?" Eva looked to the teacher.

"I don't see why not," Fran said, making a note on her list.

"Mrs. Oliver and I will work on it," Eva told them. "Go pick out your outfits."

Fran came to stand beside Eva, and together they watched the chattering girls disappear into the dressing rooms.

"They're a great bunch, aren't they?" Fran said.

Eva nodded. "They are. And next year's show will be even better. I'd like to see the set have more props. I'll talk to the drama department about that. And maybe a few more door prizes, especially if we can get a couple more sponsors." She stopped and studied Fran. "What? Why are you giving me an odd look?"

"I'm wondering if I'm hearing right. You'll be here in the fall? That's great." She put her clipboard on a nearby table and reached out to give Eva a hug. "Oh, I'm so glad you're staying."

Eva drew away. "Wait a minute. No, I'm still leaving in June."

Fran's eyes widened. "Are you? I could swear you were planning next fall's show."

"I was just making plans for whoever takes over."

Fran's mouth turned down. "Which will be no one. None of us has the time, or the expertise, or the contacts. It's your baby, Eva."

Eva held up a hand. "No, Fran, I'm not staying."

"How are you coming with ShopRite's flyers, April?" Eva rounded the counter and approached April's desk.

April grabbed another sheet from the stack of flyers. She folded it, pressing the crease with her fingers. "I'm working as fast as I can," she grumbled.

April's hair hid her profile, but Eva could imagine the frown, the pouting lips. She'd seen them often enough over the past eleven months.

"I know you are, and I know the flyers were late being delivered. But Cody will be bringing in the new edition any minute now, and if we want to be on time for our distributors—"

"I know what time Cody brings the paper."

Eva sighed. Always so difficult. Then she reminded herself that in a few more weeks she would be free of April's surly glances and her petulant tone. Every job had its personality clashes, but this one with April had strained Eva's patience to the limit.

She was about to turn away when April said, "He doesn't really want *you*."

Her voice was so low that Eva thought she was talking to herself. On the off chance that she wasn't, Eva tipped her head in April's direction and said, "Beg your pardon?"

"It's the newspaper he wants, not you."

Eva said nothing. She waited.

"We started a fund to buy you out, but we couldn't raise enough money. So now he's after you. He doesn't want to work with Boyd Carlstrom. None of us does."

Still, Eva remained silent.

"I'm willing to take second place, but I don't think you are, Eva. No, you want to be number one. Well, you're not."

All this was said without April losing the

rhythm of folding the flyers or raising her head to see Eva's reaction.

Under other circumstances, Eva would address this problem, either here at April's desk or by calling April into her cubicle for a private conversation. But with her remaining time in Willow Beach so short, she'd let the matter go.

As though she'd heard nothing, she said, "Please let me know if you need more flyers, April. I thought I brought you the correct number, but I may have counted wrong."

"I know where to get more if I need them."

"I CAN'T BELIEVE the timing," Eva said over the phone to Susan. "You're getting engaged and I'm coming back to Seattle all in the same month."

She sat in her apartment on the maroon sofa, having just checked off another day on her calendar.

"And I can't believe Greg finally proposed—I'm on cloud nine," Susan said. "And don't forget, I want you to be my maid of honor."

"I'm looking forward to it. When is the wedding?"

"The wedding. Um, I'm not sure. Greg wants to be more secure in his job before we tie the knot."

Hearing the hesitation in her friend's voice, Eva said, "Susan, are you sure everything's okay with you and Greg?"

"Of course. I'm deliriously happy."

"So where will you live in the meantime? You could stay on in my condo with me. I'm sure we'd get along."

"Thanks, Eva, but I've already rented an apartment not too far from here. We'll be neighbors."

"I'll look forward to that. I'll soon be free at last and coming home. If only I knew what I was going to do for a living."

"What about the novel you said you were writing?"

Eva glanced at her kitchen table, where her computer sat. Next to it was a stack of pages that she'd printed out to proofread. "I'm still working on it and hope to publish it, but I need a steady income in the meantime."

"But you're selling your half of the *Herald*. And when your dad's house sells, you'll have that money."

"Yes, but the money won't last forever. Besides, I want to work."

Susan remained silent a moment, and Eva wondered if she were still thinking about her own situation. But then, in a conspiratorial tone, she said, "I shouldn't tell you, but there's a rumor around the office that you might be getting a phone call from James."

"What about? Is there an opening at the magazine?" Eva gripped the phone. "I'd come back as copyeditor—anything to work for *Seattle's Best* again."

"Sorry, hon, that's all you'll hear from me. Gotta go now."

Eva sat there, stunned by Susan's news. She was to expect a call from her old boss, James. With a job offer? What else could he want to talk to her about? But, no, she couldn't be that lucky.

When two days passed without a call, either at home or at work, she decided Susan had been misinformed. She finished writing her résumé and researched headhunters.

Then, just before she left the office Wednesday afternoon, James phoned. They exchanged a few general comments, and then he said in his typically casual tone, "Got a proposition for you. How'd you like to come back to work for us?"

"More than anything!"

"Maybe you'd better hear the rest of the deal first. You'd be coming back as a staff writer, same as when you left. Margo Janovich is firmly entrenched as assistant editor. But Hannah Davis, who's on maternity leave, has decided to quit and become a full-time mom, which leaves an opening we need filled."

"I'll take it."

"Wonderful. We'll be happy to have you back."

Eva hung up with a smile on her face. True, the position wasn't the one she'd wanted, but at least she was back in the game.

"I'VE ADDED ALL my Our Town files to June's," Eva told Mark a week later, "so that the next person who writes the column will have them for review."

She sat in his office, as she had so many times during the past year. But this time, instead of making plans for the next issue of the *Herald,* she was making plans to leave.

Mark mumbled something she couldn't

make out. He was glued to his computer screen, or appeared to be, and she didn't know whether he was even listening.

"I'll clean out my desk…"

Mark waved a hand. "I don't need to hear all the details, Eva. I bet when you get done *cleaning,* all traces of you will be gone, and we won't even know you've been here."

"You don't have to be rude about it."

He went back to his reading. She sat there a moment, and when he didn't say anything more or even look up, she said, "Okay, I'll get back to work."

"You do that, Eva."

That evening, Eva started packing her belongings in preparation for her move back to Seattle. She'd finished cleaning out Seb's house and had contacted Morgan's Realty to handle the sale. Time to take a break. She gazed out the window. Now that it was June, the days were getting longer. A jog on the beach sounded good. This might be her last opportunity.

The weather wasn't quite warm enough for shorts, so she pulled on a pair of sweats. She tied a scarf around her head, buckled on her waist pouch and headed out. She hadn't been on the beach more than five minutes when she recalled that first jog she'd taken—and meeting Mark. A lump rose in Eva's throat. What was that all about?

She started off, running along the sand. Seagulls swooped. Clouds drifted across the sky. Waves broke on the shore. She tried to focus on her upcoming move to Seattle, but her thoughts refused to anchor here, always drifting back to Willow Beach—and Mark.

About a mile down the beach, she became aware of someone running behind her. The runner caught up, but instead of passing, he matched her stride. She glanced over.

Mark.

"What are…you doing here?"

"Running…same as…you."

She expected him to sprint ahead, but he stayed by her side. They ran for a while, neither saying anything, their rhythm perfectly in sync. Then, about a mile later, he grasped her elbow and pointed toward the dunes, where driftwood and logs lined the beach. "Let's take a break."

"I…" Did she really want to spend time with him? "All right, but five minutes is all I can spare."

"Busy lady."

They did their cool-down stretches and then sat on a log facing the horizon.

Without looking at her, he said, "Remember that first night when we met each other jogging, and we sat like this to watch the sunset?"

She nodded. There had been other jogs together, not many and none like that one. She sighed. "I will miss the beach."

"I'll miss you." His voice was low and husky.

"Mark, don't..."

He turned toward her. "Eva, listen, I don't want you to leave."

"Why not?"

"We make a good team."

"At the newspaper."

"Yes. I've been doing a lot of thinking, and I don't believe you want to leave, either. You like being here, and you like working for the *Herald*."

She gave a short, cynical laugh. "You're out of your mind."

"No, no, listen to me. You say you can't live here anymore because of the painful memories. But I think it's because you feel guilty.

You think you're responsible for Brett's death. You told me that yourself. But, Eva, you're not responsible. You didn't force him to take you out in the boat. He could have said no, no matter how much you begged. You didn't cause the storm to come up. You didn't make him take off his life jacket."

"We've already been through this. I don't want—"

"For years you've been living in this psychological prison. If you give up all the guilt, the pain will go away. And then you'd be able to accept that Willow Beach is where you want to be. You like it here. I know you do. You liked working with the high-school students, and you liked writing more serious stuff."

Eva stared at him, her pulse pounding. "Who do you think you are—my psychiatrist? What right do you have to tell me what to do to 'get rid of my pain,' as you call it? You aren't me. You didn't live through what I did. How can you possibly know what I really want?"

He drew back. "I'm just trying to help."

She threw up her hands. "I didn't ask for your help. I don't need your help. I don't want your help. And if you want to help someone, you might look at yourself first."

His eyes took on a wary look. "What do you mean?"

"That house of yours, that shrine to your wife. What's that all about if not guilt? Or are all those lacy doilies and fake flowers your idea of tasteful decor? Talk about a psychological prison."

Anger flared in his eyes.. "I've kept everything of Diane's for Sasha's sake. I don't want her to forget her mother. What's wrong with that?"

"Are you sure it's just for Sasha? Or is it for yourself? What about your guilt?"

"We're not talking about me. This is about you."

"No, Mark. You may be fooling yourself, but you're not fooling me. This is about you. Or, maybe I should say, it's all about the *Herald*. Because that's the bottom line, isn't it?"

Mark stared down at his feet, twisting his shoes deeper into the sand. She was suddenly aware that while they'd been talking the sun had almost disappeared into the sea. Oh, there it went, gone for another day. It wasn't the spectacular show they'd witnessed on that first night. Tonight's sunset was quick—and final.

Gripping the log for support, Eva stood. She gazed down at Mark, who had picked up a stick and was tracing patterns in the sand. His jaw was set, his brow furrowed. She reached out a hand, intending to touch his shoulder. Why, she wasn't sure. She changed her mind and drew back.

"I'm going on alone," she said and took off across the sand, heading for the hard-packed shore.

She half expected him to follow her. But he didn't. That was just as well. Then she would have had to hide her tears.

THE FOLLOWING DAY at the newspaper office, Eva's phone rang. She put down the last *Seattle's Best* cover she'd just removed from her wall and picked up the receiver.

Boyd Carlstrom's deep voice rumbled in her ear. "Hey, Eva."

"Boyd. What can I do for you?" Her question was a formality, though, because she knew why he was calling.

"I thought you might be ready for some serious discussion."

"As a matter of fact, I would like to talk to you."

"Good, good. You free for lunch today?"

Eva barely glanced at her calendar before replying, "I am."

"Meet you at the Beach Café at twelve-thirty."

"See you there, Boyd."

# CHAPTER SEVENTEEN

"So THAT'S THE WAY it is." Mark finished his speech and looked around the room at his faithful staff. "Eva will be leaving next week, when her year is up."

"And she's selling her share to Boyd Carlstrom?" Dora put down her knitting and frowned at Mark.

"I'm sure she is." Especially after the sorry scene on the beach the other evening. Man, he'd screwed up. What had he been thinking to confront her like that?

"What was it like when Boyd was here before, Dora?" Bernie asked.

Dora looped yarn around her knitting needle. "He expected everything to be done his way, no compromises. And I'm not sure he has the same interest in news that Seb had."

Cody frowned. "Maybe this is the time for me to go back to the U and get my degree."

Bernie rubbed his chin. "Maybe I should

move to California. Maria's been wanting to live near her parents."

"Josh has been after me for years to retire." Dora made another stitch, then looked up at Mark. "But we'd be deserting you." She turned to April, who sat beside her without saying a word the entire time. "What do you think, April?"

April stared at her hands in her lap. "If Mark stays, I'll stay."

Dora put her arm around April's shoulder. "Oh, honey, you're so loyal."

Mark inwardly rolled his eyes. Loyal. Yeah, right.

Holding up both hands, he said, "Please, everyone, do what you need to do and don't worry about me."

Eva peered through the windshield at the road ahead, the road that would take her away from Willow Beach forever. The fog was so thick she could see no more than a couple feet. Just as well. The sooner she forgot about this town, the better.

She wished forgetting Mark were as easy. Even though they'd carefully avoided each other during her last days at the newspaper, all too often they'd find themselves face-to-face—in the hallway, in the staff room, in a doorway. They'd both mumble an "excuse me" and go their separate ways.

The fog finally lifted, and by the time she reached Olympia, the sun shone from a clear sky. The homestretch at last. *Home.* She hadn't been able to use that word in its true sense for a long time. Now, though, her world was right again.

Seattle traffic was the usual stop-and-go from the city limits to her condo. Her slow progress didn't spoil her homecoming. Elation filled her as she pulled into her condo building's underground parking garage. Then up the elevator to the fifth floor.

Once inside her apartment, pulling her suitcase on wheels, she hurried along the hallway to the living room, then stopped and looked around. Her beige sofa and chairs, glass-topped tables and prints of city scenes on the walls were the best welcoming committee ever. She opened the sliding glass doors, stepped onto the balcony and breathed in the fresh air. Sounds from traffic below were like music to her ears. To the south lay the city, with the Space Needle landmark. To the west flowed Elliott Bay. A tug hauling a barge loaded with lumber plied its way to Canada, and a green-and-white ferry chugged to the peninsula. All so familiar, all so comforting.

By the time she'd brought everything from her car up to the condo, she was too tired to retrieve the contents of her basement storage locker. Plenty of time for that. For now, just being *home* was enough.

The following morning, amid all the work of settling in and unpacking, the one thing she'd left unfinished in Willow Beach nagged Eva. She hadn't said a proper goodbye to Sasha. She'd come to dearly love the little girl and would miss her. She'd hoped to tell Sasha goodbye in person, but Mark had carefully kept his daughter away from the office— and anywhere else the two might accidentally meet. Eva didn't blame him for wanting to protect Sasha.

Still, leaving without so much as a word was not fair to Eva or to the child. She paced the living room, thinking what she should do. She could phone. But that would be awkward if Mark answered, which he probably would.

She finally decided to write Sasha a letter. After lunch, she went to a nearby drugstore and picked out a note card she thought the little girl would like. Then she returned to her condo and sat down at her desk. When she finished writing, she sat back and read her words. Satisfied she'd done the best she could but still aching with regret, she put the card in the envelope, addressed it and stamped it.

THREE DAYS LATER, Mark collected the mail from the box in front of his house. Mixed in with the usual bills and junk mail was an envelope addressed to Sasha. When he recognized Eva's handwriting, his stomach tensed. Why was she writing to his daughter? He'd finally told Sasha that Eva had left, reminding her that Eva never intended to live in Willow Beach forever. But Sasha didn't understand. That night after he tucked her into bed, he heard her crying. He'd soothed away her tears, but the next day she was still sad.

He stared at the envelope, debating what to do. He should tear it up. Giving the letter to Sasha would only renew her distress. He gripped the envelope with both hands, ready to rip it, but then he let his hold relax. Maybe a word from Eva would bring closure to Sasha's grief.

"A letter for me?" Sasha said when he handed it to her.

"It's from Eva."

Sasha jumped up and down. "Oh, goody."

She tore open the envelope and pulled out a card. Mark looked over her shoulder. The front had a picture of a little girl holding a pink umbrella. The caption said, "Thinking of you."

Sasha handed him the card. "Read it to me, Daddy."

He scanned the message. "It's printing. Wouldn't you like to try reading it yourself?"

Sasha shook her head. "You do it."

Mark took a deep breath and read:

Dear Sasha,
You're probably wondering why we haven't seen each other lately. As you know, I planned to stay in Willow Beach for only one year. Now that time is up, and I have returned to my home in Seattle.

I hope you have a good year in school. Second grade. What a big girl you are.

I will always remember the fun times we had together, Sasha. Please say goodbye to Bella for me.
Love, Eva

Mark nearly choked on the ending words. *Love, Eva?* Yeah, right.

He noticed Sasha's wrinkled brow. "What is it, honey?"

"She doesn't say when she's coming back."

He bent down beside her. "She's not coming back. Like she said, she was here for just one year."

"But she said she loves me. Why would she leave me if she loves me?"

Good question. "Seattle is her home," he said again.

"Why can't she live here? With us?"

"It's complicated, baby. I'm afraid you'll have to get used to Eva being gone."

"No." Sasha flung herself at him and beat her fists against his chest. "Bring her back, Daddy. Please."

He put his arms around her and gathered her close. His heart filled with love. He wanted to protect her, to make everything right. But how could he when everything was broken beyond repair?

The following morning at the newspaper office, Mark sat at his desk staring at the computer screen, where a lonely sentence sat at the top. His editor's column for the upcoming edition needed to be written, but writer's block had reared its ugly head, and he'd been staring at the screen for the past half hour. He couldn't get Eva out of his mind. She haunted him at every turn. He kept seeing her words on Sasha's card, *Love, Eva*.

He rose from his chair and stretched and then rubbed the kinks out of his shoulders. He strolled to the window and gazed out. The maple tree was thick with leaves. The sun shone down on the windshield of his SUV parked nearby.

He thought more about Eva. He had no doubt she loved Sasha. The problem was Eva didn't love him. And why was that? Because she thought he didn't love her? Because she thought he wanted her to stay only because of the *Herald*?

Maybe what she'd said about him was true, that he was afraid to move on with his life. Okay, he'd admit it. Scared. Scared to trust again. Scared to…love.

Love. The key to everything.

Did he love Eva?

Images flooded his mind: the two of them locked in an embrace, working on the newspaper, sharing dinners, jogging on the beach. Yeah, he loved her. Big-time.

Was there a way to prove it to her?

The answer came almost before he finished asking the question. He could only hope and pray that it would work.

He returned to his desk, picked up the phone and called Lawrence Prentiss. When the lawyer came on the line, Mark told him his plan. Lawrence was shocked but agreed to follow Mark's wishes.

That night after he'd put Sasha to bed, he went into the living room and took a good look around at the furniture Diane had chosen, the cushions, the drapes and, yes, those doilies and fake flowers that Eva had pointed out. He'd tried to keep Diane alive by surrounding him and Sasha with things that would remind them of her. But she wasn't here. She was gone, had been for three years.

If he truly loved Eva, he would have to let go of Diane. He would have to trust again. And, yeah, that was scary. But he was ready.

He went to the mantel and picked up the photo of Diane. He gazed into her blue eyes, eyes that so reminded him of Sasha. "Good-bye, Diane," he whispered. "We loved you,

Sasha and I, and we'll always remember you. But now the time has come for us to love again."

He scooped up the other photos and found a cardboard box to put them all in. When Sasha wanted to remember her mommy, they would be available, but for now he needed them to be out of sight.

The next morning at the office, Mark looked up the phone number for Morgan's Realty. When Jeb Morgan answered, Mark said, "Hey, Jeb, how'd you like another house to sell? I've got one for you."

STANDING AT HER kitchen counter, Eva filled two mugs of coffee from the coffeemaker and handed one to Susan. "Let's sit in the living room where we can enjoy the view while we chat."

Susan nodded as she reached for the coffee. "Good idea. I like having my own place, but I sure miss your fabulous view."

Eva picked up the plate of pastries she'd arranged and led the way. She placed the tray on the coffee table and waved Susan into one of the beige side chairs.

"You really didn't have to feed me." Susan

placed her lime-green tote at her feet and eyed the tray. "I've had breakfast."

"I bet I don't need to twist your arm, though." Eva grinned and handed Susan a napkin.

Susan's laughter rang out. "You know me too well."

"I remember that when it was your turn to bring treats to work, we always had something really yummy."

Susan spread the napkin on her lap and then reached for a piece of the pastry. "Speaking of work, how'd your first week go?"

Eva made a face. "If you asked my feet, the answer would be 'Grueling.'" She kicked off one of her flats and flexed her stockinged foot. "Why did I ever think high-heeled shoes were comfortable?"

Susan touched her mouth with her napkin. "Comfort doesn't matter when you're a fashion slave. You've gone so long without wearing heels that your feet are out of condition."

Eva rubbed her arch. "I know."

"Feet aside, how do you like being on the staff again?"

Eva shrugged. "I was hoping to still get the fashion assignments, but Molly Hartman seems to have taken over those. The food columns are open, but you know how good I am at cooking."

"You don't have to cook. Just write about what other people cook."

"I know, and I shouldn't complain."

Susan selected another pastry and took a bite. "Last weekend, Greg and I and his parents stayed at the cutest bed-and-breakfast in Morganville. Isn't that about twenty or so miles from Willow Beach?"

Eva sipped her coffee. "Yes, it is. And I think I know the place you're talking about. Old Victorian, painted bright pink, pots of geraniums on the walkway?"

"Right. Lovely place, and the cook made the best cinnamon rolls for our breakfast. Anyway, when we went out for dinner, I found this." She reached into her tote, pulled out a folded tabloid-size newspaper and handed it to Eva. "Check out the publisher. Isn't he the one who's buying your half of the *Herald?*"

Eva unfolded the paper and read the banner across the top. "The *Morganville Messenger.* Yes, he's the one."

"Doesn't look like much of a newspaper," Susan said. "It's mostly ads. Oh, and check out the big Personals column. Is he providing news or running a matchmaking service?"

"Not much news, that's for sure." Eva perused the paper's contents.

Susan leaned forward. "Hey, why the frown? You are glad you came back, aren't you?"

Eva put down the newspaper and twisted her fingers together. "To be honest, Susan, I don't know. I just don't know."

A perceptive look crossed Susan's face. "It's Mark, isn't it? You're in love with him."

"No!" Then in a softer voice, "I—I can't be in love with him."

"Why not?"

"He just wanted me to stay there so that he wouldn't lose the *Herald*. Besides, he never said anything about love. And he had the nerve to accuse me of hanging on to my *pain* over the past so that I wouldn't have to admit I really liked my job at the *Herald* and really wanted to stay in Willow Beach. Have you ever heard anything so crazy?"

Susan shrugged. "Well, actually, the idea sounds like something I heard in one of my psychology classes. It probably has a big long name, but I don't remember what it is."

Eva snorted and folded her arms. "I should know my own mind, my own self, better than he does, shouldn't I?"

Susan's eyes reflected doubt. "What he said might be worth thinking about. Do some soul-searching. Do you really want the *Herald* to become a newspaper like the *Morganville Messenger?* Do you really want to be back here in Seattle? Or do you want to live in Willow Beach?"

After Susan left, Eva paced the living room. Her stomach churned, and her head throbbed. How had life become so complicated? A week ago, she was elated to be moving back to Seattle and the career she'd always wanted. Now her world had turned upside down again.

Was Susan right? Would soul-searching, as she'd called it, help her to know what to do? Something had better happen fast because at 2:00 p.m. the following day, she had an appointment with her lawyer, Nolan Cramer, to sign the papers for the sale of her half of the *Herald* to Boyd Carlstrom.

AFTER A RESTLESS NIGHT, Eva awoke still unsettled, and all morning at work she strug-

gled with her problem. She was almost late
to her appointment. Just as she was about to
leave the office, an interior designer she was
to interview called to reschedule. By the time
they went back and forth with one date and
then another, she had only a few minutes to
reach Nolan's office.

Fortunately, he was only a few blocks away,
and at last she was seated across the table
from him. He went over the papers with her
and laid out the page for her signature. He
handed her a pen.

The moment of truth had finally arrived.
Gripping the pen, she stared at the signature
line. All she had to do was write her name,
and the matter would be settled.

Eva swallowed, her throat dry. Her hand
shook as she guided the pen toward the line.

Nolan peered at her. "You okay, Eva?"

"No, I'm not," she whispered. "I can't do
this."

He leaned forward. "What?"

She cleared her throat. "I can't sign this,"
she said louder. She looked up and met his
puzzled stare. "I'm not obligated to sell to
Boyd, am I?"

Nolan frowned. "No, not until you sign. But—"

She pushed the pen and the paper back toward his side of the table. "Then the deal's off."

"O-kay…" He arched an eyebrow. "Does that mean you're keeping your half of the newspaper?"

"Not necessarily. As soon as you've straightened things out with Boyd, contact Mark Townson and tell him I'll sell him my half. He can pay me off however he likes and take as long as needed. Whatever works for him will be fine."

Nolan raised his eyebrows. "You're sure that's what you want to do?"

"Yes, I'm sure."

Later, when she was back in her condo, had eaten dinner and was settled on the sofa with a cup of coffee, Eva did some more soul-searching. She thought about the past year in Willow Beach and how she'd gone there with the idea that she could never live there again, that what had happened to Brett and the split with her father would haunt her forever.

Then she thought of the year she'd just

spent there. Okay, she and Mark had clashed over their opinions of what was important news and what wasn't. But they'd often compromised. And helping the high-school students with their show had been every bit as much fun as attending a fashion show here in Seattle. Maybe even more because she'd been so much a part of the planning.

And the times she'd spent with Sasha and Mark, especially Mark, had been wonderful.

Had Mark spoken the truth? Was she holding on to her pain and her guilt to prevent moving on in the present—and the future?

She sat there and thought about that while the twilight sky faded into darkness and the stars popped out one by one. Then she reached up, unclasped the necklace and pulled it from underneath her blouse. Laying the medal in her palm, she ran her fingers over the embossed letters as she had so many times during the past eleven years. First Place. "Yes, Brett, you were a winner," she whispered and smiled a sad smile.

She curled her fingers around the medal and then carried it into the bedroom, where she tucked it away in a dresser drawer.

MARK STARED AT the sheaf of papers on his desk, papers Lawrence Prentiss had drawn up for the sale of his half of the *Herald* to Boyd Carlstrom. He'd read them through and had seen nothing amiss. Now all he had to do was sign his name. "I hope you know why I'm doing this, Seb," he muttered under his breath. "I love the *Herald,* but I love your daughter more. And I'm hoping this will prove it to her."

Taking a deep breath, Mark grabbed the pen from its holder and scrawled his name on the line. He sat back and stared at his signature. Done.

Folding up the papers, he put them in the return envelope Lawrence had provided. He could hand deliver the document to the lawyer's office. But if he did, he might have to answer more of the man's questions.

He could send one of the staff over with the envelope. But that, too, would invite questions and speculation. He'd face them later.

No, he'd send the papers by regular mail. He sealed the envelope and, because it was already addressed to Lawrence, only needed to add a stamp. Considering the thickness of the envelope, he slapped on another one for good measure.

He put the envelope in his outbox along with the other outgoing mail.

As he left the office, he stopped at April's desk. "I'll be out of town for a couple days. I'm not sure how long, but at least overnight."

She frowned. "Out of town? Where are you going? Or is it a secret?"

"No secret. I'm going to Seattle. There's some mail in my outbox that needs to go out today. Don't forget to pick it up when you make your rounds. It's important."

"I never forget the mail."

He'd already arranged for Sasha to stay overnight with Eileen, so all he had to do was throw some clothes in a duffel bag and be on his way.

He made good time until he hit Olympia and I-5, and then traffic slowed. Finally, he reached Seattle and the exit his GPS told him would lead to Eva's office building. Once there, he pulled into the underground parking garage, where he caught the elevator to the sixteenth floor. His breath came short, and his heart thumped.

At the end of the hallway, he saw *Seattle's*

*Best* spelled out in large black metal letters on a white wall next to glass double doors. He thought of the *Herald*'s office, where the name of the newspaper was painted on the window.

The doors burst open, and a group of four or five women breezed out in a blur of colorful outfits, high heels and huge purses slung over their shoulders. Talking and laughing, they barely glanced at him as they passed by. He caught the open door before it closed again and stepped inside the office.

He headed across a thick carpet, past chrome-and-black-leather furniture to a receptionist sitting behind a counter that took up nearly all of one wall. The scent of roses from a bouquet on a glass-topped table filled the air. Abstract prints in a variety of bold colors hung on the walls. Everything shouted elegance and sophistication. He thought of the *Herald*'s office with its molded plastic chairs and wooden tables and the sorry-looking philodendron.

No comparison, but so what? Other things in life mattered more. Like love. He was here to state his case, and state it he would.

He lifted his chin, straightened his shoulders and marched toward the receptionist. He'd almost reached her desk when a woman coming down the hall to his right caught his eye. Eva? He blinked and looked again. Yes, the woman was Eva. And yet not Eva. Not the Eva he'd come to know anyway. Her hair was in the twist thing. Her light blue suit fit her snugly in all the right places, with the short skirt showing plenty of leg. He had to admit she made a striking figure. She looked as if she belonged on the staff of a high-class magazine.

She, too, was headed for the receptionist. "Claire…"

Then she saw him. She stopped. Her eyes widened.

"Hello, Eva."

"What are *you* doing here?"

"I need to talk to you."

Alarm flashed in her eyes. "Sasha? Did something happen to Sasha?"

Her concern for his daughter brought a smile to his lips. "Sasha's fine."

"What, then?"

A small group had gathered, keeping their distance but watching with undisguised curiosity. He tipped his head toward them. "In private?"

Eva raised her eyebrows at the onlookers. They muttered about having to get back to work and disappeared through doorways and down hallways.

She turned back to Mark. "There's a conference room down the hall."

## CHAPTER EIGHTEEN

HEART HAMMERING, Eva led Mark down the hallway to the meeting room. What could he possibly want to see her about? Must be the newspaper. Except for Sasha, nothing meant anything to him. Was he here to try, one last time, to talk her out of selling to Boyd Carlstrom? Or had he heard already that she hadn't? Only yesterday she'd been at the lawyer's, unable to sign the papers. Still, there would have been time for her lawyer to call him.

Thankfully, no one was using the room. She led Mark in and closed the door. An oval table and chairs filled the space. She motioned to a chair, but he shook his head and held up one hand. "No, thanks."

She remained standing, too, unable to take her eyes off him. How could she have missed him so much in only a few days? But she had.

She still didn't know why he was here. Her nerves tingled.

"Mark, why *are* you here? If it's about the newspaper, you should be glad about what I did. Now you don't have to worry."

He tilted his head and raised his eyebrows. "What do you mean?"

"Then you don't know…"

"Know what?"

"That I didn't sell. I changed my mind. I told my lawyer to contact you and arrange for you to buy me out on whatever terms suit you. That was only yesterday, but word travels fast."

"What?" He stared, openmouthed.

"Did you hear a word I said?"

"Yeah, but I'm having trouble understanding. You didn't sell to Boyd?"

"No, and now you can have the *Herald* for yourself. And I can get on with my life—here." She looked away.

"There's a little snag in that scenario."

"What snag?"

"I just sold my half to Boyd."

Now it was Eva's turn to stare. "Am I hearing right?"

"Yep. Signed the papers this morning before I left to come here."

"Why on earth would you do that? Are you insane?"

He lifted a shoulder. "I thought selling my share would prove I love you for yourself, not just because I wanted to own all of the paper. So that's why I'm here. With the hope that—"

"Oh, Mark." Tears sprang to Eva's eyes. "You really love me that much?"

"I really do. And you must care about me, at least a little,"

"Oh, I do. That's why I *didn't* sell to Boyd."

A big grin lit his face and he held out his arms. "C'mere, honey."

They both stepped forward and met halfway. In an instant his arms were around her, holding her close. She drank in his oh-so-familiar scent, felt the strength of his embrace. Nothing had ever felt so good.

"I missed you so much," he whispered against her ear.

"I've missed you, too."

He tilted her chin and covered her lips with his. With a soft sigh, she clasped her arms around his neck and returned his kiss.

It was everything she'd dreamed of since she'd left Willow Beach.

He deepened the kiss for long moments, then eased away. "Let's get out of here. There must be somewhere we can go to be alone."

"I have appointments," she murmured.

"Not anymore, you don't. Your only appointment today is with me." Clasping her elbow, he drew her toward the door.

Eva pulled to a stop. "Wait, Mark. What are we going to do about the *Herald?*"

"The newspaper is the least of my concerns at the moment."

"We have to think about the future before we jump into something we both might regret."

He leveled her a solemn gaze. "We love each other. Does anything else matter?"

"No, I guess not."

"And, Eva, if Seattle is where you want to be, Sasha and I will be here, too. It's a big city. I'll get a job somewhere."

"You don't like big cities."

"I like wherever you are. Don't you get it yet?"

She smiled and her tension melted away. "Yeah, I get it. Tell you what, since you've

signed over your half to Boyd, I'll go ahead
and sell him my half, too. Then we'll decide
where to go from there."

He raised an eyebrow. "If you're sure that's
what you want to do."

"I've never been so sure of anything in my
life."

"All right. I know we'll find a place that's
right for both of us. All I ask is that you promise me forever."

"Forever," she murmured. "Yes, I promise
you forever."

"That's what I wanted to hear." He pulled
her into his arms and kissed her again.

The door to the conference room opened
and Susan came in. "Somebody said you were
in here, Eva…. Oh, excuse me!" Her face
turned red.

Eva motioned to Susan. "Come on in and
meet Mark."

"Mark. From Willow Beach." Susan
grinned. "What took you so long?"

The following day, having spent the night at
Susan's fiancé's, Mark pulled his SUV into
the *Herald*'s parking lot. He sat there a moment, preparing for what lay ahead when he

entered the building. He must tell the staff that the *Herald* soon would belong entirely to Boyd Carlstrom. He'd no doubt they would all leave and be happy in new endeavors. Still, putting an official end to the newspaper they'd known and loved brought tightness to his chest.

Better get it over with. Taking a deep breath, he got out of the SUV and entered the building's back door. As he headed to his office, he spotted Bernie coming down the hall toward him.

Bernie waved. "Hey, man, glad you're back. How'd it go in Seattle?"

Mark grinned. "Real good. I'll fill all of you in later."

"Okay, but there's something you need to know."

Bernie's serious tone put him on alert. "What's that?"

"April left early yesterday. Then she called this morning and said she wasn't coming in. Said there's a letter on your desk."

Mark shook his head. What was April up to now? "Thanks, I'll check it out."

Mark reached his office and went in. The blinds were closed and the room was dim. He crossed to the window and opened the blinds, then approached his desk. As Bernie had said, an envelope lay there. It was addressed to him, in April's handwriting. His curiosity growing stronger by the second, he slid his thumb under the flap. He took out the letter inside and read:

Dear Mark,

When you told me you were going to Seattle, I decided that, no matter what the outcome of your trip, I don't belong here at the *Herald* anymore. You were right. I will be happier working someplace else. I'm moving to Morganville to live with my sister.

If I'm lucky, someday I'll find someone as nice as you.

April

Mark stared at the letter. He never would have thought she'd actually take his advice and seek employment elsewhere.

"I wish you well, April," he whispered.

Since she'd left early yesterday, he wondered if she'd collected his mail, as he'd asked her to do before he left town. Probably. April may have been difficult, but she was efficient and conscientious.

He stepped to the corner of his desk and

peered into his outbox. The stack of mail still sat there. On the top was the envelope to Lawrence Prentiss.

Wearing a big grin, Mark picked up the envelope, ripped it open and pulled out the sheets of paper. Clutching the documents in both hands, he began tearing them in half. He kept tearing until all that was left of the contract was a pile of little pieces of paper. He swept them into the wastebasket, then brushed his hands together, making sure every bit of the contract was disposed of.

He picked up the phone and called Eva. "You'll never guess what happened," he said when she came on the line.

"A Mr. Lawrence Prentiss to see you," Claire told Eva over the phone.

Eva frowned and glanced at the list she'd been making of all that she had to do. Her life was changing by the minute, it seemed. Today, she'd given James her resignation. He'd been understanding and sympathetic, as she knew he would be. Now her father's lawyer wanted to see her. Why? She'd fulfilled the terms of the will, hadn't she?

"I'll be right out," Eva told Claire.

She left her cubicle and headed to the reception area. Lawrence, looking as thin as ever in his lightweight tan suit, stood waiting for her.

Eva approached and held out her hand. "Lawrence, what brings you to Seattle?"

Lawrence smiled and shook Eva's hand. "I have a letter for you that I wanted to deliver in person. Is there someplace we can talk in private?"

"I think my cubicle is private enough. Come on back."

Once they were seated, Lawrence pulled a legal-size envelope from his jacket's breast pocket and handed it to her.

Eva's name was written on the envelope. "That looks like my father's handwriting."

Lawrence nodded and tucked his long legs under his chair. "He wrote the letter at the same time that he made his will. But I wasn't to give it to you until your year in Willow Beach was over."

"He was that certain I'd stay?"

"I honestly don't know. And I don't know what's in the letter. I'm only supposed to deliver it to you."

She nodded and tapped the envelope. "Which you have done, and I appreciate that."

Eva decided to not confide in Lawrence about her and Mark's decision to keep the *Herald*. The way the town grapevine worked, everyone would know soon enough. She saw Lawrence out and then returned to her cubicle. She sat at her desk and stared at the envelope, then decided to wait until she was at home to read it.

But even when she was back in her condo, she still didn't have the nerve to read her father's letter. She let it lie on the coffee table while she drank a cup of tea and stared out the patio door at the nighttime sky.

Finally, she picked up the envelope and opened it. The letter was handwritten.

*Dear Eva,*

*I'm sure you are surprised to receive this letter from me. I can just imagine the expression on your face. What's he writing to me for?*

*Well, because I have something important to say. You know it's always been difficult for me to talk about things and that I do better at writing than at talking.*

*Anyway, by the time you receive this let-*

ter, you will have finished your year in Willow Beach, coediting the *Herald* with Mark. Yes, I'm certain you took up the challenge. I know you better than you think I do, my daughter. I know you have integrity and honesty and a consideration for others. You won't let Mark lose his inheritance.

Even so, I'm equally certain you consider my bequest as punishment rather than as a reward. In truth, though, it is neither.

About your brother: your mother and I welcomed both you and Brett into the world with great joy and anticipation. But I know that as the years went by you felt I favored Brett over you. And perhaps it looked that way because I was so intent on him following in my footsteps at the *Herald*.

You were always more interested in feminine things—dolls when you were little, clothes later on. And I couldn't relate. Okay, I could have tried harder.

When we lost your mother I thought the world had ended. And when Brett died, as everybody witnessed, I went into another tailspin. But I made sure that you graduated high school and went off to college. Perhaps wanting you to come work for me was selfish, but, Eva, I never considered you second choice. Never. I thought if you came we might have the relationship we hadn't had before.

I didn't believe you when you told me Brett was never going to work at the *Herald*. But after you went to Seattle, I discovered among his things the papers from the recruiters that he'd filled out. I know his death hit you hard, too, but don't ever, ever blame yourself for the accident. It was just that: an accident.

I left you an interest in the *Herald* because I wanted to give you something that means a lot to me, hoping that you will come to love it as I did and love living back in your hometown. And if that love should happen to grow to include Mark, well, that would please me, too. He's a fine man.

I've known about my bad heart for several years now. And, yes, I've been seeing a doctor and following his advice and taking the prescriptions he's given me. But even so, nothing is guaranteed. So, I figured I'd better make a will and arrange my affairs while I still could. Maybe I'll last until we can be with each other again on better terms.

If not, know that I have always loved you and wish you only the best.

Dad

Eva sat there staring at her father's bold signature, so characteristic of the man himself. Tears streamed down her face, tears for all they had lost, she and her father. Yet, the letter confirmed that his love for her had never been lost. Amid all the arguments, the misunderstandings, the hurt, his love for her had always been there.

"How I wish I could have told him I love him, too," Eva said days later, after she'd shared her father's letter with Mark.

"I know how you feel," he said. "There's a lot I wish I'd said to Diane, would have said if I'd known what was going to happen when she got on that bus."

"I don't ever want anything to come between us," she said, gazing into the eyes of the man she loved with all her heart.

He drew her into his arms. "You made a promise to me a few days ago. You promised me forever. And now I have one for you. I promise you, my dear love, my soon-to-be wife, that nothing, nothing in heaven or earth, will ever come between us."

# CHAPTER NINETEEN

*Willow Beach, fifteen months later*

"HEY, HONEY, I'M HOME!"

Eva stopped typing and grinned at her husband's clichéd greeting. "I'm in my office," she called and then turned to watch him enter the room. He was dressed in his typical jeans and short-sleeved shirt that showed off those muscles she never tired of admiring.

Striding over to her, he placed his hands on her shoulders, leaned down and nuzzled her neck. "Mmm, you smell good."

As he straightened, she turned, and their cheeks brushed. Their lips collided, then meshed in a warm kiss. Her blood stirred, as it always did when she kissed her husband.

He drew away and looked over her shoulder at the computer screen. "How's the article coming along?"

"Just about finished. And none too soon.

My deadline is next week." Eva had been freelancing for *Seattle's Best*. Her current assignment was a feature on the coastal bed-and-breakfast establishments.

"What about your novel? Heard anything from your editor?"

"I'm supposed to get the galleys next week."

"You are one busy lady."

"I know. But don't worry about my column for the *Herald*. I'll have it done on time. We have to hold up our image as an award-winning newspaper." She nodded at the shiny trophy and framed certificate sitting on the shelf above her desk. Last month, they'd attended the governor's awards ceremony in Olympia and were named Best Small Town Weekly Newspaper.

He patted her shoulder. "I'm not worried. You always meet your deadlines."

Eva shifted in her seat. "Oh, I'm stiff. I need to stretch." Holding her six-months-pregnant stomach with one hand, she pushed her chair away from the desk with the other.

"Here, let me help you." Mark grasped her elbow and assisted her to her feet. He placed his own hand over hers. "How's our son doing today?"

"Really active. He likes to let me know he's there."

"Only a few more months and we'll welcome him into the world."

"I'm sooo ready."

"Me, too." He glanced at his wristwatch. "Whoa, almost six. We'd better head over to Bernie and Maria's."

Eva closed her computer file and turned off the machine. "You never did tell me what tonight's all about."

He shrugged. "Just dinner with our friends. Sasha and Bella are making cookies for dessert."

"I can't wait to see what they come up with. Let me freshen up a bit, and we'll be on our way. Sure we shouldn't take anything?"

Mark pushed in her chair and turned off her desk lamp. "I asked Bernie again today. He said absolutely not."

Ten minutes later, after a short ride across town, Mark and Eva pulled up in front of the Sanchez home. Eva gazed around the quiet, tree-shaded neighborhood, where everyone kept their lawns neatly mowed and flowers blooming in boxes and along walkways. "Isn't that Cody's truck over there?"

"Could be."

"And Dora's VW bug?" She turned to him. "What's going on?"

He grinned and cut the engine. "You'll see."

"Mark…"

"Patience, honey. You'll find out soon enough."

He jumped from the SUV, came around and helped her to alight. Holding her hand, he led her up the walk to the porch. They hadn't even rung the doorbell when the door was flung open.

Bernie stood there, a big grin on his face. "Hey, you two. 'Bout time you got here. Everyone's waiting."

"Everyone?" Eva said. "Waiting for what?"

"For you, of course." He led them into the living room.

"Surprise!"

Eva's mouth dropped open. She clamped it shut and gazed around the room to see the entire *Herald* staff grinning and clapping.

Sasha raced over to Eva and Mark. "Mommy! Daddy!" She threw herself at them.

"Hey, sweetheart." Eva hugged Sasha close and buried a kiss in her fragrant hair and then Mark gave her a hug, too.

Sasha looked up at Eva. "Are you surprised, Mommy?"

"I am." Eva looked at the others. "Would someone like to explain?" Her gaze landed on the coffee table piled high with wrapped gifts. "Oh, I get it. For the baby."

Maria stepped forward to stand beside Bernie. "Yes, this is a shower for you and your baby."

"How did you get the guys to come to a baby shower?" Eva asked.

"Don't worry," Bernie said. "When it comes time to ooh and aah over baby stuff, we men will adjourn for a game of pool." He gestured toward the hallway leading to their family room. "But right now, we're off to tend the barbecue."

Eva sniffed. "Smells good already. What are we having?"

"Fajitas. Maria's special recipe." He made a sweeping gesture in his wife's direction.

Maria grinned and pointed to the sofa, where a colorful Mexican throw was spread along the back. "You relax, Eva, while I bring in some sangria." She waggled a finger. "But for you, without the alcohol."

Luci rose from where she'd been sitting beside Cody. "I'll help you, Maria." She stopped by Eva, her eyes shining. "This is so exciting."

"Something for you to look forward to one day?" Eva said.

"Maybe." Luci cast a wistful gaze at Cody and then trotted after Maria.

Luci and Cody were both attending the University of Washington. Luci had confided that they'd been on a few dates. Eva wouldn't be surprised if, as Luci seemed to hope, something more came of their relationship.

Dora left her chair by the fireplace and came to sit beside Eva. "I'll keep you company while the others do all the work," she said with a laugh.

Mark brought a pillow to put behind Eva's back. "Us guys will help Bernie," he said. "But call if you need anything."

"I will, hon."

Mark gave Cody a playful punch on the shoulder and motioned to Dora's husband, Josh. "Come on, we'll see what Bernie's up to."

Maria and Luci returned with trays of punch, and after serving Eva and Dora, they headed outside to serve the men. Sasha and Bella danced in and out, talking about the cookies they'd baked and school, scheduled to start next week. They both hoped to be in the same third-grade class.

After a while, they all assembled outside, sitting on the patio while a soft summer breeze blowing in from the ocean wrapped around them. After feasting on Maria's fajitas, which everyone declared wonderful, they trooped back inside for gift opening. As Bernie predicted, when the oohing and aahing started over tiny booties and sweater-and-cap sets and crib blankets, the men disappeared.

When the gifts had been opened, the men came back and everyone gathered around for coffee and the raisin-and-oatmeal cookies Sasha and Bella had made.

"They're yummy," Eva told the girls.

Dora put down her coffee cup and cleared her throat. "Attention, everyone." When the chatter died down, she turned to Eva. "Eva, on behalf of all of us at the *Herald,* I want to tell you how very glad we are that you came back to Willow Beach. We can't imagine our newspaper with anyone but you and Mark at the helm. We will be forever grateful to you for carrying on your father's work."

"To Eva!" the others chimed in.

Tears welled up in Eva's eyes. She looked around at her friends and colleagues. "Thank you, everyone. I am so lucky. I have my wonderful immediate family—Mark and Sasha and our son, who will soon join us." She paused to smile at Mark and Sasha. "And I have my extended family in all of you. I've truly come home." She swept her gaze around the room to include each person and then raised her cup. "I'd like to add a toast to my father. Without his vision and dreams, we wouldn't be here today."

"Yes," Mark chimed in, "to Seb."

"To Seb!" everyone shouted, raising their coffee cups.

Later, on the way home, with Sasha tucked safely in the backseat, Eva gazed at Mark's profile, illuminated under the streetlights. Warmth and love filled her. How lucky she was to have found him.

"I love you," she said impulsively.

He flashed her a smile. "I love you, too.

And I can't wait till we get home and I can show you just how much I love you."

She leaned over the console to snuggle against his shoulder. "Promises, promises," she teased.

"Yep. And you know I always make good on my promises."

"I know you do." Delicious images of their lovemaking filled her mind, making her eager to get home and into each other's arms.

Home. Yes, Willow Beach was home now. Although the journey had had bumps and setbacks, she was here to stay. There was no place on earth she'd rather be.

\* \* \* \* \*

# Special Offers

Every month we put together collections and
longer reads written by your favourite authors.

Here are some of next month's highlights—
and don't miss our fabulous discount online!

On sale 6th June          On sale 6th June          On sale 6th June

## Save 20%
### on all Special Releases

# Hot reads!

These 3-in-1s will certainly get you feeling
hot under the collar with their desert
locations, billionaire tycoons and
playboy princes.

**Now available at
www.millsandboon.co.uk/offers**

# Blaze is now *exclusive* to eBook!

## FUN, SEXY AND *ALWAYS STEAMY*!

Our much-loved series about sassy heroines and irresistible heroes are now available exclusively as eBooks. So download yours today and expect sizzling adventures about modern love and lust.

## Now available at
## www.millsandboon.co.uk/blaze

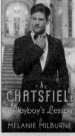

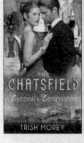

# Join our *EXCLUSIVE* eBook club

## FROM JUST £1.99 A MONTH!

*Never miss a book again with our hassle-free eBook subscription.*

★ Pick how many titles you want from each series with our flexible subscription

★ Your titles are delivered to your device on the first of every month

★ Zero risk, zero obligation!

*There really is nothing standing in the way of you and your favourite books!*

**Start your eBook subscription today at www.millsandboon.co.uk/subscribe**

Discover more romance at

# www.millsandboon.co.uk

- ♥ WIN great prizes in our exclusive competitions

- ♥ BUY new titles before they hit the shops

- ♥ BROWSE new books and REVIEW your favourites

- ♥ SAVE on new books with the Mills & Boon® Bookclub™

- ♥ DISCOVER new authors

PLUS, to chat about your favourite reads, get the latest news and find special offers:

- 🗗 Find us on facebook.com/millsandboon

- 🐦 Follow us on twitter.com/millsandboonuk

- ♥ Sign up to our newsletter at millsandboon.co.uk